CRY WOLF

Based on a true story

S. W. SYLVESTER

iUniverse, Inc.
Bloomington

Cry Wolf
Based on a true story

Copyright © 2012 S. W. Sylvester

This book is based on some true events; however, it has been fictionalized inclusive
to all persons appearing in this work. Any resemblance to real people, living or not,
is entirely coincidental. As a warning, nobody should attempt to recreate or reenact
any stunt or activity performed by the characters within the context of this story.

iUniverse books may be ordered through booksellers or by contacting:

iUniverse
1663 Liberty Drive
Bloomington, IN 47403
www.iuniverse.com
1-800-Authors (1-800-288-4677)

ISBN: 978-1-4620-6397-0 (sc)
ISBN: 978-1-4620-6398-7 (e)

Printed in the United States of America

iUniverse rev. date: 1/05/2012

In memory of my parents.

CHAPTER 1

The waning minutes of twilight bid farewell to each twin silo anchored on the Wickman family farm. Soon, the encroaching darkness would overcome the faint western glow of another passing day, and budding stars, having already made their presence known, would dominate the Wisconsin heavens. An evening breeze swept over a hayfield laid to rest, every wisp sounding aromatic notes of the duty at hand. Consorting with the chatter of crickets, a distant whip-poor-will's lullaby echoed while a porch swing attempted to keep in harmony.

Seth was stretched out crossways. One of his feet nurtured the gentle rocking; the injured other hitched a ride on an armrest. Handmade cushions comforted what remained of a body well spent. A day in the field, a hearty meal, and the rhythmic sway at dusk left him drained yet fulfilled. It was a time to cultivate dreams. For Seth, such moments were special to this end, and gazing into a flickering cosmos brought him that much closer to his dreams.

His mother pushed open the screen door. A robust woman with fine features, she carried a flour-sack towel filled with crushed ice. Soft blue eyes guided the chilly bundle over his left foot. "It'll help keep the swelling down. After all, this little piggy goes to market, and damaged goods would bring a poor return."

Although pulled from thought, he welcomed her attention and its soothing results. "Thanks, Ma. That feels much better. I don't think it's broke, just bruised. It'll go away in a few days—the bruise, not the toe." His smile broadened.

Slowly running her fingers through his hair, she returned the smile and then gathered a stack of dishes he'd left balanced on the porch railing, remnants of a man-sized slice of peach pie and brimming glass of whole milk. "I'm glad the soreness didn't affect your appetite or temperament," she said before returning from whence she came.

Seth drifted back into the sweep of early evening and wandered among the stars. A shooter briefly slashed open his view but just as quickly healed itself. For a second time, footsteps diverted his exploration. These were steps that seemed to silence crickets and quell the night bird's song, steps that creaked floorboards beneath with each dominant station. They were as familiar to his ears as the brawny figure making them was to his eyes.

His father took respite on the railing between steadfast porch columns and casually tilted his cap back, sharing in the sparkling tranquility above. Seth suspected an investigation into the mishap was imminent but was unsure of the manner in which such an inquiry would leave his father's tongue. "How'd ya cut it? Did ya burn it or step on it?"

Pa took life a bit more seriously than either his mother or brother, but at times, he'd escape into an old-fashioned humor that tended to lift a spirit rather than cause an outright belly laugh.

Seth grinned and began his tale. "Delma stepped on my foot. She scoped me with a bulging eyeball while I cleaned her teats; should've figured something was up. I swear she knew what she was doing."

Adam raised an eyebrow and asked, "Ya reckon we oughta have a doctor take a look-see?"

"Oh, I'll be all right. I yanked it out before she made full weight." Seth didn't want to imply that a tender toe would slow him down the least bit. He was to be a 1973 graduate of Oakton High School the following spring and was currently on the threshold of legal adulthood.

"We'll see how it is in the morn'n'," said his father and turned his eyes to the starry night. "Suppose'n we sell her? She'd fetch a pretty penny."

Suspecting the ole man could be in earnest about Delma, Seth piped up. "We couldn't do that, Pa. She's a mighty fine Holstein, excellent milk production and breeding stock. I was probably a bit too rough to begin with."

His father stood, strolled several paces, and then leaned over and grasped the porch railing. As he was looking over the driveway, which circled, merged, and returned to River Road, the slightest hint of a grin formed, and he seemed to be pleased about the young farmer's tolerance toward a first-rate animal. "Ya know your mother fancies a flower garden 'round the flagpole yonder?"

"Nice place to plant tulip bulbs this fall, so she said," Seth quickly added. The change of topic was a welcome relief. His opinion might just have rescued the gal from a butcher's block—not good, even for a foot stomper.

Seth knew his brother Nate would be sprawled on the sofa by now and watching the Friday-night movie. Their relationship had been strained as of late because of Seth's increased interest in hanging out with friends. They'd gone fishing only once this year and didn't even inflate their inner tubes for a summer of river rafting. Sadly, Seth's baseball glove was stiff from lack of use, and two brand-new hardballs lay still in their boxes, neither able to fulfill its potential alone. Remorse was temporarily broken by a ringing telephone, which was soon followed by his mother's voice calling him from behind the screen door.

"Seth, Wylie's on the phone. Would you like me to have him call back later?"

"No, I'll get it." Setting aside a dripping ice pack, he got to his feet and strode to the doorway with much less effort than the pain would suggest. He'd said he'd be all right, and now he'd have to show it, as he knew his father would be watching. There was a second set of eyes illuminated by the television's glow and peering out from a darkened living room. They followed his every step through the kitchen. Nate's developing talent for lip-reading made it necessary to face away from him.

"Hey, Wylie, what's up?"

The words had scarcely left his mouth when Wylie broke in, quite beside himself. "Get your ass over here right away. There's a strange light floating around out back of the pines. Ya gotta see it."

Apprehensive about his friend's intent, Seth blurted out, "Oh, you mean like last time?" A week ago, Wylie had called him, Wade, and the

Moeller twins claiming an orange light was stirring about in that same area northeast of the cottage. He and Wade had showed in minutes, while Alec and Thomas Moeller covered seven miles of winding blacktop in record time. It was a lot of excitement only to have it conveniently disappear before they arrived.

"I'm not shittin' ya, so hang up and get movin'!" These words were followed by a click and a dial tone.

He approached his mother and whispered so as not to be detected by Nate's hearing, which was as acute as his eyesight. "I'm going next door to give him a hand. Shouldn't be too long."

She motioned to the countertop nearest his exit. "There's a little something to bring over, if you please." Centered within the flowered rim of stoneware, neatly covered with plastic wrap, was a healthy slice of supper's dessert. "Don't take any unnecessary chances, your foot the way it is and all."

"Not to worry, Ma. Wylie wants me to give him a hand, not a foot." Shuffling toward the care package, he wondered how she could've prepared it so fast. He wasn't on the horn more than five seconds. Nevertheless, Nate was at his side before he'd slid the plate into his hand and pleading in a tone drenched with hope.

"Can I go?"

"Not this time, Little Brother, maybe next."

He shot back, "Where have I heard that before? It's always the next time."

Seth pushed open the screen door with his free hand, irked by the pestilence. He rolled his eyes and snapped, "Stop bugging me." As he left, a tension spring pulled the door shut with a bang, finalizing his harsh words.

The subtle limp that had gotten him inside also got him to a dusty pickup truck in the driveway. He opened a squeaky driver's side door and positioned Wylie's pie on the seat, confident that the work gloves tucked beneath would keep it level. Wheel in hand and engine running, he glanced over the porch before dropping gear. Indoor lighting had created a silhouette of mother and son, or more accurately, a concerned mother standing beside a son frozen in disappointment. Guilt briefly took its toll, but Wylie had managed to inject enough extraterrestrial venom to keep absolute shame at bay.

His father had since assumed squatting rights to the porch swing and called out above a weakening muffler, "Don't dilly-dally; ya oughta be givin' that foot a rest."

"All right, Pa!" he yelled as he drove off. Many infectious phrases had entered his head over the years, and unable to resist his father's influence, he felt natural mumbling, "There's no rest for the wicked."

Wylie Barone lived a quarter mile east of Seth's home on a small farmstead set against a stand of white pines. Some people called them monarchs of the north. Mature hardwoods complemented a swath of land untouched by the lumberjack's teeth a hundred years earlier. Willow Creek flowed along the road to the south, its timber-lined banks making it barely visible. From either direction, River Road crested in open pasture and then descended into a tunnel of foliage so thick it was reminiscent of a subterranean passageway. If not for a tilted mailbox at the roadside, the gravel driveway might go completely unnoticed. By day, Wylie's settlement was a wooded oasis in a sea of rolling farmland; by night, it was a daunting black forest defending its ground.

Seth's headlights found the Barone mailbox and an open gate. A sharp left with a little pedal spit gravel into the roadway, pushing him up and around the bend. He skidded to a stop at Wylie's doorstep, where the monarchs overlooked a small cottage hidden behind cedar and lilac shrubbery. Across the courtyard, a modest barn, machine shed, and chicken coop were humbled by the surrounding oak and maple giants. Both conifer and deciduous trees combined to the north to form a dense wood, through which a well-worn trail had been blazed to open pastures.

Wylie scurried from a dimly lit entrance and, poking his head through the open passenger-side window, forcefully whispered, "Pull the keys, hit the lights, and follow me."

They met in front of the pickup and ventured out into the looming darkness, picking their way down the cow trail with hardly enough starlight to sidestep scattered mounds of cattle dung.

Wide-eyed and nervous, Wylie continued, "While I was checking on my herd, a green light shone through the pines near trail's end. We both know any light back in here ain't normal, so I went back to the house and called ya."

Seth was leery of Wylie's story. The light had been orange the last time around. Still, he couldn't suppress the possibility of truth and hence the foreboding nature of their journey. A big part of him wanted to be proven wrong, so he matched his pace with his neighbor's, more alive than ever before and unmindful of the damage caused by Delma's heavy hoof. If Wylie was acting, he was doing a damn good job of it. The tall trees began to thin as they neared the access to open pasture. Coming to a halt, Seth murmured his first words. "So, whereabouts did you see that strange light?"

Wylie pointed to the shadowed undergrowth. "It was back in there and a lot smaller than the orange light a week ago … Take a walk through with me."

"I don't see anything, and humping through a dark woods looking for your boogeyman sounds awfully stupid to me. Hell, I was an idiot for coming over here in the first place." He spun around and began his humiliating trek back to the pickup.

"Ya don't suppose an idiot can tell me what the hell that is then?"

Allowing his friend the benefit of the doubt one more time, Seth glanced over his shoulder and was instantly paralyzed by what he saw. Slowly turning about, he inched closer to Wylie's side. "Holy shit, what on earth is that?"

"I asked you first."

Together, they stood motionless, speechless, completely absorbed by what was taking place before them. Emerging from behind several inky pillars of pine, floating over the forest fern, was a soft, glowing light. Lime green in color, it moved forward while wavering about—a little up, a little down, a little from side to side. The nearer it came, the more it took on a vaguely human form. A freakishly large head wobbled on a pale torso without legs. Long arms were joined hand in hand below the waist as though in silent prayer. Closing in at thirty yards, it abruptly stopped, seeming to have become aware of their presence. Time spent in mutual awareness was stretched to the maximum before it, once again, began to advance.

Renewed movement changed Seth's demeanor toward the thing. Excited curiosity rapidly turned to one of feeling downright threatened. In his mind, progression indicated aggression and deserved an immediate response. "I think we better get outta here; it sees us."

Wylie grabbed his arm. "Wait a minute; it might be friendly."

Struggling to keep his tone low and feet planted firmly, he questioned such reasoning, "And if it isn't?"

"Aww, come on, ya pussy," Wylie snarled. It was a classic move intended to jolt his buddy's sense of pride, and it had worked great until the creature narrowed the distance to twenty paces.

Quickly scanning what he could see of the area around him, which wasn't very much at night, Seth focused on a rusted metal fence post barely protruding from the trail. At some point, cows must've pushed it over and gradually trampled it deeper and deeper into the ground, but it was all there was to be had. Keeping one sharp eye on the creature, he double-gripped the post and pulled it free from its burial site. Stepping forward and squaring off into a batter's stance, he stated with all due seriousness, "If it comes any closer, I'm gonna lace the fucker."

By this time, Wylie was bent over, his hands on his knees, and gasping for air, convulsing in between gulps. Seth thought he was going to puke from fear. Then the unexpected happened. Wylie motioned for him to put the weapon down, and yet again, the situation became more bizarre. His noxious behavior was such that it corrupted his sense of balance; he rocked back and forth before finally collapsing, rump first, into a crusty dung heap. There he sat without care or concern as he shook violently from side-splitting hysteria.

Bewildered by the sudden turn of events, Seth's eyes darted between Wylie and the creature, not knowing what to make of it. Things became clearer when the green man-thing moved his light source from its prayerful position and began waving it overhead in a most frantic manner.

"Seth! Put it down! It's just me, Wade!"

As the familiar voice drew nearer, a glowing green halo illuminated the shirtless impression of his school chum. It was Wade Hotchner sporting a sheepish grin. Wylie's persistent laughter while seated in a pile of crap brought to bear the full extent of a brilliantly executed hoax.

"Why you miserable bastards ... You scared the bejesus out of me." Seth dropped the metal post but wasn't up to throwing his hat into their jovial celebration. He was flustered by his gullibility and wishing very much to remove himself from center stage. Continuing as soon as his composure could be regained, he asked, "What is that thing anyway?"

Wade tossed him the object of deception and then reached out to help Wylie to his feet. Seth fingered it between jittery hands, oblivious to their antics. What he had was a semiclear plastic tube about the size of a small cigar and partially filled with a glowing lime-green liquid. The light reminded him of a firefly's, only bigger, brighter, and without the flicker. He studied the new toy in half-grinning amazement while waiting for the squeals from his conniving friends to cease, or subside enough for him to be heard.

"Where'd you get this? It's absolutely incredible."

Using a twig to scrape the greatest portion of manure from the seat of his trousers, Wylie answered, "I picked it up in the city last week. It's a glow stick." After another comedic intermission, he went on, "Once a person bends and breaks the glass inner tube, a chemical reaction between two different fluids causes it to glow. It's supposed to be a temporary emergency light lasting only a few hours before fading out."

As they were traipsing back to the cottage, the air was filled with every comment he could have expected from them.

"Ya should've seen the look on your face!"

"I thought you were going to beat me to death!"

"I was aimin' to pull that metal post out with the tractor, but ya did it for me!"

"It was so hard to keep from cracking up."

And best of all, they repeated his own threat: "If it comes any closer, I'm gonna lace the fucker." This brought another round of roaring. Seth chuckled along with them, knowing Wylie needed a hearty laugh on occasion, even if it was at his expense. Besides, other thoughts were occupying his mind as the glow stick guided their return. His bruised toe had awakened from its adrenaline coma, and, more important, he needed to figure out how he could improve on the clever scheme these two jokers had hatched. It begged the question: who would be the next victim? Better yet, victims?

Walking one behind the other, they found their way to the cottage and went around back. Once they were there, a sizable deck offered ample seating to continue the ribbing or indignity, depending on the person. As Wylie popped open several aluminum lawn chairs, he solicited Wade to get them a soda from the fridge. "Cold bottles are in the back, and bring the oatmeal cookies on top!"

Seth recalled the pie his mother had sent along and parted company, flipping the glow stick onto Wylie's lap as he passed. "Be back in a sec." When he returned, they were laughing up a storm again—this time over the total success of their plot and the glow stick that made it possible. He handed Wylie the peach casserole, which had once been a perfect wedge of pie. The work gloves might've leveled the plate, but inertia didn't allow it to stay in place. Taking the corner at the end of Wylie's driveway had sent it crashing into the passenger door.

"What happened to it?" asked Wylie.

"It flew across the seat as I was rushing over to help a friend in need. Should still be good though."

"I mean your foot, Slugger. Your mom's pie is always good."

Watching as Wylie peeled off the plastic wrap and dug around for a plastic fork, Seth seized the opportunity to retort. It was sarcastic humor that tended to keep their friendship lively, and most everything was vulnerable to attack. "If you must know, Shitpants, Delma stepped on it today. Not that it would've stopped you from pulling a fast one on me anyway."

Wylie was too involved in stuffing his piehole to pay Seth any mind. The remark managed to elicit only a slight grin from Wade, who appeared equally content with oatmeal cookies. Seth yielded to the priority of their sugar break and quietly stared into the lime-green phosphorescence. He wondered how he could be fooled so completely. Although the novelty of Wylie's glow stick had played the primary role, it was evident that timing and location were also critical to the overall believability.

Even in his young life, there were plenty of things that aroused concern for him and his friends: Vietnam, civil rights, assassinations, nuclear proliferation. It could be so overwhelming. Distraction came by way of a fevered space race, and planet Earth was watching when *Apollo 11* landed America on the moon first. Who could forget Armstrong's words as he set foot from the Eagle, "That's one small step for man; one giant leap for mankind." Modern technology had launched a new era in human evolution and with it a heightened feeling that anything was possible. The likelihood of alien visitations seemed no less probable than human beings' own inclinations to do the same. Wylie's orange light was only one of countless reported sightings around the world, collectively increasing awareness of the UFO phenomena. It'd be safe to say that many more were tilting their heads upward in curiosity. Not only was the historical timing magnificent, the venue was equally so.

Wylie's unsettling location, at night, evoked the supernatural. It taunted skeptics and created doubt in nonbelievers. Over the last few years, they had spent scores of summer nights stargazing from chaise lounges huddled in the courtyard. Though reclining guests had an overhead portal to the stars, the general consensus was that it was more likely something weird would come out of the woods. Many had been caught actually looking over their shoulders. No one could deny the creepiness of Wylie's farm after sunset or its tendency to feed the imagination—whether it was with aliens, ghosts, or monsters.

Time and location were available still and waiting to be utilized again. It was clear that Wylie's dramatics were convincing, as was Wade's alien illusion. That being said, with some modification the hoax could be much more convincing. The next question seemed to be: did Wylie have any more of those glow sticks? And if not, could he get some?

Wade sat leisurely slouching, his enormous blond Afro making his head thrice the size of an average one. With a glow stick perverting any distinction between them, the creature he portrayed simply appeared to have a huge skull. Little doubt it had scored high when they were plotting their treachery. Experience informed Seth that Wade, son of a livestock auctioneer, was a good neighbor to Wylie and readily available should he need help with a herd that was obviously more cherished as pets than as a source of income. It was righteous that Wade's burgeoning recognition as Oakton's starting quarterback in no way altered their friendship or the time spent fostering it.

Like a lion's roar after a kill, lengthy and proud, a whopping, carbonation-fueled belch tore open the glutted silence. Wade beamed at the sheer volume of his feat, and facing Seth with a wide smile so customary to his identity, he remarked, "It was all Wylie's idea. I just happened to be the first person he showed it to."

"That may be true, but you were every bit as game as I was. And anyway, Seth would've wanted to do the same to either of us had he found them first." Looking at Seth, he asked, "Ain't that right?"

"Ya damn straight, and without any hesitation whatsoever. By the way, have any more of those glow sticks on hand?"

A sinister grin stretched across Wylie's face at the very thought of a repeat performance. "I know what you're thinking. The answer is yes, a whole fistful of them."

Seth went on, "Well, now that you've waded into the shallow end of the pool …" He glanced at the captivated jock. "No pun intended, what you say we take a dive in the deep end? If we use a friendly end-of-summer cookout as pretense, I bet we could round up a whole bunch of people to scare, and all in one glorious shot. My little brother could be an extra alien. It's been said two bobbleheads are better than one. Can't you guys see it? Everybody will be sitting around in lawn chairs, sucking on beers, talking about UFOs, and then bam! Greetings, Earthlings."

Wylie's excitement seemed to double with every word spoken. Chiming in at full throttle, he added, "I can rig a light behind the hill in the back forty. A few more steps down the spooky cow path and our aliens could come out of a hidden spaceship. It's perfect. I was gonna turn the girls loose back there anyway. Thanks to you guys, I already have plenty of hay in the loft."

Seth pressed on. "With a little further planning, we could really scare the daylights out of our chosen ones. That's something I can be sure of."

Wade wasn't as enthusiastic; for it was he who'd faced the business end of a metal fence post. "Great! Not just one crazy person swinging what amounts to a battle-ax, but an angry mob grabbing whatever they can find. Why don't ya pass out guns and ammunition? Then, with any luck, I can have an open casket."

Both Wylie and Seth reassured him that anything in the area capable of being used as a weapon could also be removed. As for firearms, there were only a few of them, and they'd be stashed in a safe place, far from anxious hands. It was also understood that they shouldn't pick anyone suspected of having a heart condition, like older people, for obvious reasons. Taking these precautions against potential hazards eased Wade into willing participation. The game was on.

Preliminary duties were mutually agreed upon, and thus Project

Big Scare was set in motion. Wylie would concentrate on location, securing a light source, eliminating potential weapons, and providing a clear flight path, which excluded the promising humor of slippery cow pies. Wade was responsible for costume design and the choreography of the alien advance. Nate would hopefully be his loyal apprentice. Seth's attention targeted the sequence of events during execution—things such as timing, communication, and containment. A frightened driver on the twists and turns of River Road could result in tragedy. Any further suggestions, along with nominations of prey, would be discussed when they met on Sunday at Wylie's. Consent stipulated that all decisions concerning Project Big Scare (PBS) were to be unanimous.

Seth stood and lumbered toward the patio steps. "It's been a long day; it's time for me to turn in." With a flip of his hand, he gestured for them to follow him toward the pickup. "Incidentally, did either of you see glow sticks being sold around town?"

Wylie said he hadn't, which was why he had snatched them when he was in the city. That didn't mean there weren't any in town, just that he hadn't seen any. Wade went into town more often because of football practice and knew of no place that carried them. He'd checked after Wylie showed him the original.

With a sigh of relief, Seth resumed. "PBS would be doomed from the start if any of our chumps were wise to glow sticks. It also means you can't be blabbing to anyone about the terror you put me through; that'd jeopardize our plan. We'll have enough insiders to get the job done."

"We can have fun with it after PBS. Can't we, Wylie?"

Wylie looked at Seth yet spoke to Wade. "Suppose we could, but after PBS, it won't compare. Seth lucks out."

As they gathered beside Seth's truck, Wade held the glow stick firmly and plied his trade. "Pep rally." He urged them to put their hands on top of his glowing fist and began to chant. "PBS! PBS! PBS!" With each beat of a letter, he thrust his fist downward, gathering momentum as well as team support until the fevered pitch culminated in a primal howl—unmistakably the battle cry for Oakton's Timber Wolves. Seth's tired body was revived; Wylie's youth was restored; and Wade was pumped with the excitement of it all.

In the birth of conspiracy, there comes a fleeting moment when members exchange devilish grins of overconfidence—or at least with this plan there was. The "nothing can go wrong" attitude devoured a mass of three in one chomp and then spewed them on their way. Wade slapped the glow stick into Wylie's palm and accepted a ride home with the farmer. Agent provocateur and master of deception, Wylie retired to his dusky hollow.

"Drop me off at the end of the driveway," Wade mumbled as they neared his home. "I can walk up."

Sensing his friend's rebounding uncertainty, Seth questioned him with care. "Are you okay with the project? I mean, we really haven't done anything yet."

"I'm okay with it. Why? You aren't going to weasel out on us, are ya?"

"Not a chance."

"I figure you'll be watching my back pretty close, considering your little brother will be out there with me." Gently closing the truck's door, Wade began his walk to the family ranch.

"You can be sure I'll stop it if things start to get hairy. There're football games to be won, and Nate and I want to see them."

There were many practical jokes that made the rounds in a locker room, most of which were cruel—atomic balm in the jockstrap, the snap of a wet towel, athletic tape ripping out body hair, and savage titty twisters, to name a few. PBS was something different. It'd be perceived as a life-or-death situation, and there was no telling what a person would do under those conditions. Seth knew this much: whatever it was he had gotten mixed up in, he was committed to seeing it through. And see this project through he would, right to the very end.

CHAPTER 2

Adam let his son sleep in the following morning. It provided an opportunity for him to work more closely with the youngest and for Mother to pamper the eldest. Usually, it was the other way around. Although a labor shortage slowed their pace, they'd finished milking and were marching up the porch steps to the essence of flapjacks and sausage. There was no need to say anything, a mutual "Mmmm" sufficed. They promptly kicked off their barn boots before entering. The kitchen was Martha's realm, and cow poop violations made Delma's vengeance pale by comparison. That part of the barn stayed in the barn; she'd have none of it. House slippers were provided inside the door to help save wear and tear on socks—an idea still in the early stages of development.

Socks to floor, Adam skated over to his wife and lavished her with smooches to the earlobe. Her giggles echoed approval while her hands ushered him away from the hot stove.

"You two go wash before you even think of taking something off the table. Adam, would you please call Seth down for breakfast." The strategy was simple. Father would distract while sons confiscated enough for three mouthfuls. Sometimes, she'd let them win. Today wasn't one of those times.

Nate slipped by his dad and paused at the banister, chuckling through stealth. Adam grinned and then barked up the stairway. "Seth ... Seth!"

"Okay, Pa," he garbled out of a sound sleep.

"Get up! Sun's burnin' a hole in the roof."

Seth sat up and rubbed clarity into his blurred vision. It was near seven o'clock, a shocking realization to a farmer's biological hourglass. Fastening his jeans devolved into a struggle with a zipper that refused to accommodate his occasional morning arousal. That finally accomplished, he finagled his way toward the bathroom and yelled down the staircase in passing, "Be down in a minute!" Hopefully, splashes of cold water on his face would relax his trouser trooper and save him from a potentially embarrassing approach to the breakfast table.

Pa and Nate were into a half-dozen links and a full stack before Seth pulled himself up to the table. His mother had waited for him to arrive. Rather than be first to speak, he barehanded four warm flapjacks and stabbed as many links with his fork.

Not too proud to begin, Adam passed Seth the maple syrup. "How's the foot today?"

"I should be able to work the field. There isn't much left to second-crop anyway."

Adam took a sip of coffee before handing down his verdict. "After hashing it over with your mother, I figure your brother and I can handle what's left."

Nate snickered through a heaping maw. "Pa and I'll strap on the harness until your poor little owie gets all better."

"Don't tease your brother," said Martha. "Never know who Delma might step on next."

A nose up at the assailant and Seth was ready to plead his case. "Aww, come on, Pa. There must be something I can do." Judging by the look on his father's face, he was talking to the wrong person, a suspicion that was confirmed when his mother spoke.

"Hmm, let me see ... You could read some of the books you've collected or work on your airplane model; perhaps help me in the kitchen from time to time."

"Sounds like I'm going to be down for a week." He had been kidding himself to think otherwise. She'd gotten a good look at his toe the night before and had consequently given Pa the lowdown; the patriarch had personal experience in such matters. Protest was futile. He'd be lucky if it was only one week. Fortunately, the second-crop hay was almost done and chopping corn was some time off.

Wickman and son slowly got up from their chairs. Sluggishness would soon be worn off. Giving Seth a burly squeeze to the shoulder, Adam skirted around the table and planted a kiss on his wife's cheek. This type of appreciation would never become a chore. With a belly pat and a "Good wood, Martha darl'n," he snatched his cap. "Nate, grab the ice bucket or we'll be lickin' sweat. Ya think ya can keep up with the ole man?"

"I'll give it a try; that's all a horse can do."

Watching his father push open the screen door with young Nate close behind took Seth back several years. He couldn't help but feel excitement for his brother, despite the aggravation as of late. It'd be a mistake to tell him about PBS until it was absolutely necessary. The kid didn't need anything that'd take his mind away from moving machinery, unpredictable cows, and one-on-one with Pa.

Martha began to take away the breakfast dishes, being careful not to remove portions her son might wish to devour. It was unusual for Seth to still be present, but there he sat, choosing thumb and forefinger to erase a milky mustache. He did wipe his fingers off on the napkin instead of his pants or shirt sleeve. This time, for Martha, it was close enough.

"Did Wylie like the pie?" she asked with the concern of a housewife missing a compliment and a plate.

"Wylie loves your cooking. He gobbled it down first thing. Forgot your plate, sorry. I'll get it tomorrow." He hoped she wouldn't ask what it was Wylie needed help with, because he didn't know what he'd say. Maybe if he were to offer a bit more information, she wouldn't ask. "Wade was at Wylie's last night and needed a ride home." *How dumb could he be?* he immediately wondered. Wylie could've given him a ride home.

"Hasn't Wylie found a young lady to cook for him yet?"

Seth felt like he'd just dodged a wild pitch and was quick to answer. "I suppose when the right girl happens by, although, if he gets cooking like yours every now and again, it might take awhile." He kicked back on the rear legs of his chair, haughty in his recovery.

"Once heard a story about a young fellow that liked to rock back and forth on his chair, much like you're doing now. One day, he fell backward and cracked his head open on the floor. Grief-stricken relatives buried him three days later."

He immediately leveled his chair. "No foolin', Ma?"

"It could've happened, provided a concerned party didn't say something."

"I know; if you've told me once, you've told me a hundred times, but that story will stick like a tick."

"Hope so—we don't need a head injury too. Give me a few minutes; I'd like to straighten your room."

"Have at it. I won't be going anywhere."

His room was at the top of the stairs, and even though Nate's was closer to their bathroom, he could monopolize the stairwell. The ability to slow down a fervent sibling at will was a constant source of horseplay. As far as rooms went, Seth's was quite plain. A door panel served as a workbench/desk. It was not particularly crafty; however, paint made it look better, and it was as sturdy as a hog pen. Books stacked on either side were mostly reference and had been promised a shelf all their own someday. In the breeze of an open window, two balsa-wood models teetered on strands of fishing line. The Wright Flyer and Curtiss Jenny preceded his work in progress: Lindbergh's *Spirit of St. Louis*. That'd be hung by the Cardinal pennant. Outside of these things, only a small dresser and single bed broke up the empty walls. Martha had tried to help with sheer curtains and a plaid throw at the end of his bed. Any more than that, she knew, and there'd be grumbling.

As Seth entered his room, no less than three feather pillows lay on a tightly tucked bed—two for his head and one for his foot. It was more inviting than an airplane model, so he put on a clean T-shirt and slipped into Oakton Football shorts, a confidential perk from Wade. He put his dirty jeans on the desk chair and selected a book about Charles Lindbergh. Lounging contentedly on down pillows and morning air, he wanted to believe the billowing elm outside his window wouldn't succumb to the same disease that had decimated a once tree-lined Main Street in Oakton. It furnished shade from an afternoon sun and a pleasant rustle when wind passed through its leaves. The tree was a friend—silent in criticism, generous in bounty, and always there.

With a gentle knock and a smile, Martha entered carrying the ice she had promised. Her expression changed upon examination of her son's injury. "My goodness, young man, you may lose that toenail. Can you wiggle it for me?"

"Sure can. ... See ... It's swollen some and a bit colorful, but not busted. At least it doesn't have the inner sting my finger had when I tried to barehand a ground ball."

"And here I thought that's what they made baseball gloves for. It shows you what I know."

Thanking her for the ice pack, Seth placed it as he liked. "You do all right, Ma. Always have."

His mother paused to collect his soiled jeans. "Now, if there's anything you'd like, I'll be within earshot," she said and then smartly went about her business.

Most of the morning, Seth spent reading about transatlantic flight and kidnapping, stopping at times to mull over possible victims for PBS. The problem was he couldn't think of anyone he'd want to put through what he went through. Maybe the Moeller twins, Alec and Thomas, but odds were high that Wade would choose them. They played football together. He dozed past lunch, and Martha brought soup and a sandwich to him an hour later. Having not worked up much of an appetite, he picked at it as he assembled his monoplane. It was a long afternoon, and he caught himself checking the clock often, listening for the rumble of farm machinery or the distant bellows of Delma. By five o'clock, he decided to scoot out to the barn and see how things were coming along, if he could get by security.

"And just where do you think you're going?" demanded Martha. She'd caught him trying and failing miserably to tiptoe across her kitchen floor, hobbled as he was.

"I thought I'd hop out to check on those two. There's no telling what kinda trouble they're getting into."

"Not for awhile, your father insisted on that. He'd only send you back in. You can relax on the porch swing if you like. I'll bring you another ice pack and some lemonade. How does that sound?"

"Do I have a choice?"

Removed from the picture, Seth watched father and son walk in from chores. That morning, Nate had followed the leader into field labor. Now he returned walking side by side with his father, equal in accomplishment and proud of it. He'd earned the right of passage that signified his ability to work as hard as any man, notwithstanding the need for additional body weight and a safety razor. As they climbed the steps, Seth straightened his posture and downed the last swallow of lemonade. Afternoon temperatures had molded the ice pack around his foot. He knew he must've appeared comfortable, and that made him feel uncomfortable.

Nate stood tall beside his father and, with hands on hips, proclaimed, "Well, well, well, haven't you got it made in the shade with lemonade." Initiation into manhood didn't shroud his feelings toward his big brother.

Seth would have to do something about that.

"Go wash for supper," Adam ordered and then stepped closer to Seth and asked, "Do ya mind if I have a look-see?"

"It looks worse than it is." The injury that had created more work for others offered him only these few positive words worth speaking.

"Nasty bruise. Reckon we'll give it a spell yet. Not to worry; hay's in. Your brother and I can handle chores."

"How'd Nate do today?"

Adam took the empty glass off the railing. "He did good. Don't think Delma thought as much though. When all's said and done, she just might treat ya better."

Nate was out the screen door before it could close behind Pa, forgoing an appearance of disinterest in favor of getting a peek at the injury. This was prime time for Seth to try to correct his brother's behavior. He slowly lowered his foot to the floor and pulled on the sock that hadn't a foot in it already, making sure Nate got an eyeful. By squinting in agony while attempting to stand and then falling back on his ass in failure, he brought complete attention to his disability.

Struck with compassion, Nate rushed to his aid. "Put your arm over my shoulder, and I'll help you up."

He reached out for that help and employed the necessary dead weight to persuade the younger boy of the genuineness of his need. Whimpering in a broken voice, he said, "You're such a, ka … ka … kind brother. …But you smell like shit. For God's sake, take a bath."

His arm draped in such a way as to permit a loose headlock; he finished it off with a light knuckle rub to the crown.

Easily pulling away, Nate danced around in his traditional slap-boxing offensive. "You want a piece of me? Come on. I'll give ya a piece, Gimpy."

Their rocky relationship seemed reborn through playful provocation. They thought the day couldn't get any better. Mother's pot roast would prove them wrong.

After supper, Adam thanked his lovely bride and retired to his recliner and the evening news. Martha instructed Nate to take a bath for God's sake, causing another round of laughter. Seth revived a sense of contribution by assisting with the dishes. His mother washed while he dried, and it was his dry hands that could answer the phone the quickest.

"Hello, Kelly's Bar; Kelly speaking."

Martha shook her head, another example of his father's words of wisdom that forced confusion. Naive callers usually hung up and tried calling back, assuming they'd gotten the wrong number. The experienced would humor the old crow, eventually having their request granted.

"You're beginning to sound more and more like your ole man every day. Who is this Kelly anyway?"

"I don't know." Seth shrugged as if it could be heard over the phone. "He must be crazy with the heat." Seth figured the cliché went for naught into Wade's unseasoned ear.

"Not as crazy as my ole man for letting me use the Buick tonight. How 'bout I swing by in an hour?"

"I'll be ready." He'd been cooped up all day, and as long as he agreed to stay off his feet, his parents shouldn't raise too much fuss. It was Nate he worried about, especially considering their recent bonding, but a third wheel, and a thirteen-year-old brother at that, didn't improve his odds with the ladies. In fact, it'd murder any possibility.

"Ma, Wade has the car tonight and wants me to go riding around with him. Would it be all right if I went?"

"Wade's got the car? I wonder how he managed that one." She paused before continuing. "What does a mother have to do to get you to stay off that foot, shackle you to the bed?"

"I'd sooner chew it off at the ankle." On a more serious note, he said, "It's Saturday night, and we're just going to be cruising around."

"I suppose, if your father approves."

This was as good as a yes, because his father would nearly repeat those same words from behind his newspaper.

That having gone as expected, Seth lay on his bed impatiently waiting to use the bathroom. Brother Dear had decided on an upstairs shower over a downstairs bath and wasn't setting any speed records. His cue came when Nate looked in on him, just to check, and scampered down to see what Pa had on the tube. A shave, a shower, a splash of musk, and he was set to go. His best chance of avoiding a crushing scene like last night's would be to sneak by Nate and hang out at drive's end. Relying on sneakers, one healthy foot, and handrails, he was able to skip steps six and seven. Those were the squeaky ones that often gave away his position. Once at the landing, he crept toward the living room. Ma had vacated the kitchen, current whereabouts unknown. Pa was shifting his eyes between the television and newspaper. Much to his surprise, Nate was sound asleep on the couch. Apparently, a full day's work took every ounce of energy the kid had. He eased the door shut and was off without a hitch.

Wade stopped on the roadside as Seth gingerly covered the driveway on foot. He knew Wade was accustomed to all kinds of injuries given his sports background. Anything less than a broken bone or torn ligament was to be tolerated without complaint. He didn't want Wade to think he was a whiner. Their ride into town began with elbows out windows and a "Forward ho!" They were tempted to stop in at Wylie's, but the gate was closed, indicating their friend's need for privacy. Slowing down in passing was the closest they'd come to invading that privacy. It was enough to know that tomorrow would bring them together for the detailed planning of PBS.

"I wonder what Wylie's doing tonight," Seth said as they gained speed.

"Pay no attention to that man behind the curtain; the great and powerful gonads have spoken."

Seth wasn't sure if Wade was referring to Wylie's erotic urge or his own, so he moved the conversation ahead, content that it mattered little.

"Word has it Frank is pissed that you're going to be the team's starting quarterback this year." Frank LaRue, a senior, had been last year's backup at the position. Wade was a junior, and it'd be an understatement to say Frank felt cheated after paying his dues.

"Tough shit, it was Coach Willis's call, not mine."

"I ran into Alec and Thomas at their dad's feed mill a few days ago. They seem to feel the choice was a good one."

"Most players don't think as much, but I'll take whatever I can get, and those are two of the best."

Once they got to Oakton, Seth noticed a familiar service truck riding their bumper down Main Street. It could be no other than Alec and Thomas Moeller prompting them to meet them in the pharmacy parking lot. The twins parked their pickup alongside Wade's Buick, both sufficiently far back to avoid immediate detection but able to observe others cruising the main drag.

Leaning his head out, Thomas joked with Wade. "I see your daddy let you use the family car. You must've been a good boy."

"If I were that good, I'd know how you plan to squeeze a couple heifers between you and your ugly brother."

Alec laughed and countered from behind the wheel of a working man's transportation, "That's what the back is for. Why do you think they call it a pickup?"

Seth popped the fateful question. "Where's the party? Bowling alley has league play, and the streets are deserted. Something must be going on somewhere."

"A couple quarter barrels are being tapped right about now at Smelly Run. A buck will get you into where everybody else is at."

Thomas chimed in, "Why don't you guys follow us over there? That's where all the girls are."

Wade and Seth nodded, and the two-vehicle convoy rolled out of Oakton.

Paved road turned to gravel, which became a tractor path through the woods, before opening to a clearing by a narrow brook. Whether it was rotting fish along its bank, varied excretions from partiers, or cattle accessibility upstream, there was always a foul odor lingering about Smelly Run. This made it an ideal location, because nobody in their right mind would want to go there. As property of LaRue Real Estate, privacy was assured given the political influence of wealth. Raiding a Frank Junior party on family holdings could easily get a cop fired.

They parked the car and buckboard near the exit to avoid being hemmed in. It was no secret that the sporty coupe next to them belonged to Frank. A roaring campfire guided them toward clusters of dark figures milling about a circle of vehicles and music. Some people were able to fraternize between groups, but for most, the beer had yet to blur or sharpen class distinctions. A shapely sophomore, skintight in attire, seemed delighted to exchange plastic cups for dollar bills; her position was discernibly scrutinized by two lurking she devils. Seth figured Frank had wooed her into accepting the job, which could have such dire consequences given the two jealous women in her midst.

Alec and Thomas paid their fees and, after filling their cups, decided to hang around and flirt with the hostess. Seth and Wade moseyed over to a few fillies, whose acquaintance dated back to Sunday school. Seth considered how bold they must seem to Frank and his followers, showing up uninvited and then hiding behind a flock of choir girls, as if that could possibly avert a confrontation. Be that as it may, it was just the medicine a sore toe and a bruised ego needed. The girls were as giddy as, well, schoolgirls drinking beer.

It wasn't too long before Wade parted from the group. Seth followed close behind, sensing something much more imminent than nature's call could feasibly justify. Walking past Alec and Thomas, who were still teasing the affections of the beer vendor, they wove their way around cars in search of a private place to relieve their bladders. With a couple shakes and a zip, they turned around to face Frank's penetrating glare. All except one of his cohorts were posted about vehicles like traffic cops keeping curious onlookers at a distance. It was that one bodyguard at Frank's side, that one mammoth frame tempered in his father's lumberyard, that posed the greatest threat: Talbot Sager.

"Who the hell invited you, Hotchner?" Frank snapped.

"Your girlfriend mumbled something about it, but her mouth was full at the time."

Tal moved closer only to be held in check with the back of Frank's hand. Seth in turn stepped forward, demonstrating his allegiance, yet wondering how Wade's comment could possibly warrant it.

"It looks like we got a fuckin' clown here, Tal."

"It's that pubic hair on his head. Maybe we should call him Pubie the Clown."

Wade skipped over Tal's insult and delivered a sobering threat to Frank. "I just have to hold off Tallywacker long enough for Seth to break your fingers. Would ya have a problem with that, Seth?"

"Not at all. Can I break a couple of the gorilla's fingers too?"

Visibly infuriated by the farmhand's mockery, Tal looked at Frank. Seth watched as the anger and arrogance on Frank's face melted into doubt and dismay; tension filled seconds ticked by at a snail's pace. Finally, Wade spoke up.

"Then none of us will be playing. The trouble here is that I won the position fair and square, and you don't like it. Well, Frankie Baby, that's just too bad. So it's best to get with the program if ya want any passes to come your way."

With Tal's temper on the verge of detonation, Seth silently reached out in thought, hoping to defuse a situation that would challenge his injury to the utmost. "Those two Casanovas are cutting it a bit close. Now would be a good time."

Just then Alec breeched the conflict. "What's goin' on here?"

It was an enormous relief for Seth when the Moellers showed and he suspected for Frank too by the words he'd dealt.

"It's nothing that two mill rats need know about." He pulled a wad of bills from his pocket, peeled off four dollars, and threw them at the feet of his rivals. "I didn't invite you punks, so take your money and get off my property. Come on, Tal; it stinks of cow shit around here."

Tal growled his parting words, "I'll be seeing ya in practice, Hotchner," and then pointed at Seth, saying nothing but showing plenty.

They all watched Frank and Tal withdraw to a crowd forming by the beer taps, casting sharpened eyes over their shoulders before pushing their way through.

"Damn," Wade said. "I'd hoped to resolve the problem instead of making it worse. Now what do we do?"

Seth split the oppressed silence. "Huh ... Stinks of cow shit around here? It's Smelly Run for Pete's sake. I was trying to fit in." Turning to Wade with half a grin, he said, "You just had to go and call him Tallywacker, didn't ya?" His comments lifted them from degradation.

"That was for calling me Pubie the Clown. Can you imagine that? I don't look anything of the sort." Wade fluffed his hair and flashed his big smile.

"You called him Tallywacker?" Alec laughed.

"Nobody calls him that, at least not to his face," added Thomas.

"I could be going out on a limb with this one, but I get the impression we're not welcome here," Wade joked. "Please, somebody tell me I'm wrong."

Alec somberly agreed. "Frank and Tal won't let this go. A few more beers, a few more guys, and they'll be back."

By mutual accord, and in a bold act of defiance, they'd leave the same way they came—right through the middle of everything. Four dollars on the ground were of no more importance than the urine it had paid for, so off they went. The crowd was thickening, and it hummed with excitement, not at their approach, but rather from one word shouted by an anonymous loudmouth, "Catfight!"

Alec and Thomas looked at one another and then spoke as one, "Sara." They forced their way into the hoard of rubbernecks.

Seth and Wade knew which girl the twins were referring to. It was the sexy little barmaid, and she was, without doubt, the target of those evil harlots they'd seen earlier; they had a reputation that preceded them wherever they went.

As all four barged into the arena, one girl was double-clenching Sara's long, dark hair and dragging her buttocks across the ground. Sara's hands were wrapped around the wrists of the attacker in a frenzied attempt to ease the painful jerking. Another girl was wrenching at the white T-shirt that covered her bare breasts and taking sloppy potshots at liberty. Alec was all over the hair-puller, pressing on the soft spot between thumb and index finger to get her to release her grip. Thomas bear-hugged the other and slung her aside, her dogged hold ripping Sara's shirt in the process. While the Moellers whisked their anguished friend from harm's way, Seth and Wade fended off the ranting and raving of two very nasty bitches.

The tallest of the pair shouted at the top of her lungs, "That sleazy little whore thinks she's so hot, shaking her tits and ass in front of our boyfriends. The slut deserves everything she's got coming to her, and more."

The other, who was considerably heavier, attempted to get past Wade while delivering a throaty warning, "Get outta my fuckin' way, clodhopper, or else."

Wade's steely eyed response and rooted stance backed her into submission. "Or else what?"

Seth locked eyes with Frank and Tal as they roared with contemptible glee over their chivalry before shifting his attention to the matter at hand.

Having yelled above the profanity still gushing from the girls in front of him, Wade's words hit home. "This is wrong, and all you guys know it. How could ya stand there and do nothing?"

Once again, Seth glanced over at Frank and his loyal football subjects. To his surprise, scattered here and there, was the undeniable face of shame, a noticeable breakdown in Frank's iron curtain of control. Maybe some benefit could come of this.

Keeping a wary eye on the witch in front of him, Seth quickly scanned the reactions of the others attending the evening's festivities. His inspiration was short-lived. There was a darker side of humanity that shone brighter in the blaze of a campfire. Some athletes, keepers of social order, laughed while encouraging frontal nudity. A few cheerleaders plied their trade, goading the hard women to continue their assault. The morbidly aroused lingered closest, seeking a detailed view of the action. Still others were kicked back on the hoods of their old beaters, casually sucking suds and enjoying the attack as if it were a drive-in movie, jeering at the Moellers' noble deed as if it had robbed them of their entertainment dollar. The greasers who had transported the vicious females, for whatever reason, lit up their ritual cigarettes of noninvolvement. Most disturbing were the playful girls from church, who looked down their noses at the stranger who wore no bra. There was nothing good about this scene, nothing at all.

Back at their vehicles, Thomas was helping Sara into the truck while Alec hustled to meet with his returning backup. "She's a bit shaken, but I think she'll be all right. We're gonna take her home."

"Excellent idea. I think that's our cue too," said Seth. "There's no telling what'll happen next."

"Thanks for the help."

"Same here," Wade replied. "It didn't look good for us either until you and your brother stepped in."

After Wade fired up his father's car and dropped it in gear, he spun a layer of dust along the side of Frank's baby-blue Chevelle. "The dumb ass shouldn't have left his windows open." He followed the pickup out to the paved road and then parted directions with a couple toots, taking the roundabout way to River Road. Should Frank form a posse, they'd assume that he and Seth would take the more direct route. Once they felt at ease, with no headlights behind them, Wade expressed the unusual considering his view regarding minor injuries. "So tell me, how's your foot doin'?"

Mildly taken aback, Seth answered, "It'll be all right. How could you have known it wouldn't be a millstone?"

"I didn't know, but neither did they, because you covered it up well; even I could hardly tell it bothered you. It wouldn't matter anyway. I've seen you throw a bale of hay farther than Frank throws a football."

Seth knew of Wade's intrasquad rivalry, yet he hadn't been privy to the true extent of the hostility. He'd have wanted Wade to confide in him much sooner than this. The no-whining policy must've had something to do with it. Seth let it slide for the time being. "How'd you ever think of a nickname like Tallywacker?"

"Wise guys like him need a nickname because they sure as hell got one for everybody else. That one seemed perfect for the prick."

Toning his laughter down, Seth asked, "And what name have you given me?"

A brief period of stoic observation and Wade returned his eyes to the road. "I never had cause to call you anything other than Seth, even if you are the furry-headed offspring of a Holstein humper. I love ya like a pet. Just don't go gettin' all sloppy on me."

Seth couldn't contain himself and struggled to squeeze off a feeble comeback. "Okay, Pubie."

Not many of the things that had occurred within the previous hour would have tolerated their brand of humor. Sticking to those things that did made it a short trip home and readied them for a solid night's sleep.

Door open, Seth mentioned to his chauffeur, "You shouldn't have kept me in the dark about those two. It's not whining; it's leveling the playing field."

"I'll try and work on it, Coach, and thanks for being there."

"Who's getting all sloppy on whom?" Seth smiled and took his leave.

With no one around to point out his weakness, he limped to the steps' railing and made use of it. There was a difference between him trying to hide his injury and Wade keeping such an obvious threat as Frank and Tal to himself. What that distinction was, he couldn't say, only that it was there. Seth was glad to have been at his friend's side and committed himself to maintaining his position, particularly when school started. Alec and Thomas would have to keep their guard up during practice; in this, he trusted.

CHAPTER 3

Sunday morning began like any other day of the week: up before dawn, coffee brewing, toast and juice, and then chores. Holy day or not, cows needed to be looked after. Seth was awakened by Nate's call to rise and felt rejected in his convalescence. Prior to yesterday, he couldn't remember the last time his name wasn't sounded or his brother dashing unimpeded down the stairway. It'd be smart to wait fifteen minutes for them to finish their light meal and pull on work boots. He wasn't any happier about missing chores than Nate would be about his slick move into town—left-behind feelings didn't need a visual to exist. What was he to do with two hours until breakfast? After the previous night's recreation, perhaps he'd have a nice warm bath to soak his foot in.

It was an old porcelain tub with short clawed legs and contoured for relaxation. Mother went to great lengths to keep it gleaming white. He lowered himself inch by inch into therapeutic euphoria, high tide eventually covering him to the neck. Given the fast-paced life of a teenager, he used that tub much less than he would've liked. His foot kept thanking him for it.

The aroma of bacon found an empty stomach behind a closed door. Seth didn't know how long he'd lain in limbo, but it was long enough to cool bathwater. Having forgotten to collect a change of clothes, he wrapped a towel around his waist and opened the door. There they sat neatly folded at his feet. When it came to domestic needs, his mother was always a step ahead of him. Yelling above the sizzling fatback, he acknowledged her insight. "Thanks, Ma!"

At the kitchen table were three basted eggs drained of grease, likewise the bacon, and a stack of toast. A jar of store-bought grape jelly teased his palate. Three crispy strips folded into toast and jelly was a breakfast sandwich he never grew tired of. The desired components of a salty-sweet combination was a matter of to each his own. Pa had a stash of gumdrops and Spanish peanuts in his desk drawer, and there was no end to soda and potato chips at school. His way made it easy to sop up broken egg yolks.

"That was really good." Using a napkin to wipe off his mouth this time, he decided he wouldn't spoil progress by leaning back on his chair. "Is there anything I can help you with?"

She glanced out the window before cracking half a dozen eggs to simmer. "Why yes, you could start peeling those apples on the counter." She figured a basketful should keep him occupied while she fed the rest of her family.

Adam and Nate engaged in a frisky struggle for the bathroom sink. Results were a satisfying draw. Seth kept paring his way to usefulness, and the cook began cutting those that were skinned.

"Nate, after you're finished with breakfast, I'd like you to get dressed for church."

"Aww … Do I have to, Ma? Seth doesn't."

"Once you've been confirmed, as your brother has, then you may decide if forsaking the Lord is wise. Church is where I met your father, without whom you would not be."

Seth continued peeling in silence. Like his father's, Seth's attendance was as scarce as a hen's teeth and made commenting on the subject inadvisable. With his back to the action, he thought about what she had said. Not going didn't mean abandoning religion, just the building. It seemed to him a heart of gold wouldn't confine itself within stained glass, distorting its true brilliance to outsiders; neither would it hide behind fortress doors and stone walls, being defensive in nature. Did his mother mean that good marriages began with church? He recalled the choir girls from the night before and concluded her rationale to be somewhat flawed. His parents were lucky; they just happened to meet at God's house—or man's version of it.

Nate bellyached his way upstairs; Adam went for news; and Martha resumed spreading apple slices in a baking pan. The final piece of fruit rewarded the peeler; all else was sprinkled with cinnamon and covered in a crumbly mixture of flour, sugar, and butter. An hour of cooking gave her time to get ready for church before setting it out to cool. As always, her husband would drive their car up front and see her off safe, and then he'd steal away to undertake one of the many things on his long to-do list.

Best for Seth to hold tight the couch and watch television until the parishioners had departed. Most often, he'd join his father in the barn but not this Sunday.

"It's time for us to get going, Nate." Martha straightened the waist belt of her cheerful dress. White flats and matching purse complemented her wholesome appearance.

"I'm on my way down, Ma."

She strode to the archway and looked in on Seth and *The Three Stooges*. "Don't forget to take the apple crisp I have set aside for Wylie. It's on the counter."

"Soitenly," Seth answered without taking his eyes away from the sadistic antics on TV. It wasn't a program his mother condoned because of the violent content. Slapstick mixed with idiocy times three actually reinforced the absurdity of violence, Seth thought. It didn't inspire imitation—knuckle rubs excluded. Mass media offered the real thing, warfare at home and abroad. Horrible pictures and shocking sound bites emphasized body counts and created images that lasted forever. In ten minutes, the Stooges would disappear behind daily life. "Disorder in the Court" might be foolish, but it wasn't depressing. He watched them through before he gave Wade a call. Wade's younger sister, Anna, answered.

"Hey there, Anna. How ya doin'?"

"I'm doing fine, Seth, and yourself?"

"Fine, fine as frog's hair. Speaking of hair, is Wade around?" Seth knew she was infatuated with him, yet his mind's eye still saw his friend's pudgy sibling in baggy clothes as the little sister he never had.

The few times he'd seen her over summer presented no clues to her changing body.

She called for her brother and returned for more. "We're about to leave for church. Are you going?"

"Unfortunately not today," he humbly stated for her benefit. "I'll be seeing you in school next week though."

"Yes, and as a freshman, I'll be nervous about finding my way around five hundred students."

"Don't go worrying about that. I'd be happy to show you where things are; just say the word."

"Thanks, it's nice to know you wouldn't ignore me. Here's Wade, and take care."

"You too, Anna darlin'." Only later did he realize his secondary reference to be Pa's. Wade was right; he was more a chunk off the old block than a chip.

Knowing Wade was committed to attending church, he made arrangements to meet at Wylie's afterward to discuss Project Big Scare. Their exchange was brief owing to timing and Anna's nearness. She'd be no less capable of bending an ear than Nate, and secrecy was vital to success. Wylie should be moving around by now, he figured. Why not bring him some apple crisp and get an early start on planning?

Once you were past the metal gate, a half acre of cow-trimmed lawn foreran two weeping willows either side of the lane. Their romance opened a doorway into Wylie's world. Inheritance allowed for an independent existence as well as a grim reminder of his parents' absence. Charm, wit, and good looks concealed a void created by the loss of his sole kin some five years prior. Only the very astute could detect his continued sorrow. At thirty-four years old, he seemed to have everything, and yet nothing.

Outbuildings were weathered in drab yellow without desire for a new winter coat. Ivy crept up the concrete silo, teasing an autumn sun to turn its leaves crimson. A corncrib leaned with age. Rust was fused together by a wagon wheel here, a whiskey barrel there, and a horse-drawn hand plow going nowhere. Although the homesteader preferred low-maintenance perennials, splotches of shade-loving impatiens flourished in a decrepit wheelbarrow, an old feeding trough, and the trunk of a vintage sedan.

Seth lifted his mother's baked goods from the passenger-side floorboard, a more secure placement than he'd used during his last transport, and followed Wylie's hand gesture inside. Enveloped with foliage, the cottage was predisposed to a darkened environment. Any light that did manage to get through proved inadequate to support healthy plants, a problem easily remedied with other life forms. The kitchen and what was once a dining room were partitioned by two fifty-five-gallon aquariums extending lengthwise from opposite walls. Heavy posts from floor to overhead beam framed access between rooms, parting a seascape dominated by angelfish. When illuminated, each natural setting became a moving picture of the underworld, and Wylie could sit for hours watching either flick.

Only one window faced north, and it was situated between refrigerator and aquarium. A roomy cage hung from the ceiling; it was home to Flip, a small green parrot with ruffled feathers and a stout bill. Known for vulgarity, the bird was just as apt to draw blood with his gaffed beak as with a string of rude words. It wasn't so much that Wylie intended to teach offensive language as it was that Flip impersonated his owner's lack of self-control. The parrot's recurrent squawking eventually reproduced low-tolerance phrases associated with keeping quiet. On the milder side, if they could be classified as such, were, "I'll kick your ass," and "Flip the Bird." He was a continuous source of amusement for most callers; however, the words he mimicked didn't truly reflect Wylie's feelings for him. He had a nice spot near the window, fish swimming to his left, crackers on the refrigerator to his right, and top billing among Wylie's cast of characters.

Seth made room for apple crisp on the cluttered snack bar, three stools reminding him of the once-complete family that had inhabited the place. Motherly knickknacks on the windowsill tempted a reluctant dishwasher but only to the extent of one flower-rimmed plate waiting to be returned. Foamless dishwater surrounded a mountain of bachelor's procrastination. Passing between fish tanks, he paused to tap the glass before entering the den. A small woodstove kept winter fuel bills low, and a rolltop desk opposite gave Wylie a cozy place to conduct business. A pair of inseparable lovebirds nestled in a corner cage, a charm of colorful finches in another. On exceptional days, patio doors allowed feathered friends easy transport to the deck, there to be entertained by nature's free flyers gathering at a birdfeeder and makeshift bath.

Then there was Buster, the last living terrier of a litter of five. As a younger pack, they'd strike panic in trespassers who dared set foot on their territory. Now, only Buster remained. His hazy blue eyes were blurred; gray hair speckled a brown coat; and a cyst the size of a baseball hung from his lower rib cage. At twenty-eight, he'd far outlived his family and tragically his masters as well. The crinkled snout and sharp white fangs of youth had given way to one dingy cuspid and a faint growl at a foreign scent. It was as much as he could muster from the comfort of his hairy pillow next to the woodstove. Those unfamiliar with Buster's excursion last winter considered him a prime candidate for euthanasia, never offering more than foul expressions or cruel comments. The few who were aware that Buster had fearlessly set out during a blizzard were of a different opinion. Drifting snow had piled much deeper than his legs could surmount so he'd used one of the trenches formed by Wylie's return from town. For three days, Wylie desperately searched until finally coming to the sad conclusion that Buster had simply chosen his own manner of death, like an aged Eskimo. A week later, Seth was helping Wylie push the last swath of a new snowfall away when Buster came trotting home. Obviously overwhelmed with emotion, Wylie called out for his cherished companion to come, and the dog hastened his gait. Tongue hanging from an open mouth that resembled a smile and tail wagging incessantly, the old dog bounced on stiff, bony legs about his kneeling master, affectionately licking the tears from his cheeks. Together, they returned to a blazing woodstove and as much soft food as the returning warrior desired. In seeking his death, Buster had found a zest for life. Seth honored their private moment while clearing the lump in his throat and then joined them in sublime reunion.

Upon notice of Wylie's preoccupation with watering plants on his deck, Seth crouched down to give Buster the attention he so deserved. A kind word and gentle touch brought him back upright, not the screech from that retched beast by the window. They cast evil eyes at one another, but Seth spoke first. "Flip sucks. Flip sucks." He'd been trying for quite some time to teach the little booger a new line. It hadn't caught on.

"Shut the fuck up." The parrot's insulting reply sent Seth on his way, discouraged and without a rebuttal.

Last but not least, two barn cats lounged on a cable spool / deck table, trusting Wylie wouldn't give them a squirt of water too. Elsie, sterile four years and counting, was white blotched with black. She looked like a miniature Holstein. Tony, as one would guess, was a tiger stripe with a thick neck and enormous paws. Although it had been suggested that they'd make a "Grrreat" breakfast commercial, cleaning themselves was at the bottom of their list, and hence they were not camera friendly. Forgoing appearance, they were good mousers and roamed the property at will, never bothering with birds, pets, or otherwise. Dividends were paid with fresh squeezed milk and plenty of dry food.

Especially appealing to Seth was the deck scenery. Little if anything grew beneath the lofty pines, and that was all right; it'd take something away from their strength. On occasion, a few deer could be seen weaving their way in its depth, lured by tender fruit from several apple trees to the north. A keen eye during baling last year gave Seth the insight that Wylie baited the area with block salt, corn, and pumpkins when hunting season neared. He had no qualms about using a shotgun to scare off varmints that threatened his prized chickens—raccoons, skunks, stray dogs, and the like—but a hunter he was not. Baiting served to lure the animals into a safe haven rather than a death trap.

"You're just the man I want to see," Wylie said while quenching the thirst of a fuchsia. "Where's your sidekick?"

"He's off to church, said he'll stop by later." Seth positioned a lawn chair to take full advantage of his favorite view. "So, tell me what you came up with for PBS."

Pulling open a chair, outwardly pleased with the location and inquiry, Wylie answered, "How much extension cord does your ole man have?"

"I know he has a hundred-fifty-foot cord plus a couple hundred-footers, a few smaller ones hanging around too. Maybe four hundred feet total."

"We'll need all that and my six-hundred feet to go from an outlet inside, through the pines, and onto our landing site behind the hill."

"Landing site?" Seth chuckled.

"Well, ya gotta call it something." Wylie continued, "I've got a couple florescent shop lights, each with two tubes. They have a softer glow than those glaring incandescent bulbs. I figure to lay down half a sheet of plywood and plug in the juice. I like the way they flicker before kicking in. That may be common above fish tanks or in a classroom, but not in the back forty."

"That's a great idea. I'm glad you didn't do it to me. What about guns?"

"Handguns and ammo can be stored in my safe; shotgun and twenty-two, locked in the front bedroom. It'd probably be smart to put the butcher knives in there too."

"There's a lot of things around here that could do damage."

"It's not like I'm gonna stack a cord of wood in the front bedroom because someone might use a piece to splinter Wade's skull. We'll just have to be aware of what's goin' on."

"Let's take a walk down the cow path," Seth proposed. "We can check out the scene by daylight."

"Let's do that, Slugger. See if ya can find a weapon this time around."

Cross-courtyard, a long machine shed sat forward and slightly north of the barn. It was divided into two sections. The larger sheltered farm machinery and transportation; the smaller was used for chopping and stacking firewood. On rainy days, Wylie, or whoever he could convince, had a dry place to swing an ax. Two blades were buried each in their own block. One was shiny with use; the other was rusted and wedged much deeper.

"What about those?" Seth asked.

"I'll stash them behind the woodpile. You'd need the vision of a barn owl to find them after dark. Regardless, I'm gonna slide both doors shut. Don't want anyone in my shop either."

Seth had been in Wylie's shop many times and knew it was filled with potential weapons. Old logging tools embellished walls, and garden implements were right around the corner. For a moment, Wade's thoughts of an angry mob bearing raised pitchforks while hunting down an interstellar Frankenstein crossed his mind, and then Wylie took it away.

"I'll latch both doors from the inside. I've gotta protect my babies."

His babies were a gray-on-red Ford 8N tractor and a polished, black '68 GTO, each in near showroom condition. It wasn't that he didn't drive them; he simply took good care of them. A three-quarter-ton flatbed served him well much of the time; it was as reliable as it was corroded.

Attached north of the shed was a chicken coop, whose generous fencing gave fowl room to scratch and peck in the shade of a sugar maple. Wylie was partial to the unusual when it came to chickens, and his choices reflected it. Black Polish, their heads lost in a white fountain top-notch, comically bobbed around as if blind. Black and white Cochins, both colors plumed right down to the claws, waddled amid their taller coopmates. Wylie gathered eggs for cooking, but not a single chicken would ever experience the chopping block. Plump, juicy fryers were purchased from Oakton's Country Market. At one time, two peacocks ranged freely on the grounds, alarming guests with their shrill cries until nocturnal predators silenced them. So too was the fate of several pheasants. Only a vase of feathers on his rolltop desk indicated either species had ever been there.

Cleverly hidden behind machine shed and chicken coop was the barnyard, the least attractive area on most any farm. Very little could grow inside its fencing, which was composed of four-tier barbed wire plus electric. Two dead trees accentuated the famine. Its only redeeming features were a tank full of cool water to quench pastured bovine and a feeding bin for occasional sacs of grain. Several calves frolicked around a dozen cows of mixed breed. To Wylie, they were the product of advanced genetic engineering, carefully selected for particular traits. To Seth, they were a hodgepodge of who knew what, interrelated to a worrisome degree and on the verge of spawning sideshow celebrities. Whichever opinion was more accurate, they never confronted one another for the sake of friendship.

Teddy, a one-horned bull, serviced the entire harem whenever they allowed him, and he seemed to like a human audience. Freshening could happen anytime of the year and just about anywhere. More than once, Seth had come over to help during difficult deliveries, which were never in the same place. Together, he and Wylie'd stick around to watch the matron lick her newborn clean and help a wobbly calf find nourishment. There was always an abundance of raw milk to squirt into the open mouths of Elsie and Tony. Like his chicken dinners, Wylie bought his milk at the Country Market. The herd lived a life that couldn't be imagined by other cows, if cows could imagine. Old age, accident, or untreatable illness would be their only enemies.

They walked to the barnyard gate and opened it, letting loose a famished throng. Seth thought it a late start, but Wylie didn't have set schedules and neither did his family of animals. There, Seth reminisced several years back to the time when Preacher Clarke and his youngest stopped in to visit. Since the untimely loss of his parents, Wylie hadn't gone to church, and the pastor feared he'd lost faith—and thus the church had lost donations in the collection plate. Preacher Clarke had tried to present himself more as a friend than a clergyman, yet he was what he was and in critical company.

Timothy, his five-year-old son, had been a virgin to rural life. Blond as the summer sun could make it, his Dutch-boy haircut had attracted womenfolk in droves. He was also an inquisitive and amusing child. While Preacher Clarke had been making small talk with them, Timothy gazed in protruding awe at Teddy copulating with Maureen in the barnyard. No longer able to contain himself, his excitement had burst forth.

"Look, Daddy, Wylie's got trick cows!"

"Trick cows?" Wylie had laughed out loud and then let it fly. "It's the greatest show on earth, Timmy. Stick around, and you'll witness the second coming." He had howled with ever more vitality at his own play on words.

Seth had stood gaping, each corner of his mouth turned upward as he had been unable to decide whether to laugh or shut his trap. Wylie's contagion had decided that for him. Although the minister had taken it as well as could be expected, he had not since returned.

It was coincidental that Teddy and Maureen were the last to file past their liberators and a little disturbing for Seth to see Teddy clip-clop to catch up with his fertile daughter, Isabelle. Despite the forward view, he did manage to study his surroundings. Wooded margins were free of fallen branches, governable rocks, and metal fence posts independent of their purpose. The area looked clean, irrespective of cow pies, as Wylie's pets habitually veered left and onto the northwest pasture.

"I threw the downed tree limbs as far over the fence as I could. No one will dare go in there at night. Sometimes, it even spooks me. On the day of our scare, I decided I'll feed the cows in the barnyard, one less thing to worry about."

The low point was between cow path, pasture, and hayfield. The location made the hill in front of their proposed landing site seem larger and better able to conceal a nonexistent spacecraft but not the protraction of light.

"This is really going to be something."

"Only if we can keep from laughing out loud," said Wylie as they pivoted and headed back to the cottage. "What is it you have planned, Neighbor?"

"Right now, I have all I can do to gimp around patties. When we get to the deck, I'll tell you about it."

Wylie could drink soda anytime, and offering it to guests was a natural consequence. Seth accepted the hospitality out of respect, not desire. "Thanks. What do you think about having PBS this coming Friday night with a dry run on Thursday night, weather permitting?"

"If it's good for Wade, it's good for me."

"We can have our summer's-end cookout here on your deck. There's lots of seating, and darkness settles in faster. Both favor a leading conversation like the Apollo mission in December followed by the orange light you claim to have seen last week."

"Listen, it was no prank. I know what I saw."

"Whatever ya say. Anyway, the power station down the road could serve as an electromagnetic lure for a UFO. Everybody thinks they're drawn to such things—that and military bases. By nine thirty, it'll be dark enough to get the full effect from your lights. Wade and Nate will have to hang out at the landing site for awhile, but if they have something to eat and drink, they'll be fine.

"I'll fix them a real nice goody basket," offered Wylie.

"They'd appreciate that. Then, whenever you feel the time is right, say you need to go check on a couple cows that didn't come back with the herd, and if one or more guests want to go with, all the better. This time, bring a flashlight. Wade and Nate will then know whether you're coming or going and when to plug and unplug the lights. This alone could be misunderstood as some sort of alien communication."

"I see what ya mean. When I turn the flashlight off, they can turn the florescent lights on and vice versa."

"It's up to you and Wade, but when you return a second time, that's when our little green men can come out of their spaceship from behind the hill."

"After a couple more light signals with all present and accounted for."

"Everybody except me, that is; I'll be busy." Seth pressed on, "If they react anything like I did, you should be able to keep them there long enough for me to do my thing. After you've stretched it to the limit, tell them you're going back to call the cops."

"Ain't that pushing it bit too far?"

"Nonsense, this is where it gets better. I can unplug the phone jack behind the fridge; I can also unhook the positive battery cables on their vehicles and close the gate to River Road. The only thing remaining is a complete power outage."

"I take it this is where the fuse box behind my front door comes into play. Not many people know it's there, because I hang coats over it."

"Precisely, figure it this way: after the sighting, you follow behind to help anyone who might need it, given the slippery landmines. They'll try to start their cars, and when that doesn't work, I'll guide them into the house for protection. Once they discover the phone is as dead as their cars, you'll bring up the rear and can hit the power as you slam the door shut. Put it all together, and we have a full-fledged alien invasion. Depending on Wade's costumes, I bet Nate and him could come right up to the windows."

"This is so good it's beginning to scare me. Can ya imagine what it'll do to them?"

"I sure can. That's why I'll need freedom to come and go as I see fit. Some could try to make a run for it, and I'd have to chase them down. Should that happen, you'll have to cover what goes on inside."

"And how am I to explain that one? Who knows how many would be on your tail."

"At that point, everything is improvised. I just hope I'm around when you decide to turn the power on and let them in on it. You know, to get a look at the same face I wore last Friday night."

"As if ya won't see your fill before the lights go on." Wylie snickered. "Did ya think of anybody you'd like to scare?"

"No, not so far. Did you choose anybody yet?"

"For me, it's gotta be Shea McCune. There's no need to ask anybody else because he always stops by with someone."

Shea was a tall, slender twenty-five-year-old with wit much quicker than body. His final year of graduate school would buff up his skills in mathematics, science, and the ability to teach them. Never did he question the probability of other intelligent life in the universe. It was extraterrestrial visitations that needled his skepticism. Traveling in such a vast space-time continuum was, in his opinion, "highly unlikely." Eyewitness accounts to the contrary were the least reliable of all evidence and simply couldn't satisfy his rigid criteria—actual physical evidence. Some perceived his capacity to consume and regurgitate information as a kind of cognitive snobbery and him as a Mr. Know-It-All.

Seth thought differently. He was intrigued by Shea's delivery of the facts rather than the facts themselves. Double-checking data was easy enough but listening to it was enjoyable. Once you got past a little arrogance, you found there was a friendly fellow with a good, if not droll, sense of humor. He'd make an excellent teacher for those who wanted to learn. As for Wylie, Shea stood well above any other choice. Shattering his cynical mind, even for a short time, would be glorious. One too many times Professor McCune had questioned his observations and suggested natural explanations for unnatural occurrences. Wylie was anxious to hear the college boy rationalize PBS when it defied all explanation.

Concerned, Seth asked, "Aren't you worried about who he might bring with him? What if it's a girl?"

"What difference would that make? Equality has its price. My guess is that he'll be with one of his smoking buddies. They'll stop by and munch out before heading over to the Lumberjack Saloon. It'll be Friday night, and Egghead needs to escape like anybody else."

"Hmm, a mystery guest, won't that be interesting? I think Wade will choose Alec and Thomas Moeller. They've been out here lots and play with him on the football team."

The crackle of gravel and a peek at his watch prompted Wylie's reply. "Speak of the devil. That must be him now."

"Come around back. We're on the deck!" Wylie yelled.

Wade rounded the corner and took the three steps as if eluding an imaginary tackler; he was cradling a rolled paper bag as if it were a Packer pigskin. Sitting down in the chair Wylie had set out for him, he held high the bag and let it unravel. "Guess what I got in here?"

Seth leaned forward in his chair. "Don't keep us in suspense, Crazy Legs. Show us what you got."

"I like that name a whole lot better than the one Tal gave me."

The first article he pulled from the bag was a curly blond wig similar to his real hair. "My uncle gave this to me last year as a practical joke. Said he couldn't resist. It's a clown wig." Wade flung it onto Seth's lap. "Don't even think about saying it."

Pulling the wig over his head and flashing an impersonation of his friend's big smile, Seth fluffed his new look. Wade's warning didn't stop Wylie from mouthing off though.

"Ya look like one of my Polish roosters. Walk like a chicken for us."

"Cut it out, you guys. I think it'll make Nate and me look alike, not like two different aliens. Everything in the bag is about matching one another."

Next out of the bag were two dingy long underwear tops, tattered but suitable for the purpose.

"These will be better than going without a shirt. If it's cool out, they'll be warm; if it's warm out, we'll spray them with mosquito repellent. Best of all, they'll reflect a glow stick to the max."

Then out came two pairs each of white canvas work gloves and navy-blue tights—yes, navy-blue tights.

Wade laughed. "As for the gloves, I expect us to have our hands free to move around. We'll mold some heavy aluminum foil into a reflector and use sport tape to fasten it under our bellies; toss a couple glow sticks in each for our desired effect and presto! Nate and I will have upper-body animation."

Of the two-man audience, Wylie was faster. "Okay, ya can flap your wings. Now tell us about the nutcrackers." It was what Seth would've wanted to know if he could've gotten the likeness of a quarterback in tights out of his head.

"They're the other half of the illusion. Look, Ma, no legs. We'll float like a butterfly and sting like a bee. Isn't it great?"

Seth scoffed. "You really think you're going to get Nate to put those on?"

"He'd better, or I'll kick his ass."

An open patio door gave Flip the right to his two cents' worth. "I'll kick your ass."

"They're small, but they'll stretch; cut the feet out if we have to. I took them out of the Goodwill box so they won't be missed. And don't worry; they're clean."

"I have to hand it to ya, Wade," said Wylie, "ya get the trophy for best in show. That deserves a cold bottle from the fridge. Help yourself."

Wade returned with his prize and took a slug. "I thought of white grease paint to highlight our faces, but I don't have any. My uncle should've given me some of that too, the cheap bastard."

"I'll go check my Halloween stuff; I might have some."

Sure enough, Wylie had a small jar and a suggestion in the form of two pairs of bug-eyed sunglasses. Big alien eyes were what he had in mind, whether they'd help or hinder in the dark was another question. It'd be worth a try. "I bought these at a two-for-one sale. We'll see how they look on Thursday's dry run."

"Does that mean we're going to pull this thing off on Friday night?"

"That's the plan, if you're okay with it. Come inside; we'll fill ya in while we tie into the apple crisp Seth's ma sent over."

Wylie and Seth were happy to explain their ideas a second time, supposedly for Wade's benefit, as three equal shares from Martha's kitchen were divided and eaten. Every sweet morsel thickened their plot to take over the world, and, like children before Christmas, they just couldn't wait.

After telling Wade the identity of his victim, Wylie asked, "Did ya decide who you're gonna scare?"

"It can only be Alec and Thomas. They raced out here right away last week. This time, they'll figure they're coming over for a cookout, not a fake sighting."

"Like I told Seth, it was no prank. I know what I saw."

"Who did you choose, Seth?" Wade asked.

"Nobody yet, but I'm thinking on it," he replied and then addressed his accomplices. "In case we don't talk between now and Thursday, we'll meet here at eight o'clock. I'll bring Nate with me then."

"Haven't ya told him?" they asked.

"I thought it best to wait. He's been working the farm more and doesn't need the distraction around animals and machinery. I'll surprise him on Thursday."

Wylie stood at the kitchen sink and began washing Martha's plate. "Wade, if ya have any extension cords at home, bring 'em along. We'll probably need 'em." Mechanical chatter drew his eyes to the window; nothing else sounded like a VW Beetle. It pushed its way across the courtyard and parked well clear of his neighbor's trucks. "Damn, it's Wilma Pudder. Hang around awhile, she'll think I have plans."

"Done did my planning today," said Wade, "and slept through one sermon already. The Pud Lady is your problem."

Seth held up his last guzzle of soda. "Here's to Pud in your eye, Wienie Boy. I'm with Wade on this one," he said and then quickly chugged it down.

"Just shoot me now," mumbled Wylie as he watched a woman, similar in frame to the car she drove, roll out of an open door.

Wilma's advantage was in the fellowship she'd shared with Wylie's late mother, something he couldn't deny and wouldn't. A duly appointed messenger of the Lord's Word, enlisted by Preacher Clarke, she'd carry on into eternity while godson Wylie pretended to listen. He could never get sharp with her, nor she with him.

Seth took his mother's plates and, together with Wade, slipped out the front door. Expectation of a clean getaway was thwarted by a spurt of energy from the Pud Lady. The gal could move when she wanted to. Short in stature, sharp-tongued with a gruff tone, thick glasses, support hose rolled beneath hemline—it all fit her coarse personality, unless it was Wylie she spoke to. Still, they would remain courteous.

Wilma spoke to the two doormen. "Leaving so soon, gentlemen?" She cast her fish eyes at Wade. "Mr. Hotchner, I saw you nodding out in church again. Get a haircut or sit in the back; it looked like your sister was jerking on a big yellow balloon."

Seth chuckled at her parody.

Shifting her weight in a series of waddles, she faced Seth and focused in. "Mr. Wickman, I didn't see hide nor hair of you. Following in your father's footsteps, are you?"

"I like farming just fine, Ma'am. Thanks for asking."

"That's not what I was referring to."

Wade stepped in before it went any further. "Nice to see you again today, Miss Pudder. Seth, we should be on our way. Catch ya later, Wylie."

CHAPTER 4

After the previous day's meeting at Wylie's, Seth went home to a pleasant Sunday dinner followed by several hours of torment, and then Nate had to go out and do chores. If not for that and *Bonanza*, very little progress would've been made on his model plane. This was Monday; daybreak on the third day of barn eviction, and withdrawal was becoming intolerable. At least his toe had stopped throbbing. He tried to read some while the cows were being milked, but his comprehension was nil. The best that could be done with the *Spirit of St. Louis* was to examine Sunday's work. Time had become an endless rut between bed, desk, and window; fertile ground for the type of depression that came with headline news. However, no sooner than the napalm girl came, she went.

"Seth! Come and get it."

"Okay, Pa."

Normally, he would've smelled breakfast before entering the kitchen. His mother's fried potatoes and ham were a surprise that shouldn't have been. He hoped his family wouldn't sense his blues.

"Do ya think you'd be up to doin' some errands today?" asked Adam.

Seth was all over it like butter on bread. "You name it, I'll do it."

"Your brother and I'll be mendin' fence this afternoon. I'd like ya to buy a roll a' barbwire and a sack a' staples, couple salt blocks too.

Check with Wylie, perchance he needs someth'n' from town. How 'bout you, Mother?"

"I'll make a list for the grocery store."

Just as his parents knew what to do about his sad state, so too did he with his brother's. "Pa, if you're not fixing fence until this afternoon, can Nate go with me this morning?" He could see the food Nate had stopped chewing. "But only if he wants to."

The sudden offer and open mouth couldn't keep breakfast in its place. Nate spat his reply. "Sure, I'll go."

Seth controlled his laughter and spread some frosting. "On the condition that Pa doesn't mind, we could stop and watch football practice; maybe take our gloves and shag some balls." Both practice field and baseball diamond were part of the same sports complex. They'd acted out many Big League plays when Oakton's diamond wasn't in use, and with football on everyone's mind, vacancy was assured.

Adam winked at his wife, a move that didn't escape Seth's eye. "I reckon I could rustle up someth'n' to do. Hightail it back for lunch though."

Nate cleaned his plate lickety-split, excused himself, and hastened upstairs to prepare for a welcome change. Seth remained in the company of his tickled parents. Pa casually asked about Wade and the football team while Ma flashed warm smiles having nothing to do with football. It seemed his parents' shrewd manipulation of events had reversed a sticky situation between brothers and gained private time for themselves, a double victory.

With the breakfast table cleared and Adam entertaining the dishwasher, a self-employed bonus, Seth went to see what his brother was doing. Nate's room was bigger than his and in stark contrast. Athletic heroes wallpapered everything except ceiling and window. Sports magazines—minus choice photos—were scattered beside his bed. Seth kept the clothes he owned in his closet and dresser, both of which were smaller than Nate's. Still, number-two son couldn't keep his stuff organized. The hamper was really a basketball hoop that saw much action and few points, waste basket too. Underneath the bed was a landfill of whatever—sentimental playthings unwilling to disappear, school papers worth keeping, single socks of different breeds, sports equipment, candy wrappers—and all of it collecting dust bunnies. It was a place Nate alone would enter, and that was exactly where Seth found him.

"What you digging for? Truffles?" Given the number of times Nate had been told to clean under his bed, Seth normally would've stepped on his rear and held him there a minute, saying, "Looky here, it's Nate from Down Under." A sore toe prevented it.

Nate ejected his glove and two new baseballs in crumpled boxes and then wormed his way out. "No foot on the ass this time, huh, Chester?"

Seth popped a ball out of the box and looked it over. "This ball is good. How's yours?"

"Mine too, although my glove needs to be punched a little."

"We'll give them a hard workout this morning. Team bus leaves at eight thirty, any sooner and we'd embarrass the football team."

"Are you bringing your cleats?"

He stopped at the doorway. "It wouldn't be the same without them. A player needs to dig in."

Seth opened the closet door and took his glove from an old beer crate. He slapped the new ball into its pocket and dropped it in a mill sack containing the catcher's mitt, bat ring, helmet, and a dozen practice balls. Of two bats, one was designated for general play and one for the Green Machine, a pitching contraption at Pinewood Mini-Golf. The first would meet its objective; the second remained for another day. His uniform was created for comfort. Cutoff gray sweatpants posed as knickers; red three-ring tube socks as knee stockings; white, loose-fitting T-shirt as jersey; and a Cardinal cap as itself. With the bat slung over his shoulder, cleats and mill sack dangling from behind, he used his free hand to take hold of the stair railing.

Nate squirted around the slow mover. "Caught ya sleeping, Hopalong."

"Hold your horses. We won't be leaving for another half hour. I still have to call Wylie yet."

"I know, but I thought we could loosen arms out in the yard, unless you don't feel up to it."

"Don't feel up to it? You're too much, Little Brother." Seth dumped the equipment off on him with instructions to pick out a decent older ball and to put the rest in the pickup; he didn't want any grass stains on the new ones. "I'll be out in a few minutes."

The grocery list, along with funding, was on the kitchen table. Seth tucked them between two pairs of socks, a temporary solution. Through the window, he could see his parents strolling garden rows. They looked happier than pigs in shit.

"Hey, Wylie, I'll be going into town. Is there anything I can pick up for you?"

"Could use a couple sacks of chicken feed. I also need to buy some lumber at Sager's, but I'll get that myself on Thursday. The owner's kid always gives me a deal, and he's only around in the afternoon."

"Do you mean Tal Sager?" He couldn't imagine the louse doing something nice for anyone except Frank.

"That's the one. Said he's in your class and plays football with Wade."

Seth evaluated the situation. Although Wylie knew many people, he wasn't always privy to the affairs of others, particularly the inside scoop of a high school football team. There was no local paper delivered to his mailbox, and it didn't bother him the least. Not feeling a need to bring him up-to-date on current controversy, Seth kept it short. "Wade knows him better than I do."

"Anyway, if I'm not around the buildings, put them in the machine shed. Cash will be on the kitchen counter ... and thanks."

Neither baseballs nor bats by themselves ever threatened windows; it was when they met one another that they created problems. One of them had to go. Martha's ban on bats might've driven part of their game further from the clubhouse but allowed another part to thrive. Within the generous strip of lawn separating home and driveway was a natural pitcher's mound and, sixty feet six inches away, home plate. Even the most unruly pitches were destined to roll on harmlessly. A backstop wasn't included in landscaping, so stopping the ball anyway they could saved steps. Each could see their folks watching from the porch steps with an armful of sweet corn as they developed a kinship never to be forgotten.

It went without saying that Seth took to the mound; squatting at home plate wouldn't go over well with cornhusker fans. Three-quarter speed was as fast as he'd throw to Nate at his age; to do otherwise would be detrimental to their mutual best interests. It also didn't require full range of motion, which was easier on his toe. This aside, he could still give Nate a fastball with some zip, a snappy curve, and a couple off-speed changeups. With a wrist twist of the ball, he'd always let him know before throwing breaking pitches.

"Last three were right down the pipe. A batboy could've walloped them into the upper deck. Try to throw me something that moves around a bit."

"Why, that smart-ass," Seth said under his breath. "I'll give him some movement." Although Nate hadn't caught for him since June, others had. More speed and better control of his knuckler, which by its very nature was aimed unpredictability, had given the pitch a mind of its own. His brother would be expecting a curve while this pitch tended to dance and dive.

The ball without spin dropped like a rock on the inside corner. It was clearly a strike as it had crossed home plate, but Nate was unable to snatch it on the short hop. Knocking it down in front of him was the best he could do. "That's one badass pitch. Ya gotta show me how to throw it."

"Do you want to see what a screwball looks like?"

"Just don't go taking my head off."

Like a knuckler, the screwball required an awkward grip and release; it was difficult to control without a fair amount of practice. Seth considered it another off-speed pitch. Major Leaguers could throw them near fastball velocity. The point was it curved opposite that of a natural right-handed curve and without as much of a downward pull. It was a good toss when a pitcher was ahead in count and had no ducks on the pond.

As the ball whizzed in, braking sharply at final entry, Nate moved with it, backhanding it square in the doughnut hole. He jumped from his crouch and fired a quick return. "That would've brushed back a right-handed plate hugger. Now nail the outside corner with your fastball."

Seth took the catcher's sign, wound up in dramatic fashion, and let loose with moderation. "That was a bit down and away. An eager beaver might've chased after it though."

"And after that last pitch, look really lame doing it," Nate added.

"You'll have to show me how to throw a screwball too, when we get on the dirt."

Twenty minutes of warm-up and baseball chatter ended with them walking in tandem to the truck. They tipped their caps to loyal fans sitting on the porch steps and climbed in. Seth peeled his mother's grocery list and money from between his socks, stashing them in the glove box. The list was smudged but legible; the money, damp but acceptable. Nate sat smugly in his seat, elbow hanging out his window, donning a Mona Lisa smile and matching country uniform. It was the good ole days once more.

Bright sunshine and fresh morning air rated much higher than top-forty on a scratchy radio, giving Seth cause to double travel time. A number of major habitats could be seen along the winding stretch of River Road, and seasonal changes were speaking. The lush green forest of midsummer had grown pale, a few smidgens of autumn color beckoning others to follow. Only pines could ultimately deny the summons. Patches of mature goldenrod and budding asters permeated fallow ground. Tawny prairie grass slumped in retirement. By the river marsh, a red-winged blackbird wavered tiptop a plump cattail, purple loosestrife upstaging his acrobatics. Blue-flowered chicory, aged Queen Anne's lace, and lemon trefoil garnished the roadside. The starlings' yellow bills had gone gray, and their cackles were many. Soon, they'd number in the hundreds. Some would stay, and some would go, like the crows.

"Seth, what's that stuff that looks like tall dandelions?"

"It's called hawkweed. Folklore says hawks ate the flowers to sharpen eyesight."

"What do you say?"

"Ever see a hawk wearing glasses?"

Nate smiled while rubbing the sheen from a new baseball. "Only in cartoons; that's where I learn most everything."

Humored by the response and pleased with his brother's willingness to self-criticize, Seth paged back in time. "In that case, I'll gladly pay you on Tuesday for a hamburger today?"

They'd mimic their animated television stars until the grocery store came into view, for it was still business before baseball. A short and nonperishable shopping list was bearable; the near-empty parking lot, a blessing. It was a fast in and out. With Alec and Thomas at practice, service at Moeller's Feed Mill was slower. Given a choice, it beat the pants off standing in line at the Country Market. By nine o'clock, they were lacing their cleats on bleachers behind the backstop. Even without bases and chalk lines, the field was beautiful. The boys of summer had a mind to replace distant cracks of football pads with that of bat and ball. They'd have their way.

Seth sent Nate into center field. "I'll hit you some fly balls, but lob them in. I don't want you to throw your arm out before getting on the mound."

"Try and keep them inside the fence!" he yelled back. "This is baseball, not a steeplechase."

After one round with worn baseballs hit deep into center field, Seth called his brother into shallow left to take a few short pop-ups. From there, Nate moved to shortstop. It had long been known to Seth that his protégé tolerated the outfield, but he loved the action on dirt. Of the dozen or so hard grounders and line drives, not a single shot escaped his glove. If only they had another player to cover first base, then Nate's timing wouldn't be interrupted by having to drop the bat and put on a glove to take his throw at home plate. Nonetheless, his throws were crisp to the target. There was little doubt that the kid had a strong arm and a knack for playing the ball off the bat. It was his hitting that needed improvement.

The previous year, Nate had had to choke up on his stick to stay with the ball. This year, he had a quicker swing with a grip tight to the knob. The problem was he took his eyes off the ball in an attempt to kill it. Watching the ball into the bat was a concept that needed constant reinforcement. In a total of ten at bats, Nate made playable contact with six pitches; two of these were safe hits. The other four at bats were strikeouts. If he wanted to pursue organized baseball, which was what Seth suspected, he'd need help with his hitting and chores. There wasn't any reason why Seth couldn't provide that help.

After collecting the scattered baseballs, they met at the pitcher's mound. Seth showed Nate the basics of his knuckler and screwball, and a more devoted student could not have been found anywhere.

"Practice throwing them during warm-up, real easy like. Takes time to get used to the grip. Speed will come later." Seth tucked a new ball into Nate's glove. "Right now, you get twenty-five pitches, and all I want to see is your fastball, slider, and that split-finger changeup you have." The hard curveball wasn't a pitch Seth encouraged; if not thrown right, it could damage the young superstar's elbow before his dream could materialize.

Squatting down for the first ten pitches was pushing it; the next few demanded an upright stance with bent knees. Nate was quick to release him from his commitment.

"My arm is getting sore. Do you mind if we go and watch football?"

"Good idea. I need the break."

They gathered their equipment and headed to the truck. Seth changed into his sneakers while Nate decided to leave his cleats on; he wanted to extend baseball fever as long as possible.

The practice field wasn't that far away and could've been walked. But Seth parked in front of several cars along the street a short jaunt from the west-end goalposts. There were some fans standing outside the end-zone markers, talking among themselves. It appeared to be a scrimmage between first-string defense and second-string offense, with defense protecting the near goal. A select number of players were part of both A-teams, so when first-string defense was on the field, the offense was considerably depleted. It seemed odd that Wade was directing second-string offense and spared the hard-hitting football that all the other participating players were subject to. Logic would have it that as starting quarterback, he was too important to risk being hurt on defense, and to lessen the chance of injury, the defense had received instruction to hold up on tackles involving him. It also seemed reasonable to assume Coach Willis wanted to give his fledgling recruit as much play time at the position as possible.

Players not directly involved in the scrimmage were standing along the north sidelines waiting for their opportunity to get in the game. This gave the south sideline an uninterrupted view of Oakton's offensive backfield. As Seth and Nate walked behind a group of men, they drew little attention away from the critical commentary. Easily recognizable, Frank LaRue Senior and Buck Sager dominated the conversation. Although the farm boys thought they'd chosen a safe distance from the slander, the boisterous tone would carry and take a nip out of their otherwise fine day. They could understand how coach and quarterback felt and were biting tongues along with them.

Wade was in his element; an uneven playing field honed his skills. Coach had given him license to call plays with second-string offense, and many times, he preferred them to that of first. Players were motivated by his leadership and, given their lack of experience, ready to repeat the pounding down after down. Across the way at middle linebacker, Tal was exceptional. He followed the ball well and was rarely fooled by play-action pass. Frank patrolled deep at strong safety and was talented in his own right. It was an overzealous desire to make the passer look bad that made him vulnerable to the pump fake, a weakness Wade would exploit every so often. At defensive corners, Alec and Thomas respected Coach's decision to use restraint, but that was it. Slackers, they were not.

Waiting for his team to return to huddle after a sweep left that Tal had obliterated, Wade took note of Seth and Nate next to the bigwigs. He wanted to wave but didn't want to acknowledge the rude bystanders. A couple of nifty calls should do the trick. There were five running formations Coach wanted him to work into the offense; when he'd use them was his choice. They were plays the Lakeshore Pirates ran with great frequency. The reasoning behind running them was to prepare the defense for their first game. This time, he'd call a strong right option pass and hit the tight end on a ten-yard out. As with the last play, Tal would blast through the lineman to get at the ball carrier. If backs could slow him down, he'd have time to let go the pass. He also needed to have Alec, at right corner, commit to the run. A convincing run fake was essential.

Wade gathered his teammates into the huddle. "Strong right, option pass on two. Tight end, do a square out at ten. Backs, take out those linebackers. Flanker, the safety will jump on the short pass, so get in his way or I'll change my mind about the next play. Ready and break." The huddle broke apart with a hand clap, and they trotted to the line of scrimmage.

With a flick of Wade's wrist, the ball nosed itself smack dab into the numbers of a charged receiver, and there it stuck. Johnson turned up field and gained another twelve yards before Frank pushed him out of bounds. Although it was only practice, the sophomore tight end signaled an excited first down. Others didn't fare as well. One running back had to double on a determined defensive end and the other, an outside linebacker. Tal was free to make good his threat from Saturday night. Ignoring Coach's instruction, he slammed into Wade at full gallop and drove him hard to the ground. The late tackle brought a variety of reactions. Frank Senior and Buck hooted with delight at the bone-crushing hit as Seth and Nate did with the pass completion. A few defenders slapped low fives with Tal, including Frank Junior, but the majority of players from both units weren't happy about his blatant disregard of Coach's orders. Wade's scolding at the beer party had indeed made an impact. The tide was turning.

Sprinting toward a grinning Tal and grabbing his facemask, Coach Willis spit his rage, "If you ever pull such a stunt again, you'll have more slivers in your ass than Howdy Doody! Now get it to the bench and sit on that awhile." He turned and faced the rest of the team. "And that goes for everyone else here." Looking to an anxious sideline, the drillmaster barked his final words in the matter. "Redecki, get in here at middle linebacker."

Wade had shaken off the tackle, not the opportunity for a big play. He brought the huddle together. "Strong right thirty-two play-action pass on one. Johnson, do a buttonhook at ten. Collins, do a post pattern. Ready and break."

His plan worked perfectly. Redecki was hungry for contact and fell for play-action, leaving Johnson momentarily open. A pump fake and Frank was had. Wade lofted a patient spiral as the flanker streaked by a stunned safety, catching it in full stride at the goal line. Those B-teamers who weren't sprawled out on the ground were jumping up and down with arms raised high, howling like Oakton Timber Wolves should. The ragtag crew believed in themselves against the mightier starters, and Wade was glad to be part of it. Collins was swamped by teammates when he returned to huddle after the catch. Maybe Coach would reconsider his second-string status, for it was LaRue who had the position he wanted on A-team offense.

While Frank was being chewed out for blowing coverage, Seth glanced at Tal, who sat on the bench, likely stewing in his own juices at a play that he could've prevented, or so he probably thought. Buck, Tal's father, was of the same opinion as his words reached Seth's ears soon after the play. "That was just a fluke because my kid wasn't in there." The other men in the group nodded agreement. This didn't stop him or his brother from shouting approval along with the substitutes who helped make the play possible.

"Get a load of the farm club," said Frank Senior in a condescending tone with his thumb hitchhiking in their direction.

Buck was less forgiving. "I'll have their tractor pulling my homecoming float after the bank forecloses." Within the clan, his malicious comment drew the most unsettling chuckles.

Seth watched his sibling closely. Verbal suppression wasn't one of Nate's virtues, and the mere mention of such a thing was fighting words. "Don't say a thing, Nate," he warned, fearing it wouldn't be enough. Presumably, it wouldn't have been if not for unexpected company. Music wasn't alone in soothing the savage beast.

From amidst the parked cars on the street, Sara walked her bicycle over to where they had made their stand. "Hi there, Seth. Mind if I watch practice with you and your good-looking friend?"

Seth could see Nate's knees almost buckle at the weight of her compliment thrashing around in his head. Here was this brown-eyed beauty, with an alluring smile and a tempting body wrapped in a tube top and faded cutoffs, a field daisy tucked behind her ear, and she had noticed him. The evil men evaporated in her aura.

"Hey, Sara, do I mind? You'd squash my heart if you didn't. This here is my brother, Nate."

She laid her bike down and took the spot that opened between them. "It's nice to meet you, Nate. It sounds like I missed an exciting play. What happened?"

Even though Sara directed her question toward Nate, Seth could see he was awestruck into speechlessness. "Wade completed a couple passes, one for a touchdown." Nate managed to smile and nod.

"I don't know much about football. Can you show me where Alec and Thomas are playing?"

Seth pointed out her interest and continued with other players she might've met while beer tending, some good and some not so good. "Those men over there, that's—"

Before he could finish his sentence, Nate interrupted. "Helmet Head and Buzz Cut. They think their shit doesn't stink."

Seth knew it was too good to last. Nate had cranked his volume with each word, unflinching in motive. Fortunately, they were engrossed with Sara's appearance and deaf to Nate's growl.

Sara's soft tone eased the tension. "I've met Frank's dad. He's our landlord. We moved in a month ago, and he's been over a number of times to check on I don't know what. He gives me the creeps."

"The big guy, Buzz Cut," Seth snickered at repeating his brother's snide remark about the saw miller's receding hairline, "is Buck Sager, Tal's ole man."

Sara glanced at him. "How did I know that?"

They spent the next half hour watching practice in friendly gab, completely removed from the concerns of the fathers. Alec and Thomas were switched to offense for the last ten plays from scrimmage. With Tal riding the bench and two rookies at corners, the field opened up. From fifty yards out, it took four handoffs and three passes for Alec to do his jig in the end zone. First team defense minus three starters caught hell after that series. The remaining three plays reviewed conversion attempts. Coach Willis put his trust in a freshman soccer-style kicker, a bold move on each count. Most conference teams opted for two-point conversions, while teams that didn't were toe kickers. Regardless, his recruit sure could put the foot into football. Morning practice ended with the team gathering at midfield, except for Tal. He was to take five laps as punishment.

Seth was convinced Frank Senior wanted to get close and personal with Sara, loitering stares and twirling luxury car keys a dead giveaway. Between his son's treatment of her at the party and his sinful ambition, they'd have her beaten and raped within a week. He knew that neither his presence nor that of Nate would stop Frank Senior from running his own play. As Oakton's army retreated to the locker room, three gladiators stepped forward to greet them. From the trampled earth of midfield came Wade, Alec, and Thomas, a move that foiled the elder Frank's intent.

"You fellas looked pretty decent out there today," said Seth.

Nate was more specific. "That long pass was the best. It faked the safety right out of his jock."

"Sure did, didn't it?" Wade smiled at his young fan.

Alec and Thomas tried to keep from gawking at Sara and were fooling no one. "Hi, Sara," came forth in unison.

"Hi, guys. I thought I'd take a ride and see what football is about." Sara looked over her guardians' war-torn bodies. "It's a rough game."

"Keeps us out of trouble," said Alec, before last Saturday night could come to mind. "Well, most of the time anyway."

"Ya got that right," added Thomas.

"I'm happy you all took the time to come out and watch practice," said Wade. "It was just the push I needed with those assholes bitchin' about my every move."

"Sara, suppose you'll be going home the same way you came?" Thomas eyeballed her bicycle.

She snuck a cautious peek at her landlord taking his sweet time getting to his car. "I guess so."

At the risk of upsetting the Moellers, Seth offered a lifeline. "I don't think as much, not when I can throw your bike in my pickup and get you home in five minutes. Maybe these two big, strong football players can do that."

"That'd be wonderful, Seth. Thank you."

"No problem." It was something Nate would've enjoyed doing; sitting next to her in the cab should console him.

"Aside from watching you play today, I came hoping for a chance to talk with both of you," Sara confided to the twins. From her hip pocket came a folded gum wrapper pressed thinner yet in tight denim. She handed it to the closer of two equals, which was Thomas. "This is my phone number. I've washed your shirts, and you can come and get them anytime."

He took the wrapper. "Aww shucks, ma'am, they're just a couple ole rags. I thank ya kindly all the same."

Alec followed suit. "Likewise, ma'am, I'm sure."

She giggled at their combined humor. "You two are just as charming without a beer in your hand."

"Don't go telling anyone," said Alec. "You'll ruin our reputation."

As the group made its way toward the pickup truck, Seth noticed Frank Senior dawdling at the driver's side door of his expensive car, fumbling through his keys as if he didn't know which one would open it. He was glad he'd offered to take Sara home.

After the bicycle was loaded and Sara seated inside, Nate jumped in next to her, pronto, pushing Alec aside in the process. "Get outta my way, muscle head, and make room for the man."

Alec was amused but didn't show it. He recognized the clickity-clack of baseball cleats on pavement and went with it. "I see you got your tap shoes on, Ginger."

Nate slipped out of his game shoes, not bothering to unlace. It'd be a really bad move to accidentally step on Sara's sandaled feet. He held one shoe to Alec's face. "They'll tear into flesh a lot deeper than the nubbies you have on."

The others laughed out loud. Alec joined them. "I guess he told me where it's at."

He pulled his door shut and spoke past Sara. "Seth, we promised Pa to be home for lunch, and we have to stop by Wylie's yet."

"What's up at Wylie's?" Wade asked Seth.

"We have to drop off that chicken feed in the back."

Wade whispered, "Does he know?"

A hard stare and slight head shake made it clear that Nate was still unaware of the secret fright night.

Before the players turned toward the locker room, Wade threw Seth a bullet to dodge. "Hail to PBS."

"What does that mean?" asked his teammates.

He looked at Tal circling the far goalpost and gave a persuasive explanation. "Payback sucks."

Sara guided the farm truck down a road on the outskirts of Oakton, a place where curbing ended and stagnant ditches began; there were no sidewalks or blacktop, just gravel and dirt. Homes in this area were small, unkempt, and rented by the week or by the month. Locals called it Shanty Town. It was an eyesore for nearby residents and a lucrative investment for La Rue Real Estate. There were always people living in them. Of all the times country roots labeled Seth and his family lower class, nothing could prepare them for the heart-wrenching reality of Shanty Town. It was one thing to know of this place, quite another to be in its grasp. Poor was redefined, and, contrary to opulent belief, theirs was a kingdom of prosperity. The brothers noticed one shack looked better than the others—no dog squat, junk cars, or empty beer cans, but rather clean windows, a litter-free yard, and red flowers by the stoop.

"This is it, till my dad finds work," said Sara. "Leave me off here. I want to check the mail."

Nate took her bike from the truck and rolled it to her side. "Tell your mom the flowers look nice."

"My mom passed away last year. She liked geraniums, so I try to plant some wherever we happen to stay."

"I'm really sorry about your mom. I don't know what I'd do without mine."

"Thank you, Nate." She gently touched his shoulder and then leaned forward and spoke through the truck's open window. "It seems you helped me out again, Seth. I think I've fallen into the right crowd for a change."

"Our number is in the book under Adam Wickman. If you need anything at all, that's where we're at."

Seth dropped it into gear. Nate hopped in and waved good-bye.

"What's her last name?"

"Taylor … Sara Taylor."

It wasn't until he was halfway home that Nate needed more answers. "How is it that a person can feel so good about someone and yet feel so bad?"

"It's called love and compassion, the foundation of most religions, written and spoken often, practiced much less. Although I suspect your hormones run thick in the mix."

"So it's a good thing?"

"Yes, it's a good thing."

"Wish there was something we could do to help her out. I mean … her neighborhood is a hellhole."

"We've done it. She just has to pick up a phone, and we're ten minutes away. Besides, Alec and Thomas will be on duty, and they're even closer." He knew that eventually, Nate would quiz him about Sara's comments to the twins regarding the laundered shirts and beers. The beers he was aware of; the laundered shirts were probably to replace the one she had torn from her at the party. When the time came for his brother to ask, he'd play dumb.

While Nate unloaded chicken feed into Wylie's machine shed,

Seth staggered to the house and knocked on his door. No response. In keeping with their agreement, he entered and collected the cash from the kitchen counter. Without the aquarium lights on, the room was dark; the air was saturated in bubbling water. Buster didn't budge from his pillow or Flip utter one loutish phrase from his repertoire. He wondered if Wylie was also taking a siesta. All for the best, lunch would be ready, and his toe bothered him. They left as they had come, giving peace its due.

"You better get inside and wash," said Seth. "We'll clean out the back later." His brother's hesitation urged him on. "Well, what ya waitin' for, Christmas?"

Nate took his time. "Winning isn't much fun if you know it beforehand. Of course, you wouldn't understand that because ya hardly ever lose."

"Is that so?" He reached for the leader's shirttail and, with a firm tug, flung the body behind him. Painfully hopping two steps at a time, he got to the door first. "Then you won't mind if I win. Now go back and get the groceries you forgot."

Martha heard the commotion and hoped it was positive. She never could tell when it came to horseplay. Adam, sitting at the kitchen table, didn't risk it. "You boys settle down and wash up; soup's on."

Lunch was all the grilled cheese sandwiches that could possibly be dunked into a bowl of steamy tomato soup, a custom they enjoyed to their parents' toleration. Pa and Ma seemed more concerned with how the morning had gone for them.

"Did ya get anyth'n' for Wylie?" Adam asked.

"We sure did, two sacks of chicken feed. Nate forgot the money in the glove box."

Martha questioned Nate. "What about you, young man? How did your morning go?"

"Not too bad, Ma; I played some baseball, watched some football, and met one of Seth's hot girlfriends."

"And what name does this girl go by?"

It was time for Seth to intercede. "Her name is Sara. She's a friend of Alec and Thomas. We watched practice with her, and she's not my hot girlfriend."

Nate looked at his father. "Not hot? I may be young, but my vision is twenty-twenty. She's the babe that flyboys paint on their B-29s, a real bombshell."

Adam snickered.

"I think we've taken this conversation as far as I want to go," said Martha, "so if you please, Adam."

Nate helped it along. "I'll get the baseball equipment and money after lunch, Seth." He looked to his father. "I might as well leave the fencing supplies in there."

"I reckon so. Drive it to the machine shed after lunch, and toss in a few cedar posts, the digger and wooden toolbox too."

"You got it, Pa." Sometimes his father would let him drive, not so much on the road as in the fields or courtyard. He never turned it down.

The afternoon went better than Seth had expected. He did have a yearning to be on the fence line, but it was also a relief to be off his feet. Hours flew by as the Ryan NYP began to take shape. In between actual construction, he reflected on his readings. The *Spirit* had been built in a record sixty days by a small company in San Diego. It was powered by an air-cooled Wright nine-cylinder radial engine called the Whirlwind. On the twentieth of May 1927, Lindbergh took off from Roosevelt Field in New York. Thirty-three and a half hours later and about thirty-six hundred miles, he landed in Paris. This was the first nonstop transatlantic flight and, in Seth's opinion, was bested only by the Wright Brothers at Kill Devil Hills, North Carolina, in December of 1903, the beginning of powered flight. Even in his day, Lindbergh's voyage would be a big feat for a single-engine monoplane and, in Charlie's time, as impossible as a trip to the moon. There was no forward visibility, so he used a periscope. Without a radio to communicate, failure of any kind would mark an icy death in the turbulent North Atlantic waters and a footnote in the pages of aviation history. Instead, the lanky country boy, who looked like he could fall through a flute and not sound a note, gained world fame. Eight months before his famed flight, he'd parachuted from an ill-fated plane and lived to tell about it. That alone would've made many a pilot gun-shy at the prospect of a trip across an ocean.

After he had grown weary of the model, sometime during his urge to read more about Lindbergh, Seth dozed off into the wild blue yonder.

Nate brought him softly out of the clouds. He realized he'd slept straight through afternoon chores, something he thought could never happen.

"Seth … Seth … It's time to eat. We're having meat loaf and corn on the cob."

When he arrived at the dinner table, everyone was seated, including his mother. Sunday's big meal generally started with a family blessing, not Monday's. For some unknown reason, his mother insisted on prayer. He knew how hungry Pa and Nate were after digging post holes and milking fifty Holsteins, yet they waited for him to sit down. Grace having been said, the feast was on and over in fifteen dedicated minutes. As always, Pa thanked the cook and took to his chair. Nate was instructed to take a shower; most times he had to be told or he wouldn't do it. Mother began to clear the table.

"I'll give you a hand with the dishes," said Seth.

"I appreciate the offer, but there isn't much to do. Pots and pans were done before you sat down. Why don't you go see what your father has on television?"

He scanned the sink and counter; she'd been truthful. "As you wish, and, by the way, the flowers look nice."

Martha smiled. She'd centered a few garden favorites, cosmos, at the dinner table.

The Republican National Convention on three networks left no choice in programming. Pa couldn't be sidetracked from all the hoopla, so much so the newspaper lay folded on his lap. Seth would be eligible to vote when election time rolled around. Whether conservative or liberal, he thought politics to be a dirty business; it was difficult to get at the real truth, and thus it was a crapshoot. His father was partial to Nixon, and he'd back the ole man till his belly caved in, like many other sons his age. Possible campaign finance violations and the link to the break-in and alleged bugging of the Democratic National Committee, according to Pa, were merely preelection mudslinging; a political ploy designed to gain momentum in the home stretch. Why should Seth believe him? The title of father carried much clout in a son's eye. For this reason, he'd watch the celebration on television and not necessarily listen to what was being said. There were other important issues on his mind, such as financing of a more personal nature. Buck Sager's remark about the tractor was burning a hole in his brain. He knew their real estate was paid for; it was their machinery that was bankrolled, and he had no idea for how much. Buck was hitting below the belt with that one. Part of him wanted to tell his father about the incident and part of him didn't. The latter held sway. As with politics, he trusted in Pa's decisions.

CHAPTER 5

Each dip in the driveway held a shimmer of yard light off an overnight downpour. It was too early for sun but not fish; they were always awake. Seth put a peanut-butter-and-jelly sandwich in one jacket pocket and a thermos of milk in the other. His fishing tackle waited truck-side. With rain, collecting bait required no more effort than to bend down and pick it up. As he dropped the last of a dozen night crawlers into a tin can, he knew fishing wouldn't be on the agenda if not for a poor night's sleep, probably because he'd crashed yesterday afternoon. No matter, he was awake now and doing what he wanted to do at four thirty in the morning. A note on the table would let his rising family know of his intent. Nate would know where.

A little past Wylie's was an entrance to a wooded roundabout and, like his neighbor's driveway, a person would hardly know it was there. Matted grass indicated an occasional vehicle, although it couldn't be considered popular among fishermen. This was where Willow Creek joined the Oakton River, and a ten-foot ridge oversaw their union. Anyone privy to it could tailgate fish in the ambience of Mother Nature.

His bobber fixed at twelve feet, bait would squirm just above the riverbed. Maybe he'd tempt a perch or two grazing the bottom, but more likely, it'd be bullheads. After dropping line, he unscrewed his thermos and took a big gulp. Sandwich hastily shoved into a paper bag; he used it to separate fingers from meal, trusting that pants didn't remove everything left behind after baiting a hook. Hidden in darkness, early birds chirped the coming of a new day. Nate would've wanted to be there with him. It was five years ago when a feisty eight-year-old brother joined Curtis and him on opening day of trout season.

Seth was introduced to Curtis Delano on a dreary Tuesday morning barely a week after Wylie's parents became traffic fatalities. They both arrived with condolences—he delivering a jar of chicken soup by way of bicycle, and Curtis, heartfelt sympathy by way of a beaten station wagon. Several times that summer, they had fished the same spot, and a friendship developed. By spring the following year, plans were made to try their hand at rainbow trout. Nate was a last-minute addition.

An hour's drive north brought them to a secluded stream near an Indian reservation that Curtis was historically tied to. The indigene parked his wagon near a small bridge and said it was the best place to access shoreline. Two other cars agreed. Dreams of satisfying legal limits pushed them through heavy brush, primordial light giving just enough to make their way. Three other fishermen were strewn downstream keeping a respectable distance between them. As newcomers, they certainly saw more spots available than their predecessors, and each of them nearly climbed over one another for first dibs. Eventually, they settled down into chosen hot spots and began casting. It was then that Seth noticed there was more to the picture. Their counterparts were obviously serious about the sport. They stood still in waist boots, casting fly rods with utmost precision into a rippling current. Lure-studded headgear, multipocketed vests, and creels twitching with achievement—*professional* was the word that described it. The advent of three amateur anglers crackling through underbrush must've gotten their blood up, and he thoroughly expected the zinging of cheap reels to bring them to a boil.

Less than half an hour into fishing, Curtis snagged his hook four feet shy of the opposite bank. Roaming up and down shoreline in an effort to jerk it free resulted in nothing more than wet feet. He secured footing at the closest spot nearest the snag and had at it with a heave-ho. His pole soon reached its breaking point sending a loud crack echoing in both directions. Everyone there watched as most of the rod slipped down his line and disappeared beneath whitewater; the snag held firm. Curtis was left holding what remained, which was a rod handle and dangling reel. He looked upstream at his fishing buddies and then downstream where the pros tended to drift further and further away. Native hair swayed from side to side as he shook his head at the decision to use brute force rather than cut the line. As if tossing a rose into an open grave, he let go the rest, unconcerned with what could be salvaged.

They were unsure of the big man's emotional state when he passed behind them but positive the fishing trip was over. Even if there had been an extra rod and reel, they doubted Curtis would've returned with it. Nate reeled in his line and followed; Seth brought up the rear. Once again, they fought brush, this time with one less pole. While the brothers loaded fishing gear, Curtis stood on the bridge and stared downstream at what had ended before it began. He hardly noticed the approach of his companions. They spent a few minutes watching real fisherman. This didn't help. Two of them sat on the shoreline, unable to continue casting in their hysterics. The other casually waded over to the scene of the mishap, probably to claim ownership of what could be recovered. Seth didn't know what to say. Nate did.

"Don't feel bad, Curtis. I kept getting lures stuck in tree branches. Lost three of my best, and they didn't even touch water."

Realizing there wasn't any possible way he'd get home without being discovered, Seth confessed. "I slipped and fell trying to squeeze in a couple more casts before leaving. I'm soaked to my skivvies." He turned around to reveal his soggy backside.

A hard life didn't give Curtis much to smile about and less to laugh about, but this was too potent for stoicism to endure. His hair danced, his beer gut jiggled, and a big, open-mouth grin formed unnatural lines; yet nothing much came out. It was sort of like panting and exactly what was needed to release the farm boys from a cage of uncertainty.

"Let's get outta here," Curtis said laughing. "I think we've had enough humiliation for one day."

Just when the elders had thought humor gone after about fifteen quiet minutes on the road, Nate brought it right back. "We must've looked like the Three Fuckin' Stooges to them guys." He only said what they'd been thinking, but it kept them in stitches all the way home.

Seth sat on the tailgate waiting for his bobber to dip below the surface. He chuckled at the memory of the trout expedition and then shoved the last bite of sandwich into his mouth. On that particular morning, it was laughter that filled empty stringers; he hoped today it'd be fish.

The first light of day was about to break without so much as a nibble. It had to be quarter of six, and half the herd would be pumped dry. He was lost in chores of which he wasn't a part until headlights tore through his melancholy. Shielding his eyes from the glare, he heard the low rumble of a big-block engine and decided it was likely Martin Hoffman, his part-time friend and a summer transplant from the big city. His pickup was louder because of a worn muffler, but Marty's motor was raw muscle. The monster closed its eyes, growled some, and then fell silent. Huge tires upheld four hundred horses of midnight blue. Total confirmation came as the window slowly rolled down, revealing the chiseled face and deep-set stare.

"Hey there, Seth. Mind if I drop a line with you?"

"Not at all; there's lots of room. Maybe you'll change my luck."

As far as Seth knew, Marty's parents' income afforded them dog days of leisure in a cozy cabin twelve miles due west. It was a forested setting that lent itself more to hunting than fishing or farming, so it was ideal for Marty's primary interest. Had he been given the ability to see deeper into water, Seth suspected he would've preferred shooting fish. However, fishing was where it had all begun two years past, and fishing was where it'd probably end. Till then, listening to Marty while the river flowed by was as good a way to pass time as any.

Without words, Marty hopped on the tailgate, baited hook, and fastened bobber at twelve feet. He'd fished this spot before. After his line was set, he asked, "What you been up to?"

"Farming can keep a fella busy, except for the last three days. A cow stepped on my foot, and the folks saw fit to bench me. Nate's been filling in."

"A Holstein has got to weigh half a ton. It must hurt."

"Oh, I'll be all right. At the time, I wanted to run Delma through a meat grinder though. How you been killing your time?" Somehow, discussion with the hunter often took aim on said subject. Seth was strangely drawn to that which he never had a particular desire to do outside the city dude's influence. It was more confusing than anything, so he just fell into place.

"I've been hunting and fishing all summer. It's been great."

Seth jerked his line to give the bait some action. "Too bad there isn't a college for hunting and fishing."

"There is. It's called the U.S. Marine Corps, and my parents aren't too happy about it."

"You mean you've joined the service?"

"Either that or get drafted."

"I'll have to register in a few months," Seth admitted, "but the numbers are way down, and there's talk of ending it by December. I could luck out."

"That's where we differ. I wanted to join."

"I suppose I'd enlist if the country needed me; otherwise, farming is what I'm signed up for." He didn't want to imply a lack of patriotism toward a necessary evil.

"Don't get me wrong. It's not so much honor and duty as it is an ultimate challenge."

"One might say a challenge that could thrill you to death. Doesn't that bother you?"

"Not really. It's what I like to do, so I might as well do it up good."

"The paper said our last combat troops have been pulled from Vietnam. Who are you going to fight?"

"The paper said." Marty rolled his eyes and went for the kill. "Seventh Fleet is off shore, Air Force is carpet bombing, and Marines are still on the ground in terms of advisors, logistics, technicians, and security, not to mention covert missions into Laos and Cambodia. Besides, I'm sure Uncle Sam can find a place for me somewhere on this war-happy planet."

"I bet he could too, but if you want to fight now, tug on your line. Something's nibbling. See the bobber move?" Seth was glad to shift gears. Talk of joining the service to quench bloodlust was going beyond his willingness to understand. It wasn't chitchat anymore.

Marty pulled quick and hooked into a scrapper that wasn't going belly up without resistance. The fish took a few seconds of light drag, crisscrossing lines before battle. Seth cut his bobber free and grabbed the net while Marty reeled to keep his line taut. It was one minute of pure excitement as they worked to bring in the catch, which looked to be better than a foot of yellow perch. Normally, the species didn't argue that much. They wasted no time basking in glory; for where there was one, there were others. Baited hooks were into water before the fish had stopped flopping. An hour later, they were backslapping at the sight of ten that had succumbed to their teamwork. The last fifteen minutes netted zero, so they ended content with what the river gave.

"What do you say I take them home and clean them for lunch? My parents are gone for the day, which means we can eat in peace."

"Evidently, they're a bit more than unhappy about you joining the service."

"Pissed would be more like it, and the closer it comes to reporting, the worse it gets."

"They probably prefer you go off to college and get a different kind of education. Losing a child to war would be difficult for any parent, especially an only child. There'd be nobody to carry on the family name, no grandchildren, no future beyond themselves. Isn't that sad?"

"No more sad than the many that have gone before me. Just as you're inclined to stick with farming, I'll stick with the hunt. Both can have deadly consequences. Don't tell me you haven't noticed what farm machinery could do to a body, and it's often just a toehold away."

Seth was humbled by Marty's words. It'd been three days since he decided not to let Nate in on PBS because of the distraction it could cause around machinery and cattle. "You've made your point … Weren't you saying something about cooking these for lunch?"

"Now you're talking."

"Ma will have breakfast on the table about this time. Would you like to join us?"

"Thanks for the offer, but I should take care of these and nab a few winks. I didn't get much sleep last night."

"Neither did I. Too much R & R, I think."

"For me, it's too much story to tell right now. I'll fill you in when I pick you up at eleven thirty."

"You're going to leave me hanging, aren't ya?"

Marty put their catch in a cooler secured to his truck bed and then climbed behind the wheel and fired her up. "I sure am … But it'll be worth every minute of it."

The black wall cat indicated it was later than he'd thought. In between shifty eyes and swinging tail, it read seven fifteen. Why his mother had such an attachment to it was a direction of thought Seth cared not take. She was finishing breakfast dishes; only last night's vase of cosmos adorned her table. Father and brother were nowhere to be seen. When there's nothing around to feast eyes on, hunger runs rampant. Wait, what's in that pot on the stove? Could it be?

There were four basic types of hot cereal, and each fell under the general heading of bup. Normally, it'd warm and fill the tummy during winter months and save cool, damp days when its hardiness could sure hit the spot. According to his father, any of them would put hair on your chest. Wheat and oatmeal were most common. Both required a slab of butter, two heaping teaspoons of sugar, and a splash of milk. What Pa called cornmeal mush had the texture of creamed wheat and needed the same doctoring; it was the yellow color that took getting used to. Finally, there was bear food, his favorite, and another with a Pa-given name, which probably came from the picture of a bear on the packaging. It had oatmeal's bulk with a multigrain theme. Maple syrup replaced sugar and was stirred in with melting butter before adding milk. Bear food was "good wood."

Martha heard him kicking off his shoes at the door as she was stepping stove-side to stir her potted concoction. She'd succeeded in keeping it clump free for thirty minutes and was relieved Seth had come in when he did. Any longer and it wouldn't be the same. He tried to sneak a peek, but she playfully turned him away. "Wash and be seated, Oh Great Fisherman, that I might sooner hear of your exploits at sea."

"Don't tease, Ma. Tell me what's in the pot … It's bear food, isn't it?" The slightest smile didn't escape his eye. "Ah-ha, it is bear food."

Martha looked closer into the porridge she'd churned for so long. "What's this I see? Could it be lumps? And they seem to be getting bigger and bigger."

Seth didn't take these words lightly, for they could be true. There were few meals he disliked more than lumpy hot cereal. "Then stop stirring and plop it in a bowl. Be back in a flash in the flesh."

Wallowing in belly-busting satisfaction, Seth commended the cook in his own way. "Thanks, Ma. The bear is full; now it's off to the woods." He laughed.

"Where's the fish, old man? Did sharks eat it?"

"That's Hemingway. Good one, Ma. Fact is, Marty and I caught ten perch this morning, and he wants to fry them for lunch. He said he'll pick me up at eleven thirty. I hope it's okay with you and Pa."

"Did you ask him over for breakfast?"

"I did, but he had some things to do before lunch. You shouldn't take it personal though; he's a loner. Come to think of it, he hasn't really met any of my friends and doesn't talk of his. It could be I'm it, and I don't even see him that much."

"Everyone deserves at least one friend. I'd say Marty made a wise choice. Now if you'd be so kind as to remove that sock and let me look at your toe …"

They were in agreement about his injury. The swelling had gone down, but bruising was extensive. Stress on it should be minimized. Much to his good fortune, this didn't affect the fish fry or an afternoon of tooling around in Marty's fire-breathing Chevy. He'd have to stay off it until then, a more than fair exchange between active son and caring mother. Seth peg-legged it to his room before the nurse could change her mind.

Three hours passed in a heartbeat. He remembered lying down with a book and wondering what it was Marty had lost sleep over. Everything other than that had vanished; he couldn't even recall turning a page. His recuperation had infected a sleeping pattern years in the making, and he didn't like it. There was more time being spent in sneakers than work boots and yet again more in stocking feet than sneakers. Next stop, those awful slippers by the screen door. Glancing out the window as he laced up his canvas, he saw the elm cast a bleak shadow. Cloud cover hadn't broken, and if it looked like rain, Pa wouldn't be fixing fence. Chances were they'd switch to calf pens, something else that needed attention. It was fun to work around young calves. Underfoot and curious, they pestered for neck scratches and head rubs or tried to nudge an utter that wasn't there. Seth felt he'd have to take a walk in the barn sometime soon; as for now, Marty's story was less than a half hour away, and Seth suspected he was the type to show early. How right that was.

"Ma, he's here. See ya later."

"Do you think you'll be home for supper?"

"I expect so. If not, I'll call."

"There's always room for one more at our table."

"I'll see what he says, no guarantees."

Once in their driveway, Marty eased his gas pedal around the flagpole. He tipped his cap to the nice lady standing in the doorway and reached over to crack open the door for Seth. "I hope you're hungry because we got lots."

"Hungry for that story you skipped out on."

"Wait till we get on the road. I've got to figure out how to start without sounding psycho." Marty took a deep breath, turned onto River Road, and began his tale between third and fourth gear.

"Last Friday night, say around nine thirty or ten, I was fishing the same spot we were at this morning and—"

"You caught a whole mess of them, didn't ya?"

"No, and don't interrupt. Save your questions till after I get this off my chest."

"Go ahead; you have my complete attention."

"I was sitting on the tailgate and had just dropped a second line when something froze me up like a possum. ... An orange light came cruising over the water from upriver, right down the middle. It was huge, twenty feet across if an inch, and didn't make a sound. Looked like a giant basketball. When it hovered a stone toss off shore, I damn near pissed my pants. Then it slowly rose above the tree tops, and as it did, its color began to fade. I knew it was still there because it blocked out stars. Great camouflage but not invisible, until it disappeared northbound ... I couldn't tell you if any fish were pulling on bobbers because my eyes were glued to the sky for twenty minutes; almost wrote it off as swamp gas, and then it came back. It's hard to brush off a second time. I'd calmed down some and was focused. Basically, it backtracked to perfection, and all I could think about was not having my shotgun with me. After what seemed like a one-hour minute, the light moved back upriver, and I haven't seen it since. I was there at the same time on Saturday as well as Sunday and tried drinking it away last night, which didn't work. Going back there this morning was a must."

"And you'll keep going back to Fisherman's Ridge in case it returns?"

"I don't know. It's beginning to feel like a waste of time. I just thought you should be aware because you live close by." Marty cocked his head for a look at Seth's face. "Well, aren't you going to say I'm crazy with the heat?"

"I believe that you believe you seen something, and seeing is believing." All Seth knew for sure was at about the same time last Friday night, while he was being duped by Wylie and Wade, Marty was supposedly seeing the real thing less than a quarter mile away. He could empathize with how Marty felt during his encounter and speculate on coincidence with Wylie's gag, and that was it. A few more questions couldn't hurt though. "Was it a bright light?"

"No, it was more of a dull glow. In fact, it barely lit up its reflection on the water."

"How did it move?"

"Its movement was smooth and deliberate; didn't wobble or waver, in motion or not."

Seth pressed on. "You say it didn't make a sound; are you sure? Maybe in the frenzy, you didn't notice."

"Hell, frogs stopped croaking. The only thing I could do was watch and listen ... Except ... I didn't want to talk about this part because it's loonier than the rest, but I've gone this far, so here goes. Before it left for good, when it hovered over water for that long minute, that's when I heard something. Two beeps, one after another, and not very loud. The strange part is that they made me feel like it knew I was there."

"You mean to say the hunter felt hunted?"

"Unarmed and vulnerable would be more accurate."

Marty had taken a defensive posture with that last question, which should've made it the last, but still Seth wanted to cram one more in. "Is there anything else you remember, perhaps an unusual odor?"

"An unusual odor? Maybe a couple raunchy farts, although that's not unusual. I told you everything I know, and if you pass it on, I'll deny, deny, deny."

"You should know that's not my way. I just want to get the facts straight in case it happens to me."

"Okay, Inspector. You'll have to continue the investigation from here; my vacation is almost over. Now let's go eat some fish." He slipped in an 8-track tape and cranked the volume.

When it came to music, Seth could easily adapt to the tastes of others. He liked classical best, which he admitted to no one, but could usually find something to appreciate in all types. Hard rock was on today's menu, and it was as aggressive as the truck he was in. The pounding beat kept them company till they reached their destination.

A fieldstone chimney took first notice when confronting the Hoffmans' cedar cabin. From another point of view, porch chairs overlooked property that required little maintenance. It was as if their home had sprouted in the wilderness and a dirt driveway eventually discovered a road. This was quite the departure from big-city life. Inside, it was humble without sacrificing modern conveniences. A woman's touch was evident amongst the leather furniture and wildlife pictures, yet most would consider the house more of a sportsman's lodge than a summer vacation home.

Everything was set to go: fry pan, cooking oil, and a bowl of famous coating. When the fillets came out of the fridge, Marty worked it like an assembly line—fast and efficient. The hunter was also a fine cook, and this knowledge lured Seth into trying things that weren't part of his normal diet, like venison, rabbit, squirrel, and even grouse and pheasant. In the handful of times he took to hanging out with Marty at length, something different usually met his gullet. If it wasn't a fresh kill, it was fresh out of the freezer. A year had come and gone since he'd last sat down to Marty's panfry, and Seth thought he was long overdue. No one could make perch smell or taste any better.

"Get a plate and load up."

Seth pounced on the invitation. "Holy snortin', Nellie, I didn't expect all this!" The coleslaw, tartar sauce, and rye bread had, until then, escaped his roving eyes.

"Check the fridge and see if there's something you'd like to drink. It's past noon; think I'll have a beer."

After feasting, they rinsed off their plates and neatly stacked them in the sink. With the exception of this act, the kitchen was left as it had been found. That was what the woman of the house expected and what was delivered without complaint.

"Come up to my room. I'd like to show you what I bought."

He'd been in Marty's room once before and was honored to be asked again. It reminded him of their similar interests, which needed reinforcement from time to time. An open stairway led to a loft. This was Martin's Lair—the sign said so. Much like Seth's own room, it wouldn't win any awards for interior design. A White Sox pennant hung above the bed, two World War I flying aces dangled from the rafters, and abundant literature was stacked randomly about. Baseball, biplanes, and books wouldn't be topics of discourse on this Tuesday afternoon, such lay in a gun cabinet at the far end. As host thumbed through the keys on his key chain, Seth took note of a single book on the wrinkled bed covers. The author was Nietzsche, and what little he knew of his writings was enough to raise concern. It didn't ease his mind when the cabinet doors swung open and exposed an arsenal capable of bringing joy to any gun enthusiast. There were two with scopes, a bolt-action deer rifle, and a semiautomatic twenty-two. Other long guns included a Winchester lever action, an M-1 carbine, and a musket. Of the six spaces available for long guns, only one was vacant.

"I can't believe you didn't fill that spot with something," said Seth as he studied the collection.

"I did; that's where my twelve-gauge pump belongs. Right now, it's behind the truck seat along with a box of slugs."

"Has this anything to do with the UFO you've been stalking?"

"Maybe," Marty replied with a half smile. "It'd be one hell of a trophy to bring down."

"Do you really think a few slugs could do that?"

"You never know unless you try."

Marty knelt down and opened the first of four drawers. In it was a revolver so large an average man could stick his finger into the muzzle. He removed it from a foam bed and spun its empty chambers before twirling the butt in Seth's direction.

"I bought this at a gun show two weeks ago. It's a forty-four magnum; you know the rest."

"So, this is the same gun Dirty Harry used."

"Not exactly, different make but same kick. You want to shoot it?"

Hesitation moved the hard sell forward. Marty opened another drawer that displayed more handguns. "How 'bout this twenty-two target or the twenty-five pocket pistol? They're both great for beginners."

"I know what you're trying to do." Truth be told, a twenty-two was the largest caliber handgun Seth had ever shot. Would he bend to Marty's unfair tactics? "What do you have in the other drawers?"

Eagerly, his host opened yet another. "In here, we have two classics: a thirty-eight special and a forty-five auto. It gets better. Shall I go on?"

"You might just as well."

By the sentimental expression on Marty's face, Seth knew the final drawer held a piece that was highly favored—and rightfully so. It was an icon of the American Wild West, a Colt Forty-five Peacemaker. The nickel-plated six-shooter with ivory handle was tucked into a black leather holster, which only the fanciest gunslinger would strap on. The belt was adorned with a silver buckle and a full complement of cartridges looped around back; a leg strap would secure the holster to a shooter's thigh. Appearance suggested that it was right out of the movies, and he marveled in its reality.

"You like it, don't ya?" Marty traded him weapons.

Seth pulled the beauty from its form-fitted sleeve. "What possessed you to get this? It's not really for hunting. In fact, none of these pistols are."

"They could be; the question is do they have to be? Sometimes, I shoot for fun. I'm not always beading in on live game. That particular gun I've dreamed of since blasting caps with the Lone Ranger."

"You're lucky there. I had to use thumb and finger … my own sound effects too. The folks wouldn't buy toy guns for us."

"Don't you have any guns?"

"Pa has an old double-barrel shotgun and a twenty-two semiautomatic pistol. He taught me how to use them but not for food or fun. It was sort of a precaution against the unforeseeable."

"Well dad-blame it, Paw," Marty said as if speaking for Seth. As for him, he added, "I reckon we oughta slap some iron then, Sodbuster."

Before Seth could comment, Marty stuck the magnum in his belt, snatched up a box of shells for each revolver, and was leading the way. Seth followed behind carrying the Peacemaker and holdover thoughts from Marty's current reading material, *The Will to Power*. There had been two other occasions on which Marty had asked him to shoot and he'd declined. On this, the third, Marty had tried with a magnum but knew the irresistible charm lay with the notorious Colt glistening in its rootin'-tootin' splendor. Such an opportunity might never come along again, Seth reasoned, and he was with an experienced gunman. If Marty could do it, so too could he.

After exiting through the patio doors, they paused to pick out some tin cans from the garbage, selecting those not already riddled with jagged holes. A short walk away was a ridgeline that served as backstop for a pair of four-foot posts supporting an equal stretch of plank. Marty placed six cans and returned to a well-worn firing line, which looked to be a manly six paces.

"Are you going to stand there holding it or buckle up? Tie it to your leg too. How does it feel?"

"It sits comfortable on the hip. I feel a bit foolish though."

"It isn't loaded, but check it out anyway; always double-check. Now practice pulling it from the holster. Remember, this isn't a fast-draw competition; pull it out slow, steady, and firm."

He withdrew the gun carefully and one-eyed the first can at arm's length. "How's this?"

Marty was all over him. "Wait a minute there, Cowboy. We'll shoot from the hip with that gun. Don't aim it. Point it like you would your thumb and finger. It's single action, so you'll have to cock the hammer all the way back and pull the trigger for each shot. Do not cock the hammer until you've leveled off the barrel. You don't want to shoot yourself in the foot. Is that understood?"

"Yes, Master." He continued to practice.

"Now you're getting it. Let's load 'er up."

Marty dropped six cartridges into Seth's open palm. Seth carefully slipped each into its own chamber, one chubby slug at a time. What a power rush! He slid it into the holster and waited for final instructions.

"Okay, face your targets. Remember to draw your weapon slow, steady, and firm; then level the barrel, cock the hammer, point—don't aim—and pull the trigger. It'll be loud and kick some. Don't let that scare you. Hold firm. And one more thing, shoot all six, one after the other. No stopping in between or you'll lose concentration." He stepped off to one side while keeping a close eye on his student. "Fire when ready."

Seth followed Marty's introduction to the last detail, and in less than ten seconds, his rounds were spent. Only one can flew from its stand, and he was sure that was luck. Slipping the pistol into its holster, he turned to find his instructor laughing to the point of tears.

"What the hell's so funny?" he demanded.

Marty tried to say something, but he simply couldn't get it out.

"Come on, was I that bad?"

Eventually, Marty came around and spoke his mind. "I'm sorry for laughing. It's just that I'm so damned happy for ya. Never thought I'd get you to pull a trigger and then to step into it like you did. It was good, real good. It almost makes me want to milk a cow to see what gets you off."

"I'm sure that can be arranged. Maybe I could teach you a few things."

"I said *almost*. Here," he said, handing Seth six more bullets, "I know you want to do it again."

He fared better though he went more slowly with his second set, as Marty decided to give advice between rounds. By the third set, his confidence in his ability to control the weapon had grown. Determined to best his previous attempts, he took time dispensing empty cartridges, sniffing the depleted gunpowder, and trading for another half-dozen fat boys. With each click of the cylinder, he looked at his targets before putting in another round. With some last-minute encouragement from Marty and a deep breath, he was ready for action. Shots three, four, and six each took a can. Seth holstered the smoking gun and wrinkled his brow at his proud teacher.

"You're a natural, Seth. Took me a lot longer to do what you did." Marty retrieved the cans, inspecting each and replacing all except one. "You winged the other two. This one, you have to keep. It was your last shot and dead-on."

"Thanks. I have to admit shooting this gun is pretty fun. How 'bout showing me what you can do with it?" He unbuckled and swapped his gun for the magnum in Marty's belt. He would've liked to click off a few more but knew cartridges wouldn't be cheap at half the price.

"I will if you put another can on the plank; must have six."

Seth thought it amazing that Marty had time to eject, reload, and twirl the six-gun snug into its leather pocket before he returned. He noticed it was pulled loose of a tight fit. Marty stretched his fingers and laid a relaxed palm on the packed holster. If the sun had been out, it would've been to Marty's back. From what Seth could gather, the preliminaries were textbook gunfighter, Hollywood-style.

Once his student was behind the firing line, Marty rolled his shoulders and spoke without taking his eyes off the targets. "Say when. And for all those young cowpokes in the audience, don't try this at home."

Quick to the punch, Seth immediately said, "Go," and it was over in a streak of flashes. The first round was cocked within the motion of the draw, not what Seth had been taught and wisely so. By fanning the hammer, five others automatically followed. A tricky finger spun the gun home. Of the cans, two were left standing, and Seth believed that to be intentional. Whether it was an expression of modesty or baiting the hook of inspiration, he wasn't sure. It was odd that he could be one can shy of equaling a master in accuracy, if not speed. A greenhorn shouldn't be able to do that.

"Marty, you're incredible. It must've taken a lot of practice."

"It did, and that's why you can trust me when I said you did very well for the first time. Much better than I expected."

"Do it again. This time, I'll try not to blink."

"Why not shoot the magnum instead?" Marty knew repetition would serve the same result. What he really wanted was for Seth to try a forty-four while still primed with pistol madness.

"Suppose I could give it a whirl." It was weightier than the Colt Army with two more inches of barrel length, though both shared single-action mechanics. The slight difference in caliber by no means hid the fact that the magnum meant a bigger charge and therefore a bigger kick.

"That's the spirit, Deputy."

"Wow, from Sodbuster to Deputy in twenty minutes. I must be doing something right."

"You line the cans; I'll load 'er up. Check the hits for me. I'd like to know how I did."

Seth aligned them sideways to expose clean metal. If they could be transposed over one another, a book of matches would cover the pattern. It was very impressive and supported an earlier theory of his. "You aced all four."

A few steps back from their original firing line, Marty handed Seth the cannon. "We'll give this one a little more room. You can aim, but use both hands until you get familiar with it."

The heavy metal, which Seth thought bore a striking resemblance to Marty's choice in music, was as brazen and bold as its name suggested. Without delay, he held it outright, cocked the hammer, and zeroed in. Detonation hurled flames from the muzzle and sent a jolt deep into his forearms. Each successive round was ever more exhilarating, and the session ended with two having found their mark. It was fortunate that Seth's inexperience dwarfed any expectations of accuracy. He even went one-handed at the last.

Seth passed the gun off and reset his triumphs. "I only hit two out of six; hardly counts."

"They all count. With practice, you'd surprise yourself. I figured those mitts to be good for something besides pulling utters."

"We don't pull utters, City Slicker. A machine pulls and squeezes the teat which is attached to the utter."

"This, that, or the utter, call it what you want. I call those can-cans history."

One by one, Marty blew them away single-handedly. His proficiency with handguns left little room for doubt that he'd be any less accurate with long guns, and if there was any, there was a freezer full of wild game to dispel the notion. His passion for firearms would serve the military well.

"What time you got?"

Whereas most would glance at their wrist, Seth didn't. "It looks to be about one thirty, maybe two."

"Don't you have a watch?"

"Sure, just don't find much use for it. When you don't wear one, it feels funny when you do."

"I can't get along without one in the city. When I come north, it's different; it's like you say. Anyhow, we have a couple of stops to make before we call it a day. We don't want to cut ourselves short."

Given the activities thus far, Seth wondered what could possibly be in store for him. Marty's basic instincts seemed to be covered. What other driving forces were about to make themselves known? The question was of no consequence. His friend had the wheels, and that was where their next adventure would begin.

They hit the road with too much audio for yakety-yak which didn't bother them. Bobbing heads to heavy percussion filled the gap. Several miles from Seth's home was another desolate stretch. There couldn't have been more than a few homesteads on three country miles of ill-budgeted repair. He'd traveled down Muck Road before and saw nothing of any great significance. Why Marty chose it was a mystery to him.

Taking the liberty to lower the volume of the music, he asked, "What's down this way?"

"Do you know Jake and Penny Finley?"

"I know who they are; never met them though."

"I met them two summers ago. The woods back of their house is thick with beechnut and white oak, prime habitat for gray squirrel. One day, I decided to stop by and ask if they'd allow me hunting privileges. It's been good ever since, and returning the favor is even better."

"If returning the favor is better than squirrel hunting, then it's not really a favor; you're not giving anything up."

"Oh, I give it up all right. Tell you about that some other time. We're almost there."

"Going to leave me hanging again, aren't ya?"

"I sure am … But it'll be worth every minute of it."

Finley's place was a newer home, but nothing fancy; in fact, it was smaller than the big-rig garage next to it. With a couple acres of grass to cut, somebody was spending considerable time on a lawn tractor, and it wasn't Jake, as he was a long-haul trucker. The last thing he'd want to do after a run is hop on a mower. It didn't make sense to think Marty found more pleasure in mowing grass than squirrel hunting. Seth refused to think about it any longer; that was what the guy wanted him to do.

Marty was out of the cab and between buildings before Seth could close his door. Feeling stranded, he slowly wandered in the same direction, rounding the garage as a screen door clapped shut. Penny was being pulled by the hand toward him. Tall, lean, and fair, everything about her swayed with the freedom of the times—from a male's point of view. Sandy-blond hair bounced on her shoulders. A shear gauze pullover left nothing to the imagination, and a full-length floral skirt shifted in the breeze. Freckled across the nose, her colony was sheltered from broken sunshine by a straw garden hat with an emerald ribbon the same color as her eyes. One friendly smile later, and Seth was convinced this flower child wasn't much older than Marty. Two thoughts would pass before he'd be compelled to speak: Who was cutting the grass? and Why did he even care?

"Penny, this here is Seth Wickman—farmer, fisherman, and friend."

"I'm pleased to meet you, Penny. I trust the day has been to your liking … It seems to like you." Seth followed with a wink and a smile.

Beginning with a crinkled nose giggle and sparkle of green, she answered, "A gentleman and a sweet-talker. Did he tell you I was a sucker for that stuff?"

Marty laughed inappropriately.

"He only said that you and Jake let him hunt squirrels in the woods yonder."

"With one rule, he can't use a shotgun. They're loud and scary."

Marty cut in. "A twenty-two is more sporting anyway … And wasn't there something else, Penny?"

She folded her arms, astonished that he'd take privileges with the details of their arrangement. "When Jake's on the road, sometimes for a week or two, he insists that Marty check in on me regular. My husband says he's okay with it, because it's better than the alternatives."

"Why can't he take you on the road with him?" Seth asked.

"I've done that a few times, and it didn't do much for me. I guess I'm more of a homebody. Why don't we go inside and talk about it over a cold beer? I sunburn easily."

Penny led them into the house. A quick scan of the premises before sitting down at her kitchen table and Seth was silently piecing things together. Big cushy furniture, a huge stereo system, plants in macramé, a beaded doorway, lots of candles, a hint of incense—these things, along with her appearance, added up to hippie-chick, and a good-looking hippie-chick. It couldn't be easy for Jake to accept Marty stopping in while he was away.

Coasters in place, she sat down with her guests and proposed the first toast. "To Jake, may his journey be safe and successful."

Marty and Seth chimed in, "To Jake."

Over an hour had slipped by as they shared a dozen beers and as many stories. It was curious to Seth that Marty and Penny got along so well when they clearly had fundamental differences. Marty was a hawk and looked forward to plying his trade wherever the man wanted him. Penny was a dove and mistrusted the man. She'd be the one to stick daisies in the barrel of his assault rifle. This was probably why serious conversation steered away from politics and smack into personal heartache. Penny was unable to bear children and had a poor relationship with her side of the family. When he was eight years old, Marty had lost a younger sister to the ravages of cancer. He'd loved her very much. A foot injury just wouldn't compare to these tragedies. Seth relegated himself to the role of listener. When talk was lively, which it was for the most part, there was plenty of interest in a farmer's follies.

After abruptly standing, Marty walked his empty bottle to the sink. "Well, Penny, is there anything we can do to you today … I mean *for* you?"

She laughed with the aid of a wee beer buzz. "You've already done it. I don't mind being alone, but it's also nice to have company." Turning to Seth, she casually put her hand on his. "And it's been especially nice to meet you."

Marty had matched their combined efforts of six beers and seemed completely unaffected. "What's nice is that blouse you're wearing."

Penny blushed. "Honestly, Marty, don't you ever think of anything else?"

"That reminds me, we should get going, Seth. There's another stop to make before you tucker out on me." Marty went sincere on the hostess. "Thanks, you've been great. I'll stop back tomorrow and restock your fridge."

Each received a complimentary hug and a wave as they left. Seth wasn't going to let Marty push in the 8-track tape until a few questions were answered. "Your favor to them, is it cutting grass?"

"I did that once, and it was really boring. She doesn't mind; it gives her something to do. There's a garden behind the house she putters in too."

"May I ask a more personal question?"

"Go ahead."

"You're rather carefree around her. Does that mean you and her are … you know?"

In answering, Marty repeated Penny's words. "Honestly, Seth, don't you ever think of anything else?" It quickly ended that line of questioning.

"Then can you tell me where we're going?"

"The Lumberjack Saloon where we can drink from mugs and shoot pool."

"I'm not eighteen yet. Private parties like this afternoon are one thing, a bar is quite another. We'll put it on hold for a few months, after basic training."

"I can respect that. Chances are a drunk would step on your bad foot anyway. Tell you what though, how about we meet at the same time and place on Thursday? We'll catch some perch for you to take home, and I can tell you the rest of the story."

"And it will be worth every minute of it, right?"

"Now you're getting the hang of it, ole boy. Next stop, Wickman's Dairy Farm." He gave two long blasts of the truck's horn and pushed in the tape.

CHAPTER 6

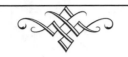

Seth couldn't believe his eyes, yet there it was, in black and white, buried fifteen pages into last night's *Greenbrier Journal*. It read; "After Car's Systems Shorted, He 'Saw' UFO." Feature articles melted away in the company of a squib stuck among advertisements. According to the piece, an eighteen-year-old had been driving home at two thirty Monday morning after visiting his girlfriend. He was on a lonely county road when suddenly, his lights went out, as did the entire electrical system, and he skidded to a stop in the middle of nowhere. Getting out of his car, he looked up and saw a large orange sphere hovering above the tree tops. It went "beep, beep" and then disappeared from sight. Even with the water in his car boiling over and the fuse box blown out, the lad was still able to drive home and call the police. Dispatched officers said evidence seemed to fit his story: twenty-three feet of skid marks, a blown fuse box, he hadn't been drinking, and he was clearly shaken. It couldn't be discounted as a hoax, nor could it be confirmed as real.

Although the events of the story took place over a hundred miles away, it bore a striking resemblance to Marty's version. Throw in Wylie's claim, and all three were within eleven days of one another. Wylie's alien prank deemed his sighting questionable. Marty's account had no such stigma; neither did the newspaper report. It was easiest to pay mind to Shea McCune; eyewitness testimony meant diddly-squat in science.

The beeping orange ball wasn't anything other than a coincidence or a natural phenomenon .... or was it?

Most of what he'd read on flying saucers came from magazines Wylie had lying around. As captivating as words and pictures could be, suspicion judged them according to entertainment value. He didn't have any material of this kind in his bedroom stacks. That was it; a Wednesday morning trip to the library would get him out of Captain Kangaroo's Treasure House.

"Hey, Ma, you think Pa will let me use the car? I'd like to go to the library in Greenbrier, and the pickup's muffler might get me a ticket in that town."

"You can ask him. He's in the machine shed. Send your brother in while you're out there, if you please."

Seth slowly wandered across the courtyard and through the open doors of the machine shed. There she sat; she was ten years old but still cleaned up good. It was obvious why Buck Sager would want their International Harvester 460 pulling his homecoming float. If Wylie's itty-bitty Ford wasn't penciled in every year for the FFA wagon, their tractor would be. Seth pulled himself from admiration to find father and brother watching him from behind the baler. It too was being cleaned and serviced, but for next season's harvest.

"Well, look what the cat dragged in," said Adam.

Nate chipped in. "We're pretty busy. Why don't you go tell your mother she wants ya?"

Nate's follow-up to his father's poppycock was expected and, as it turned out, handy. "Funny you should say. She asked me to come out here and send you inside."

"Are you serious?"

"As a heart attack, so get the lead out. She's waitin' on ya."

Nate wiped his hands on the front of his tattered county fair T-shirt and made tracks. No matter how involved men of the family were, requests from the cook were tended to in a timely manner, unless it was Nate being told to clear out the junk from under his bed.

Adam put his foot on the baler's tire; his elbow rested on his knee, a work rag dangling from his fingertips. "What's on your mind today, my boy?"

"I was wondering if I could use the car to go to the library in Greenbrier."

"Why didn't ya say so before ya spoke? … The truck's muffler does need fixin'."

"That and Greenbrier has more books than Oakton."

"I figured to get at it sometime this week … Evidently, what ya hanker for must be somethin' special if ya can't find it here or in town."

It was unusual for Pa to dig deeper into his choice of reading. Did the ole man miss him? Never mind that, the subject matter was as clumsy as his stride and needed to be shortened. He reflected on the moments shared with him last Friday night. "Star-gazing sparked an interest."

"I take it astronomy and astrophysics is what ya fancy."

Seth was taken aback. He didn't think those words were part of his father's vocabulary much less an understanding of the concepts. On second thought, he was troubled about the first. Had he stereotyped his father's agricultural generation as uneducated? It quickly brought him down a peg. "Thanks for the tip. Does that mean I can use the car?"

"I reckon so. Take the caboose and turn him loose. He could use a breath'r."

It wasn't a giant leap to suggest Pa was the one needing a break, and Seth complied without so much as a frown. Whatever could be done to lessen the burden was fine with him. "Is there anything I can get for you while I'm there?"

"Come to think of it, there is. After you've taken your rips at the pitchin' machine, mosey down to the flower shop and buy a red rose for your mother."

"You got it, one red rose." His father knew him all too well. When he was younger, he'd pester his parents to stop at Pinewood Mini-Golf on their travels to Greenbrier. They'd putt the course while he beelined to the pitching machine. When Ma wasn't with them, Pa would watch him swing away to his heart's content and then buy a rose for the mother of two fine sons.

Back at the house, Seth found his mother at the kitchen table looking over newspaper ads. "Where's Nate?" he asked.

"He's getting washed. Come over here; school is scheduled to start next Monday, and I'd like to show you some things in the paper. You can get everything that's needed at one place. Pants, shirts, socks, underwear, notebooks, pens, and pencils, it's all there."

Seth literally had a lame excuse. "Don't you think all that running around will aggravate my condition?"

"If it isn't too stressful, you could squeeze it in between library and batting cage."

To deny her request in relation to the other activities would not be fair. "I suppose we could give it a shot; last Monday worked out all right."

Twenty minutes later, Nate was in the kitchen raring to go. He'd even shaved the peach fuzz off his lip and chin without incident. Pa had the car in front and was back to work. With money and school list in Seth's pocket, they were almost ready to go.

"We can't take batting practice if we don't have our bats. Snatch both of them, batting helmet too."

"Wow. Library, clothes shopping, and the Green Machine, I must be dreaming." Nate made haste at hearing his brother's next surprise.

"And lunch at Mac's House."

Martha used his absence to put across her concerns. "Drive carefully, and don't let Nate pick out his own clothes. Use your better judgment."

"I'm glad I'll have some leverage with lunch and Pinewood. He can be downright bullheaded about some things."

Greenbrier was a less than an hour away, giving them lots of time to work out the details of their day: two hours for the library, a half hour for lunch, an hour at the department store, and the same for the Green Machine and the all-important rose before heading back to do chores. Seth had Nate jot down their last mission in bold print on the crumpled list, lest it be forgotten. Fifty minutes also gave inspection to his brother's idea of getting cleaned up. Sad to say, he required more time than it took. Nate preferred longer hair. A ball cap cleared it from his face much of the time but not today. His shirt wasn't tucked in; his sneaker laces were untied; and he should've dug the crud out from underneath his nails. Aftershave overwhelmed the breathable air to the point of requiring the cracking of a window. Seth somehow had to find a way to get this kid's act together.

"Pa and Ma said I should take you to get a haircut." It was a noble lie in his view.

"That's one thing we can accidentally forget."

"There's a salon a couple blocks from the department store, and they take walk-ins. We'll go after lunch."

"A salon! That's where women go to have their hair cut by other women. No frickin' way."

"Men go there too. Marty goes to one in the big city. He said who knows more about what women want than a woman? The alternative is a barbershop where a bald guy will run his turbocharged clipper over your skull."

"Oh, man." Nate put his hands over his face. "This is going to be embarrassing."

"No, it isn't. I'll go in with you. Lots of pretty chicks come and go from salons, and I'm not going to miss out on that. Besides, you're getting a haircut, not having your nails done, although they could use it."

"I suppose, as long as you're there, then maybe I could deal with it. We'll see what happens."

Seth slipped in one more plug before letting it rest. "Just think, the stylist could be as hot as Sara Taylor." That brought a smile and proper adjustments in shirt and shoelaces. A small pocket knife spruced his nails.

At the library, as expected, Nate rifled through the card catalogue for baseball, and they split with the understanding they were to meet at the library's front desk in two hours. Seth browsed the A's as his father had suggested but moved the instant his brother left. He found a few books and a quiet corner and then proceeded to absorb what he could in the time allotted.

The most notable sightings included those of pilot Kenneth Arnold over Mount Rainier, Washington, in June 1947, from which the term "flying saucers" was coined; a supposed crash site near Roswell, New Mexico, the following month; the lighting up of the night sky above Washington DC in July 1952; and one in and out of water at Shag Harbor, Nova Scotia, in October 1967. These were all very interesting, yet barely scratched the surface. Thousands of reported encounters, many by reputable people, were investigated by the U.S. Air Force under Project Blue Book, an understaffed and poorly funded program to provide rational explanations for waves of sightings. It concluded in 1969 that there wasn't any tangible evidence to support the flying saucer theory and therefore these phenomena posed no threat to our national security. Descriptions varied as much in size, shape, color, and motion as the project's justifications did: aircraft, balloons, astronomical bodies, weather anomalies, birds, kites, and so on.

Prior to the modern era, during World War II, they were called "foo fighters." Scores of military flight personnel reported seeing discs or round, glowing objects while on missions. There were instances when ground troops and wayward seamen had reported similar experiences. All were professionally trained observers compelled to focus on the real enemy while in the thrall of global warfare, which in Seth's opinion, meant sound judgment of the lack of UFO aggression. Even before powered flight, mysterious airships had been sighted across the United States, but none surpassed the volume of reports that came with supersonic jets, guided missiles, and the decimating atom.

Some would suggest UFO sightings began as far back as man's ability to record the event—and likely long before that. Whether it was on prehistoric cave walls, dated papyrus, or ancient stone ruins, homage was paid to celestial gods and often through great human sacrifice. Archaeological mystique regarding interpretation fostered alternative theories, less acceptable ideas in the realm of scientific and religious probability. This included extraterrestrial intervention in both technical and biological development.

As Seth read on, it became more apparent the topic was a controversial one, pitting believers against nonbelievers, those who had seen them or thought testimony and evidence overwhelming versus those who hadn't seen them or had rational answers if they had. Somewhere nearing the end of his two-hour directive, he was forced to find common ground rather than take sides. The fact was he didn't know. He'd never seen anything outside the scope of recognition. Even with abductions, which were initially thought to be a psychological disorder, he couldn't be absolutely sure. There was one thing he was sure of though, and that was that he didn't want to be caught by Nate with this information spread out in front of him. The harassment would be never-ending. Fortunately, neither of them had library cards for this place—it was too far away—or he would've been tempted to slip a couple books past him. That'd be a big mistake.

Five minutes past the appointed time, Seth found Nate near the front desk, idle but fidgety.

"Finally! I'm so hungry I could chew the warts off a toad."

"Keep it down," Seth whispered. "You know this is a library."

"Oops, sorry."

Seth hustled him out the door, inwardly humored by his backwoods remark. The reactions it provoked among those around them was priceless. It could've been much worse; Nate's backup was "hungry enough to eat the rear end out of a skunk." Thank you, Pa.

The family car didn't get to the big town much, and when it did, it avoided congestion. Suburban sprawl lent room for shopping outside Greenbrier's core—not that there were skyscrapers downtown, but there was a shit load of one-way streets and parking meters. Those who chose to deal with bumper-to-bumper traffic could keep it; the Dodge boys had plenty to see and do on the fringes. They walked from the far corner of Mac's parking lot to get their burgers and returned to eat them.

"Check out the marquee downwind," said Nate. "*The Godfather*, *Straw Dogs*, and *A Clockwork Orange* are playing this afternoon. If we didn't have to get school stuff, we could go to a matinee."

"Not any of those. Two are rated R; the other, X. You wouldn't be allowed past the ticket booth." Over summer, Seth had seen the first two. He was doubtful about *Clockwork Orange* because of its rating. It'd be uncomfortable to see with another person and even more going solo. "We're getting your hair cut, then school supplies."

"Nuts. So help me, if she screws up my head, I'll stomp on your bad foot."

"You worry too much. They're professionals and won't screw it up. Now finish your burger, and let's get it over with. We're taking away from the Green Machine."

The timing was excellent. Aside from a lady with her head in a milk bucket, the place was empty. A couple of twenty-somethings quietly argued over who would cut his hair. Full-figure Becky got the job. She adjusted the seat and fastened a neck cape around Nate and then lowered his head into a deep sink. After testing a sprinkler hose for temperature, she soaked his head, rubbed shampoo between her palms, and began massaging his hair into a lather. Damned if Nate didn't look like he was enjoying it and for good reason. Becky's jugs were swinging in his face. That wasn't all. With rinse, repeat, and conditioner, he figured Nate would be cross-eyed when she sat him up. It didn't happen, but he did look to be in La-La Land.

Becky patted the mop dry and combed it out. She'd cut while it was still wet. "How would you like your hair cut today, Nate?"

"I don't rightly know. Haven't been in a place like this before."

"I think a shag would look very nice on you. It's what many guys have been requesting."

"I've shagged a lot of baseballs, never a haircut. Reckon we could give it a go."

"You won't be disappointed." She smiled and let her scissors do the talking, for the most part.

After the cut came blow-drying and primping—Seth's interpretation of Becky's final touches. He watched her remove the bib, swing Nate's chair around, and give him a handheld mirror to inspect the back. His brother's new hairdo was acceptable. It didn't hang in his eyes without a ball cap, and that would please their parents. Seth had fed him money before they strolled in, so Nate was able to hop out of the chair and pay for it himself, plus a 10 percent tip—an important matter when seeking one's independence.

He waited for Seth's comment as they walked to the car and got nothing. "Well, what do ya think?"

"It looks like Wally cut the Beaver's hair again. We'll buy a cap for it at the store. Maybe we can find something from the Jane Fonda collection."

"You're just jealous."

"No, just pulling your leg. It looks all right. Pa and Ma will be surprised."

"You mean they didn't tell you to get my hair cut?"

"Not really. You wouldn't have done it if I asked. Aren't you happy you did though?"

"I guess so, but I should still stomp your foot on principle."

The department store was more challenging for both of them.

There were lots of people and long lines. Some faces were blurred in motion; others were tranquilized in succession while holding fast to their bargains. Sales clerks relentlessly offered service, driven by the sound of money-changers. Flashing blue-light specials, narrow aisle merchandizing—it was stifling and too much to see all at once.

"It seems like everybody and their brother is here today."

"That includes us … Follow me; men's department is this way. The sooner we do it, the sooner we'll be outta here." The accidental passage through the women's section was a result of Seth's edgy confusion with collective masses.

Nate pinched the shirt sleeve in front of him. "Look at these humongous bras, and they're here on the main aisle for everybody to see. You'd think they'd put them back a ways."

"You should be used to it after Becky washed your hair."

"She probably bought it here. The size is on the nose. Get it, on the nose?"

"Yes, I get it. Come on; you're freakin' people out."

The men's section was less crowded. Socks and underwear were prepackaged in triplicate, an uncomplicated purchase. In Seth's case, he didn't need to try on shirts and jeans because his size had remained constant for over a year. Nate was in a growth spurt, so a trip to the fitting room was necessary. Although he was drawn to current fashions, such as big collars, bell bottoms, and bold colors, an exciting day in Greenbrier curbed his demands. He settled on only one "cool" shirt and a wide belt in white. His remaining choices were mother-friendly. Toss in a couple new St. Louis ball caps, and they were off to school supplies.

The aisle was packed with shoppers. Nate agreed to hold the clothes while Seth wove his way into position. *Twelve notebooks in six modest colors, pencils, and black pens should suffice,* he thought. Their teachers would recommend whatever else they needed on the first day of class. He left in clammy relief only to have stress return when they reached the checkout lines; there were eight of them, each as many people deep. It took forever.

"So that's what hell is like," said Nate on their way to the car.

"But we're free at last; thank God Almighty, we're free at last."

"I have a dream too." He pulled the tags off their new ball caps. "It's batting five hundred today."

"And we have better than an hour to swing away. I have at least five bucks in quarters. That'll keep us busy."

At one time, Pinewood Mini-Golf would've been outside of town. Not anymore. Land development had crept up on acres of manicured lawn, and its days were numbered. Beyond gravel parking, a picket fence led golfers to a small clubhouse, putting course to the right and driving range to the left. Neither was of interest to Seth and Nate. What they wanted was tucked in the corner behind poplar windbreaks. No picket fence there, just a path between gangly trees, and, best of all, nobody was using it. Swapping their shopping bags for bats and helmet, they closed the trunk lid. What more could two brand-new Cardinal caps ask for than to be initiated at the Mean Green Pitching Machine?

"Did you notice that red Chevy van with moon windows and chrome rims parked by the clubhouse?" asked Nate while swinging windmills with the practice bat; he wasn't allowed to use his brother's Louisville, supposedly because it was too big for him.

Seth nodded and continued with their mutual warm-up.

"It looks pretty nice, hey? Anyway, after me, you come first."

"Wrong'o. I'll start out, after we go over hitting fundamentals at the plate."

"Give me some credit. I've gotten hits off you and that ornery machine."

"One fifty is a pitcher's batting average, not a golden glove shortstop's."

"I can play either."

"But you can't win without hitters."

They walked to the plate where Nate struck his batting stance under a critical eye. "How's this?"

"You've outgrown that bat. Try mine."

"For real? Far out, man."

"Line the middle knuckles in your grip. Loosen your fingers; don't strangle it, but hang on to it. You want to whip the bat around, not muscle it."

Seth observed several of Nate's swings with his Louisville. Basics were fine, he decided, noting Nate's position at the plate, his balanced stance, his back elbow down while pushing into his stride, which was smooth through hips and pivot foot. "Your worst enemy is lack of concentration. Focus on the ball when the pitcher shows it during release; spin lets you know what he's throwing. Follow it into your bat. Your head should be down during the swing, not looking into deep center field. A good rule of thumb, chin against front shoulder at the start of a swing and back shoulder at the end. If you commit to swinging, always follow through. Nothing looks worse than a half-assed attempt. You'll only have a split second to decide whether to take a swipe at it or not, so concentration pays off."

"You're right about that, and the grip does seem to put a snap in my swing. Maybe you're smarter than ya look."

"Give me that bat, girly-boy. Here, go drop a quarter in the slot, and let me show you how it's done."

"Was that a crack about my hair?"

"Just put the quarter in and let's get on with it."

Neither of them knew what the pitcher looked like underneath its green exterior. From the batting cage, it looked like an armored catapult. One could hear a tension spring "twang" right before the mechanical arm cut loose, which it did every six seconds for a minute. Because of a natural underspin, most pitches were whizzing fastballs and a bit quicker than Seth would've thrown to Nate. There was always a fraction of worn balls recycled into play, open stitches that grabbed airflow and went cockamamie in flight. Most times, they could sidestep a wild pitch, but in the event of a bean ball, their code was strict: duck away, and protect your head with your body.

The Green Machine had aliases, all given free of charge from Nate's baseball trivia. He'd been in the cage a half-dozen times and on each occasion, came up with something new. There was Cyclone, Big Train Walter, Gentleman Christy, Grover, Dizzy, and Daffy, not necessarily in that order. Today, it was Rube. Of three settings on the coin machine, it was fastest that reigned supreme. Nate fed in two bits and scooted behind the cage for an umpire's view.

Adjusting hardhat and squaring off for the delivery, Seth looked over the field. There weren't many baseballs lying around, and that meant the robot's belly was full—more than what was needed to stretch ten rounds each plus trash talk in between. Then, there it was, screaming by a late cut; Seth was guilty of daydreaming. Hypocrisy is such an ugly word. He did manage to get a piece of it, but a foul tip is still a strike as Nate made clear.

"Steee-rike. You're behind the pitch, concentrate."

Most cowhides were scuffed and dirty, hard to see when they briefly showed themselves. Baseballs in this condition wouldn't be allowed in a real game. Once in a while, a new ball was brought to bear, and such was the next pitch. This time, Seth zeroed in on a straight path over the plate. With his fundamentals in order, it didn't stand a chance. Jumping off the Louisville's sweet spot was a direct shot over the three-fifty mark in left field. There wasn't time to stand and stare, another would soon follow.

When his minute had expired, Nate blurted out the score. "Five hits. The leftfield line shot was a homer, and so was the four-hundred-foot floater in center. If not for your foot, the one in right-field corner might have gotten three bags. The other two were solid singles. You had a pop-up, a ground out, two strikes, and a foul tip. In the lineup, you'd be batting fourth. That's where the power is."

Seth walked his bat to an anxious statistician, took off the batting helmet, and handed them both over. "It's your turn. Say when, and I'll drop a quarter. Who's on the mound today?"

"Let's call him Rube."

"And what can you tell me about this Rube fella?" He didn't have a compulsion for baseball facts like Nate did. This, however, didn't stop him from inviting the stories. It was probably fresh out of the library.

"His full name is Rube Waddell, and he's listed in the Baseball Hall of Fame. He played mostly with Connie Mack's Philadelphia Athletics at the turn of the century. I read he was a left-handed farmer's son, who led the AL in strikeouts six straight years; had a blazing fastball, wicked curve, and oddball personality. That's to say he sometimes did cartwheels on the mound after a win. Opponents could distract him with puppies and shiny toys, and he liked to watch fires. Teammates had to hold him down during a game to keep him from chasing after distant fire bells."

"No kidding? Being a farmer's son, you'd think he'd be leery of fire."

"That's not all. He wrestled alligators in off-season, was married four times, and carried a pistol. I wonder if they're connected." Nate grinned.

"Whatever happened to him?"

"He drank himself out of baseball, contracted tuberculosis, and died on April Fool's Day in 1914 at only thirty-seven years old."

"That's a nine point five on the tragic scale … Regardless, Rube's cube throws nothing but fastballs. Unless they're well outside your reach, take a swipe at 'em; the machine doesn't give refunds."

Nate strolled to the plate taking leisurely swings. He stepped into the batter's box, patted his helmet down, and set himself proper. "Ready when you are."

At the drop of a coin, Seth was taking the same view his brother had when watching his stroke. The benefits of his advice were immediate. Nate slapped a base hit into right field. He couldn't stop himself from commenting, "Choke up on the bat a little."

There wouldn't be any more coaching between pitches; it affected the following two in terms of concentration. Recovery came on the fourth swing with a double into the left-center gap. The last hit was questionable; it struck Rube low and hard. It'd be an out with a fielding pitcher, a hit if he wasn't. Seth called it as he saw it. "You have two, maybe three hits; a double, a single, and the line-drive. I think it dented Rube. On the downside, you had an infield fly, two ground outs, three strikes, and a wild pitch.

"That liner at Rube shivered me timber." Nate rubbed his hands together vigorously. "You think we should get batting gloves?"

"That's a personal choice. They do tend to ease stingers. I deal with it; the feeling keeps me alert."

"Gloves or not, two out of ten sucks compared to what you did."

"I'm four years older, and this is only the first round. What's important is that you made contact with six of nine pitches; the wild one doesn't count. Of those six, three of them were good wood. You should be happy."

"Should be, but Rube doesn't throw breaking pitches. They're part of the game too, even though you don't want me to throw them."

He traded a quarter for the equipment. "Nate, you're getting way ahead of yourself, so slow down. It's also a game of patience. Your four strikeouts last Monday came on cheap curves. As to you throwing them, we're playing it smart. What we could use is a closer practice field, and I've been thinking about that."

"What did you come up with?"

"Well, we have those few acres next to the house, between our barn and River Road. It's five hundred feet of flat, grass-covered playing field. Considering we don't really need the hay off it, why not use it for batting practice?"

"That's a terrific idea. What about a backstop?"

"I bet we could make one with what Pa's got lying around."

"That's all well and good, but don't you think he'll have something to say about it?"

"What a worrywart. Pa used to play ball too. Our biggest problem is whether or not you'll keep the grass cut."

"You can count on me. Now why won't you let me throw curveballs?"

"Then can we do what we came here to do?"

"Hitting will be my obsession, Coach."

"I know you can toss a curve, you've squeezed them in enough times for me to notice. It's because of your age. Snapping the wrist while throwing hard for top spin could cripple a young arm forever. Stick with your slider another year; it's a great pitch and can only get better."

"What about the knuckler and screwball you showed me the other day? Won't they hurt my arm?"

"It's not the same release. Keep in mind that they're meant for warm-up, half-speed finger control, nothing more." Seth turned to the plate, indicating his desire to cut the jibber-jabber and have some fun.

Three rounds into the hour, and his toe had met its limit. Using it to set down thirty strides was biting off more than he could chew. Nate didn't have that drawback and went a full six rounds, wanting to push it further still. A father and son had been patiently waiting for the machine, and first come first served also had limits. Seth felt it only fair to give it up.

With the arrival of another vehicle, their car was shielded from a commotion going on at the clubhouse entrance. Two couples were making their way toward the red van, brisk in a rowdy departure. Much to their dismay, it was Frank, Tal, and their girlfriends. Tal assumed the wheel of what had to be an early graduation present. In light of last Saturday night's vendetta, Seth hoped they wouldn't notice his presence—something he couldn't rely on.

"Nate, go back to the batting cage and get those frayed baseballs I set aside." It wasn't unusual for him to gather defectives and return them for replacement.

"I know who they are, and I'm not going anywhere."

"Do as I say, and everything will be fine."

While his brother disappeared between poplars, he kept his Louisville and closed the trunk lid. Setting it inside an open driver's side window, with arms folded, he watched. Wound in self-absorption, they cared nothing for the batting cage. A fishtail, a cloud of dust, and they were gone.

"Did I miss anything?" Nate huffed from his mad dash.

"Nope, they didn't even know we were here."

He saw the bat handle sticking out the window. "Damn lucky for them."

Seth drove to the clubhouse and relieved Nate of the baseballs. There was no telling what he'd be walking into, and he didn't want his brother to be a part of it. Any other time, Mary could be seen through front windows graciously tending to her customers' needs. Where was she?

Mary had worked at Pinewood for as long as Seth could remember. She was the gal who made change for him. Her choice of attire never varied; she always wore a plain dress and white apron with large pockets. A tiny gold cross accented her button-down look. He often thought lowering her chestnut hair and applying a little makeup would bring about a world of change, but she had her reasons. Some said the loss of her right hand was due to a lawn machinery accident. He didn't see a scar; the stump above her wrist was baby-bottom smooth. A birth deformity seemed more likely. Genetically marred, perhaps Mary preferred rumor over the alternative. Either way, it didn't matter to him; she was a kind person.

He entered to find Mary on her knees trying to one-hand golf balls scattered across the floor. Working diligently to replace two bucketfuls, she didn't see him until he closed the door and then only gave him a glance before continuing her task.

"Here, let me give you a hand," came out faster than common

sense could register. Scrambling after loose golf balls was a convenient diversion from his oral blunder. He later attempted to wipe egg off his face while funneling them into the lesser bucket. "There we go. That's the last of them."

She sat up, head bowed, mythical hand set deep in her pocket. After a moment of silence, she spoke. "Thank you for your help, Seth."

It was hard to miss her glossy eyes and particularly her sniffles. Could his thoughtless words be the cause of her grief? "I'm so sorry if what I said ..."

Mary half chuckled and then plucked a tissue from her pocket and dabbed the corner of each eye. "It hasn't anything to do with what you said."

Somewhat relieved yet not fully convinced, he prodded for more. "Then what is it?"

She was unresponsive, so he was forced to draw his own conclusion from what he knew of her. The dexterity she had accumulated over the years made it doubtful the mayhem was of her own doing, and even if it had been, she'd long since learned to cope without getting emotional about it. Concealing her disfigurement wasn't normal either. Normally, she tolerated gawking patrons, using her stump freely. Mary was very much hurt, and the last people to see her were Frank, Tal, and the hussies they'd brought with them.

"Those people that just left, they did this, didn't they?"

Mary timidly nodded and proceeded to appeal on behalf of her tormentors. "Please don't make any more of it ... Let it go."

His fire fueled all the more by her "turn the other cheek" mentality, Seth delivered his own brand of brimstone. "Why those rotten sons a' bitches." Jaw tightening, he stared into an angry abyss; her sniffle tore him away. "They'll have theirs coming, and soon."

"Vengeance is mine saith the Lord," she preached as Seth took hold of the doorknob.

He looked at the frail creature huddled behind the counter and met her faith head on. "I guess the apple doesn't fall too far from the tree."

Seth stomped his way back to the car, jumped inside, and aggressively drove toward the florist's shop without saying a word. His attitude must have disconcerted Nate, but his brother remained quiet. Gathering as much benevolence as would be expected when buying flowers, he requested as his heart demanded. "I'll have two roses, one red and one pink, both with greens and each wrapped separately, if you please." Excluding his mother, Mary would have the first flower he had ever given to a girl. Mary liked pink. He waited at the counter, seething over what Frank and his band of bushwhackers might've said to Mary after, he believed, kicking over not one but two buckets of golf balls. They could've sadistically twisted his innocent words, offering to give her a hand. Those menacing demons were forty miles from home. Was there no boundary to their reign of terror, no deed too low to satisfy their sordid pleasures? He was hot as hell, and all he could do was console the victim with a flower. It seemed so feeble in the wake of the devastation. There must be something else he could do, but what? Having made payment to the florist, he returned to the car and started to backtrack.

"Where're we going?" Nate asked, knowing chores waited in the other direction.

"We're going back to Pinewood."

"Did we forget something?"

"No."

"Then why …" Stopping before he could finish his question, Nate looked at the packages. "The pink one's for Mary, isn't it?"

"Yes. She's had a bad day, and don't go thinking I'm sweet on her or rat me out to Pa and Ma that I'm doing this."

"Mum's the word," said Nate.

Seth entered the clubhouse to find Mary, tears dry but wearing the most forlorn expression he'd ever seen. His approach forced a smile from her, which quickly evolved to joy with the realization of what he had brought with him.

"For me?" she asked before shedding a few more tears, this time accompanied by a smile.

"For no other but you, Mary." With no desire to revel in her gratitude, Seth turned to leave.

"Thank you so much, Seth. This means a lot to me."

He looked back at her, smiled, tipped his hat, and left.

During their trip home, Nate held back for some time before finding something to say. "Why don't you try out for baseball next April? You'd start every game."

Seth smiled. "For me, baseball is a pastime. Something I like to do when not farming."

"Then tell me what you like about it, as a pastime."

"In some ways, it's like farming. It begins brand new in spring and ends with fall harvest. There's lots of elbow room whether working infield dirt or grazing outfield pasture. It can be made to look easy, but it isn't, and the job gets done when it gets done, not when the clock says it's done."

"I never looked at it that way. I like it because defense controls the ball for a change. I love pitching and fielding."

"It shouldn't be a mystery why we'll focus on hitting then. As a freshman, you'll need to be an all-round player to make varsity."

"Do you really think that's possible?"

"By all means: this time next summer, you'll be swatting my best pitches over River Road. I'll need to order a case of baseballs and a couple more bats to keep up."

"If that's so, I'll have learned from the best. You must've had ten homers off Rube."

"It wasn't that many."

"Let me see … There were two in the first round and three in each of the others. You really laced that last fucker."

Although the accurate count came two shy of Nate's calculations, Seth was more concerned with his brother's phrasing. The words were similar to his on the night Wylie and Wade had spooked him. He was ready to spill the beans when their farm came into view. PBS would have to wait one more day, as planned.

"Okay, eight homers not ten. I only had two in twice as many swings of the bat."

"And that's two more than the last time we went to Pinewood. Don't kick yourself; you made solid contact today, not near as many whiffs."

After they pulled up to the house, they each gathered an armload of packages, climbed the steps, and entered the kitchen to be greeted by their smiling mother stirring something in a mixing bowl.

"You got a haircut," Martha stated with surprise.

"Seth conned me into it." Setting the bags down, Nate pulled off his new ball cap. "What do ya think?"

She set down her bowl, ran her fingers through the cap ring, and then stepped back. "It looks very nice." Anything was better than the way it had been. "Where did you get it cut?"

"You're going to be shocked, Ma. At first, I was petrified. It was a beauty salon. Can you believe it?"

"Was it that place by the department store? I think it's called The Last Tangle."

"Yup, that's the place. Turned out it wasn't all that bad. Becky massaged my head with shampoo, twice, and then put some smelly stuff in and cut away while it was still wet."

"Becky did an excellent job. What did it cost?"

"Only a couple bucks more than Joe's barbershop, and worth every penny of it. I even gave her a tip."

"I'm sure she appreciated that. Now show me what you bought."

"Seth can do that. I have to change and get my butt out in the barn before Pa flies into a hissy fit."

While Seth was going through the day's purchases with his mother, Nate raced by them with clothes changed and a mind to milk cows. Pa was way ahead of him. Seth briefly thought how strange it was to be relieved that he didn't have to join them; it was quite a different feeling than he'd had the first few days into his injury. With their new clothes laid out on the table, his mother searched for her crystal vase especially reserved for the red rose she received every so often.

"Sounds like you and your brother had a wonderful day. The rose was thoughtful, so was the haircut."

"The rose was Pa's idea; the haircut was mine."

"Well, you both get a gold star. I'm not so sure about that shirt and white belt."

Seth answered her ambiguity with a tired smile. "Sometimes you just have to let him be himself."

"I guess so, as long as he doesn't want to wear them to church."

"Want me to take these things to our rooms?"

"No, thank you. I'll wash them first. You may take the school supplies though, if you please."

Flopping down on his bed, Seth envisioned Mary opening her pink rose. He hoped she wouldn't read any more into it than an attempt to cheer her up; otherwise, it could be rather awkward in the future. This train of thought swept him back to his reason for getting her one to begin with: Frank and Tal. As with the seventh pitch in the third round, he wanted to lace those fuckers for what they'd done to poor Mary and another swat for what they might have said. Then it dawned on him. Those smutty words that almost gave away PBS became a catalyst for revenge. He hadn't chosen anyone to scare yet; why not them? Last Monday, Wylie said he'd be buying lumber at Sager's on Thursday afternoon, which was tomorrow. He could stop by Wylie's after fishing with Marty and ask if he'd invite Tal, who in turn didn't go anywhere without Frank. He'd have to make sure Wylie wouldn't tell Wade and the Moellers about the invite to avoid a conflict of interest, but it could be done. As Jackie Gleason would say, "How sweet it is."

CHAPTER 7

Looking out his window at the predawn elm that had somehow survived an evening tempest, Seth felt grateful it had been spared. Only small branches were strewn beneath its spread, while its strong arms held victory high. Having avoided the fungus plague thus far, it'd be a shame if it were taken by lightning. Half the state had been ravaged by Thor's magic hammer, which had felled trees of lesser courage, downed power lines, and left debris scattered in its wake. He knew inclement weather was looming on their trip home from Greenbrier yesterday. Sure enough, it struck during chores and continued into the land of Nod. Thunderbolts flickered lights a few times but didn't affect progress in the barn or on the *Spirit of St. Louis*. He'd worked out the bugs in his plan for Frank and Tal while working on his model airplane, the distraction of which could've allowed some details to slip by, so he thought it wise to rehash them for cohesion.

Wylie was unaware of the football feud, so Seth'd simply tell him it was to be a surprise, his plot within a plot doomed if Wade knew of Frank and Tal or vice versa. It'd probably be best if Wylie didn't mention him and the Moellers to Tal either, lessening the chance of rejection. As it stood, the town bullies would eventually be disturbed that he and the Moellers were present. But he was confident they wouldn't start anything on foreign ground; they'd either stay and be sociable or turn tail. He was betting a thirst for partying would conquer their hard feelings as long as Wade wasn't there.

Seth pulled on his high tops and wondered what it was Marty had in store for him that day. Fishing was a given, but there was more to it than an angler's outing. What was it about Jake and Penny that Marty had saved for this morning's rendezvous? Anxious for an answer, he overrode his appetite, bypassed breakfast, and left a note for his family: "Gone fishing." With the exception of worms, which he'd pick up en route, everything else was in the truck. Fifteen minutes from shaking out the cobwebs, he arrived at Fisherman's Ridge. Marty was already there, two lines in the water and sucking on a bottled beer.

"It's four thirty in the morning. Isn't that a little early for a brewski?"

"Beer is the real breakfast of champions. Get a cold one for yourself; they're in the ice chest."

Having a beer to start the day was something he'd never done. What the hell? he thought. He hadn't had anything to eat, and Marty always said a guy could live on beer. "You need one?"

"Absolutely," Marty said as he chugged down the last of what he held. "Take a peek in the fish cooler."

Inside were two yellow perch and a giant walleye. "Holy mackerel, he's a big one! What you using for bait?"

"I caught him on a minnow jig. Another like him and you can feed the tribe."

"I couldn't take your catch home; it wouldn't be right. I'm sure they never had walleye before anyway."

"There's plenty in my freezer, and if they like perch, they'll like walleye; they're related. In a blind taste test, you couldn't tell them apart." He made room for his friend on the tailgate. "Cast thirty feet from mine. Here, take this black jelly bean, chew it, spit some on the jig, and rub it in."

"You got to be joking."

"It's my fishing secret. Just try it."

As the line was set to water, Seth took the second of two heavy guzzles; the first came with a toast to mark their opening. He needed them to begin another round of questioning, which Marty had induced on Tuesday. "So, are you ready to tell me about Jake and Penny?"

"I suppose you've earned it, but first I should say that I'll be leaving next week. That's why I'm talking to you about it."

"Why did you choose me?"

"For the same reason I told you about the UFO."

"Is it because I live close by?"

"No, it just happens to work out that way. Fact is, I trust you with the information—a blue moon event in my life."

Seth was flattered. "I'll try and live up to your expectations."

"Jake and Penny are into the whole peace, love, dove thing. Basically they're good people with an added twist to their liberalism. Bottom line is that Jake needs the security of having someone check in on Penny when he's away. I know they approve of you; take it from there."

"What do you mean by 'added twist'?"

"You're not going to make this easy for me, are ya?"

"I have a right to know what you're getting me into."

"I thought you could fill in the gaps yourself … Guess not. … What do you want to know?"

"Why would Jake allow you to hang out and drink with his foxy wife when he's away? What about relatives or a woman friend? It doesn't make sense."

"Welcome to the seventies, Clem. It's called free love. Jake lets his ole lady have a boyfriend when he's away and, come to think of it, a few times while he was home. Now those were some parties."

There wasn't the slightest crack in tone or quiver of lip as Seth searched for signs of a jest. "You're not kidding me, are ya?"

"Nobody's saying you have to throw the clobber in her. What Jake really wants is a guardian, whether you use the bed pass or not. He'll even try to give you money for it."

"How does Penny feel about all this?"

"It can't be just anybody. I was lucky considering our differences. She liked you straight away. What took me several months, took you a couple hours."

"I could handle looking in on her; don't know about the rest though. Is there anything else I should be concerned about?"

"Yes, your tight collar, Pilgrim. Try and loosen it up. You already know she digs you and can't have babies. What you don't know is that she's discreet, clean as a whistle, and can send you to the moon."

Seth couldn't help fantasizing. "She's also beautiful."

"Best looking forty-year-old I've ever seen, and I see a lot of them in the city."

"No shit? I didn't think she was much older than you."

"Her body is even better. It must be all that health food and not having any kids."

"Don't you get a weird feeling about sharing another man's woman?"

"At first, I did, but you'd be surprised what beers and bongs can do to inhibition. Ask your buddies from the feed mill; they know something about sharing."

"Now you've lost me. I didn't think you knew Alec and Thomas. What's their connection to this den of iniquity?"

He laughed at the reference. "You're a funny guy, Seth. I never met them, and they have nothing to do with it."

"I still don't understand."

"You don't think I've been running around the countryside with blinders on? They're hard to tell apart, but as a pair, they stick out in a crowd."

"I didn't mean to imply—"

"I know. Here's the scoop. Remember that swimming hole you showed me last summer?"

"Do you mean Turtle Cove?"

"That's the one. How many people know about it?"

"Not many. Including us, I'd say my brother and a handful of friends—those with a pickup; a car would get stuck in there."

"Are Pete and Repeat two of those friends?"

"They are; been there lots of times."

"For me, only a few times with Penny and couple times fishing downstream. Instead of going ahead at field's end, hang right and follow along the tree line. Not more than fifty yards down, there's a small clearing underneath those trees. It's very private; can't see a vehicle in there from the cove or the road. I caught some nice fish just this side of the little island. You should try it."

Seth grew impatient, a rare disorder brought on by a long-winded orator. "Where're you going with this?"

"I'm getting to it. Tuesday night, I was at that spot. Fooled myself into believing I was going someplace different when less than a mile separates it from the ridge. After dark, I wanted to give it another hour, you know why. That's when I heard voices."

"Shouldn't you be telling this to your shrink?"

"You want me to finish or not?"

"Yes. I'm sorry. Keep going."

"It sounded like some people were having a party at the cove. At the very least, one of them had to be a girl; no mistaking her squeals."

"Didn't you hear them when they came? You weren't that far away."

"I should've, but after dropping you off Tuesday, I bought a six-pack at the Lumberjack Saloon. Four cans and two fish later, I passed out and woke up in the dark with warm beer all over my crotch. If I didn't feel that happen, then anything could've slipped by."

"Are you sure it was warm beer and not piss?"

"Another wisecrack and I'll leave ya hanging again. Anyway, I reeled in and took to the woods as quiet as possible; had to see what was going on. I finally made it to that big willow on the bank without being seen. Pretty close, hey?"

"Sneaking up on things is your specialty. What'd ya see?"

"I saw your two friends with a little brunette. They were sitting around a campfire sucking suds and having a good time of it."

"Nothing strange there. Her name is Sara. They helped her out of a jam last Saturday night. Three friends out for a beer is no big deal."

"Is that so? Well, after about fifteen minutes, they got all touchy-feely, stripped off their clothes, and went splashing into the water."

Is this what Marty meant by sharing? He had to know more. "And then what?"

"They fooled around in the water for awhile and then chased her back to the pickup, boners pointing the way. There was a makeshift tent over the truck bed. Inside it was a bed—foam mattress, sleeping bags, even pillows."

"How could you see that in the dark?"

"Their campfire lit up a wide-open tailgate. It seems to me they came prepared; when it started to sprinkle out, the den you spoke of was ready and waiting."

"I'm finding it hard to swallow all of this, Marty."

"Sara didn't have a problem. I watched into round two when rain began to douse the flame and then snuck back to my truck and bided time until they left. All hot and bothered from the porn show, shouldn't have to tell you who I went to see."

"I haven't done it yet. Are you disappointed?"

"On the contrary, I was a babe in the woods before Penny came along. Now it's time for me to go; in that way, I feel like Jake."

Silence fell upon them. Seth didn't know what he'd do if seduced by Penny, and ignoring a commitment wasn't an option. Those chips would fall where they may. The threesomes suggested were shockers, particularly the Moellers and Sara, however, not so much as to make them unbelievable. From what he'd seen over the last week, both liaisons were quite possible. But what about the UFO incident? Marty was returning to the same place, at the same time, night after night, with a twelve-gauge behind his seat. A hunter staking out a fishing hole? Why would he do that unless there was cause? Random ball lightning or swamp gas didn't seem to fit his detailed description. An urge to become a storyteller was pulled from the brink. Marty was the last person he'd want to scare and including him in PBS would violate secrecy. Such a pity, orange and green lights were flip sides of the same coin: UFOs, fact or fiction.

The storm willed the morning sky overcast and threatened to keep the day in a drizzle. Seth hoped it wouldn't disrupt his evening plans; tonight would be the practice run for PBS, and Nate would have to be informed soon. His stomach growling for breakfast was the motivation to reel in. Between idle talk, they caught three more walleye, not as big as the first, yet together, they could provide for a family of four. "I'd like to stay, but Ma will have food on the table, and I'm hungry."

"Give me a few minutes." Marty secured his poles, took a fillet knife from his tackle box, and began honing the blade on abraded whetstone. "Bring me that cutting board behind the fish cooler and those walleyes." Other instructions were to put some chunky water from the ice chest into an ice-cream bucket.

While at task, he noticed an NRA sticker on the rear window behind the driver's seat; in itself, it was not out of the ordinary. It was the smiley face sticker opposite that formed a paradox. "What's up with this?"

"That's Penny's doing. It's some sort of duality yin-yang thing. I had all I could do to not draw in a bullet hole with blood oozing out."

One by one, with surgical precision, boneless slabs were taken and placed in the bucket. They wouldn't fry up to look like golden butterflies; nevertheless, there'd be no bones to spoil the taste of an equally great sport fish. Remains were tossed into the flowing path of undiscriminating scavengers; for them, it would be a banquet without effort.

He snapped the lid on the bucket and handed it to his confidant. "I would've filleted the perch too, but that'd be unfair to the walleye."

"I know what you mean."

"There's something else." Marty opened the truck door and reached inside. Out came the tin can bull's eye from Tuesday afternoon. "You forgot your trophy the other day."

"I'm glad you hung onto it. For an hour, I was Marshal Dillon, can't buy that for a silver dollar."

"You still have to come over to shoot the Winchester. That's the gun that won the West."

"Let me see, you're leaving next week and school starts on Monday. Sunday should be for the folks. How 'bout I give you a call Saturday morning? Maybe we could go visit Penny too."

"That's the spirit." A firm handshake accompanied Marty's next words. "I knew I could count on you."

"Is it useless to ask you over for breakfast?"

"Another time. Thanks anyway. Look, my bobber's moving."

The farmer called out from behind a scrambling enlistee. "Just once you should take me up on it. Ma's beginning to think you don't like her cooking."

Back at home, Seth strutted across the checkerboard tile as Martha flipped hash in her largest skillet. He opened the refrigerator door and looked for enough space to accommodate his bucket of fish.

"You're not going to put that dirty scuttle in there. Put it in the sink and find another place for your worms."

Seth did as he was told with the bucket and flashed an empty can, wrapping his palm around the bullet holes. There'd be hell to pay if she saw the holes or caught a sniff of beer breath. He smiled and left with a passing comment. "I'll go wash up." A firm tongue brushing, a little mouthwash, and breakfast should take care of his breath. The can would become a pencil holder to be explained at a later date. Beer and bullets wouldn't make good conversation with anyone's mother.

Talk at the table began with fish. She'd replaced the bucket with something more suitable and was curious. "What kind of fish is it that was cleaned so well?"

"Walleye. Marty did them in half the time I could've. They don't look like perch fillets, but they'll taste like it."

"I'll fry them for supper. Doesn't that sound delicious, Adam?"

"Indeed, it does." He winked at the fisherman.

Nate contributed in his own way. "He doesn't work a lick but can still bring home the bacon."

Adam took the last gulp of his coffee and loosened his belt two notches. "Have to run the truck into town this morn'n' to get the muffler fixed. You boys can go with or dig post holes for a backstop."

Nate's eyes lit up. "No offense, Pa, but I'd like to start digging."

"That's if rain holds off. Dig 'em deep though. I'll mark the spots, and before ya start, drag the storm branches to the burn pit."

Seth had dropped a hint regarding a backstop last night, and it had received no response. The delay suggested his father enjoyed keeping them in suspense. The next problem was getting over to Wylie's before he went to buy lumber; his choice of scare victims depended on it. Calling him on the phone would be a dead giveaway. Nate would want to follow, and Seth's preference was to wait until after chores to tell him. Should he tag along, PBS and his private retribution would be revealed. He'd use the only angle that stood a chance this side of a blatant lie.

While he and his brother gathered the weakest members of a defiant elm, Seth watched his father pick up two small branches and push them vertically into soft ground, designating the desired location of where the post holes should be dug. He continued the cleanup with Nate, pleased by Pa's choice in the matter. Well back of their machine shed was the burn pit. It took five round trips to clear the yard. Two white ash trees took up three of those trips, though the lightning and wind had pardoned their thicker limbs from becoming homemade baseball bats, which both boys had secretly hoped for. By this time, Pa had gone into town. Seth threw Nate his best pitch.

"Baseball and Sara on Monday, shopping and Rube on Wednesday, backstop today, I'd say you've had a pretty decent week so far."

"Okay, what do you got up your sleeve?"

"I need a favor, no questions asked."

"The favor I can handle; it's the no questions part I have a problem with."

"Promise to tell you all about it tonight. Right now, I'd like your bicycle and a half hour."

"Guess I could find something to do. Don't forget you gave me your word."

As soon as Nate stuck his hand out the screen door, indicating their mother's preoccupation with something else, Seth was pedaling down the lane. Five minutes later, he stood knocking at Wylie's door.

"Howdy, Neighbor. Nice bike." Stripped to bare essentials, Nate's bike was modified with high handlebars and a banana seat. Growth hormones on a country diet reduced it to a ridiculous size.

"Pa's getting the muffler fixed."

"Come on in, and take a load off. What can I do for ya?"

"I can't stay long, so I'll get to the point. Are you still going into town for lumber this afternoon?"

"That, and some party supplies."

"I decided who I'd like to scare tomorrow, and you can help. After you're done swinging a deal with Tal, would you ask him over for the cookout?"

"I thought ya didn't know him very well."

"What I said was Wade knew him better than me; apparently, you do too. Considering Wade's going to scare Alec and Thomas, another football player would be fitting. Maybe two if he brings a friend. The catch is I don't want you to tell any of them Tal's invited; likewise, don't tell Tal that either me or his teammates will be at the party. It's going to be a surprise."

"Let me see if I got this straight. Alec and Thomas will think Wade's a no-show. Tal won't be expecting the twins or they him. And finally, Wade and Tal won't know about each other until it's all over."

"You made it complicated, but yes. The key is not to tell Wade, Alec, or Thomas that you invited Tal and vice versa. It'll be a double shock."

Seth was gambling the feud would keep teammates from sharing party information at practice the next morning. Odds were with him.

Wylie pondered the scheme. "Is this to get back at Wade for last Friday?"

"Don't you think I deserve it?"

"It just seems underhanded."

"You mean like last Friday?"

"Say no more, I get the picture."

"There's one more thing: call before eight tonight. It gives me a reason to scoot out with Nate."

"Didn't ya tell him about PBS yet?"

"No. Almost did yesterday and glad I didn't. It'll make tonight's rehearsal all the better."

Seth straddled his bike and prepared to ride a wheelie, a bad foot goof sure to end in disaster. Fortunately, his plan was interrupted by an old station wagon climbing up the driveway. Out of the rusty bucket of bolts with no hubcaps and plastic taped over a broken window hopped Curtis Delano and Shea McCune—the Indian and the professor. Seth knew Shea was Wylie's choice for the scare, and Curtis, well, neither his brother nor he would ever forget their trout-fishing excursion. Was Curtis to be Shea's guest at the party? A couple minutes of socializing should solve the riddle.

After initial greetings were swapped, Curtis homed in on Seth. "What brings you here, Easy Rider?"

"Nate wanted to make it look like a chopper. A couple years back, he'd tie a balloon to the back frame so it would vibrate against the spokes when he rode. Made it sound like a little Hog."

"We used a playing card and a clothespin. How's the young trout fisherman doin'?"

"Growin' like a weed. He loves baseball and girls, in that order. I can help him with hitting; the scoring he'll have to do himself."

Shea was more direct. "Will you be attending the cookout tomorrow night?"

"I wouldn't miss it for anything. Are you coming, Curtis?"

"As sure as the Great Spirit made little green apples. We stopped in to see if there was anything we could bring tomorrow."

"Talk to the mastermind. I have to get back. See ya later, Wylie. And thanks."

While they poked fun at his bulk on a minibike, he thought it a small price for the reward. His short visit completed their list of victims for PBS. Wylie had chosen Shea and Curtis; Wade had chosen Alec and Thomas; and, if all went well at the lumberyard, Frank and Tal would be his choice. It'd serve them right for the damage they'd done to Wade, Sara, and Mary. What of the consequences though? He was confident Shea, Curtis, and the Moellers would laugh it off and possibly want to schedule a fright too. It was a given that Frank and Tal would crave payback, and they were evil enough without incentive. Humiliation should keep their fathers ignorant, so what to expect then? He alone would be exposed as the sole culprit and be considered their primary target, an unavoidable result. Indirectly, his football friends could become consolation prizes in a war of revenge, and Wylie might lose future lumber deals. It all sounded so asinine, but to do nothing was far worse.

Nate was twiddling his thumbs in the machine shed when Seth finally returned from his secret mission. It'd been twenty minutes of eternity, and the posthole digger was calling his name. Rain or not, the holes were destined to be dug. The ground would be soft and much easier to dig in than dirt sunbaked into bedrock. "Did you get your business taken care of?"

"Uh-huh. Hope Ma didn't see me."

"You're safe at home. Five minutes ago, she started to iron her pleated dress."

"Well then, let's put on our work gloves and dig those holes."

After they had finished digging, they sifted through the woodpile and found several sixteen-foot four-by-four's; they were old and gray but straight as arrows. Once the corners had been lapped and bolted, the chain-link secured, and white paint applied; it'd be ten by twelve feet of baseball advertising. No sooner than they had dragged the timber into open ground, the ole man quietly arrived in their restored farm truck and hopped out.

Seth looked up. "Muffler sounds good. If not for the creaky door, I wouldn't have known you were here."

"We can put a muzzle on that too. I reckon you and your brother might yearn to spruce it up before school next week."

"You mean I don't have to take the bus?" Nate asked.

"Nevermore, might have to stomach the ole truck though; least till I can haggle the dealer down some."

In all its grandeur, Seth didn't see it coming: a new truck. His father wouldn't suggest such a thing unless finances allowed for it. What Frank Senior and Buck had alluded to during football practice wasn't so; he secretly longed to PBS the whole lot of them, fathers and sons alike. "Talk about making my day. We'll still keep the old one, won't we?"

"Till her wheels fall off."

The remainder of the morning, they spent working as a team. Parts were measured twice, cut once, drilled, and pieced together. Along with tools and hardware, the parts were loaded into the pickup to be assembled on-site. Nearing lunch, they stood admiring their handiwork; it didn't look half bad.

"Pa, can Seth and I work on it after lunch? There's much to be done yet."

"What'd ya have in mind?"

"For starters, we can dig up the mound and bring it out here, pitching rubber and home plate too. I'd even seed the old spot afterward. Ma would like that."

"Anyth'n' else?"

"Hell yes. We have to paint it and outline a strike zone somehow. If the field were dryer, I'd go over it with the lawn tractor. Wouldn't it be the best ever to have chalk lines and markers too?"

Adam winked at his eldest. "Take'r easy. Rome wasn't built in a day."

Nate scanned the birthing of his own personal ball park. "It isn't Busch Stadium, but it's all mine."

The afternoon saw Nate's way. Relocating the mound and painting were mixed with discussions on limited upgrades. They could lay down rubber bases as reference points; however, a dirt infield was out of the question, time and resources notwithstanding. Grass maintenance alone could interfere with priority. Chalk lines were out too, unless the school had an old machine they wanted to get rid of. Markers could be made as easily as Nate's promotional idea, which was brilliant. A block lettered sign attached to a crossbeam would read: "Wickman Field," and written in cursive, much smaller below it, "Home of the Fighting Holsteins." The suggestion led to a world series of baseball comedy: patchy black-on-white uniforms complete with protruding pink utter, ball caps with Delma's smiling mug, Cow Pie Day at the park, a bullpen for Seth and a calf pen for Nate. The game was eventually called due to chores, not rain.

It wasn't Pa and Nate's bathroom ruckus or the dinner call that drew him away from his model plane. Although the *Spirit of St. Louis* was coming together, frying fish had nosed its way in. Seth was washed and on his way down as the message came. Yesterday's red rose spread its petals at the center of an angler's feast, and everybody wanted to give walleye a try. In the event the main course wasn't agreeable to all, his mother had prepared side dishes aplenty. For dessert, a plate on the counter held an overflow of chocolate chip cookies. As it turned out, the meal was a big hit. Pa summed it up.

"Good Wood, Martha darl'n'."

"Thank your son, the fisherman, and his elusive partner."

Adam took note. "I reckon she speaks of Marty?"

"That's right. We hooked up at the ridge early this morning."

"If you weren't obliged to farm'n', I'd shoo ya off couple times a week."

"And I'd go, just not with Marty. He joined the service and is leaving next week."

Martha knit her brows. "I can only assume it's what he wishes. I'll pray for his safety."

"I'll take his place," said Nate. "I haven't gone fishing with you for a long time."

As he'd done for much of the week, Seth helped his mother after supper. Nate hovered over his father's living room chair. Front-page news about swarms of killer bees northbound from Brazil briefly presided over the *Three Dog Night Special* on television, a hard-fought battle, whose treaty was negotiated with Pa in exchange for *Ironside* at eight. In any case, they were minor distractions that'd ultimately fall to Wylie's telephone call. No sooner said than done. The ringer marked Nate's involvement in PBS.

"Sure ... See ya in a few."

Nate's reaction was immediate. "You promised."

"Get your shoes on then. We're going over to Wylie's."

Martha dried her hands and piled a dozen cookies on a plate. "Don't keep him out too late."

"Not to worry, Ma. I'd say ten, ten thirty at the latest."

Though a short trip, Nate managed to ask many questions. He went nonstop all the way. Seth kept putting him off, figuring there was no reason Wylie and Wade shouldn't enjoy the moment as well. Wade's Scout indicated talks were already in progress. Seth guided his brother to the deck.

Taking lead up the steps, Nate went for answers elsewhere. "Wade, I should've known you'd be involved. What's this all about? Seth wouldn't tell me a thing."

"I'm having a costume party tomorrow night," said Wylie. "We'll grill some brats and burgers, sort of a last shindig before school starts. Would ya like to come?"

"Why are you having a costume party? It's not Halloween."

Wade spoke above the chuckles. "It's going to be. I even brought a costume for you."

"These two jokers aren't helping," said Nate. Turning to Seth, he asked, "Could you explain?"

"What they say is true."

Wylie rose from his chair. "You guys can fill him in; I'll get us a soda to go with the cookies."

Between them, they tried to give Nate the lowdown in short order; it took about a half hour. They started with the first scare a week earlier and ended with their chosen patsies, minus Seth's closet skeletons.

"Never in a million years would I have guessed what you were up to. Count me in one hundred percent." Nate turned to Seth. "Why don't ya scare Marty?"

"Who's Marty?" Wylie asked.

"He's a friend from the city. I met him a couple years back while fishing. His parents have a place west of here where they spend summer months. Marty's not the type to be messed with though, more of a hunter than a fisherman. No telling what he could be packing."

Wylie bailed him out of commitment. "I think we'll have enough people to keep an eye on."

Relieved, Seth moved on. "Why don't you two put on the alien getups? By the time we fine-tune them, it'll be dark out."

Moving into kitchen light, they dipped into Wade's paper bag while finches chirped and Flip repeated his desire for a cracker; Buster remained as quiet as the tropical fish. Off came sweatshirts, and on went long-underwear tops. Nate quickly pulled the blond wig over his new haircut, smiling at a developing resemblance. As Seth had figured, the navy-blue tights required a bit of encouragement. It wasn't until their feet were cut away and the quarterback was prancing about that Nate caved in. Next up was a makeshift belt for their glow stick illusion; aluminum foil was fashioned to hold two apiece and sport-taped around their waists. White grease paint could wait another day; even a tiny smudge overlooked in removal would raise questions on the home front. With costumes nearing completion, each of them activated a glow stick. It was too bright under kitchen light to fully appreciate, so, taking the white gloves and bug-eyed sunglasses, they all went outside.

"Seth, run down and close the gate," said Wylie, "I don't want anyone sneaking up on us."

"I'll walk fast; can't run very well yet. Send our aliens to the chicken coop. We'll have them move toward the house when I get back. I'd like to see them come at us from a distance.

Gate latched, Seth minced his return, each step drawing him closer to Wade's imagination. It was a sight not to be denied. Nothing could ever top what he thought he saw last Friday; that had key elements of shock and inexplicability, but tonight's demonstration was by far more convincing. Seeing would be believing, ten times that with him. When he reached Wylie's side, a two-fingered whistle signaled the spacemen to come forth. As Wade intended, dark tights made them appear to float in midair and wing-flapping brought out-of-this-world animation. They shared smiles, nods, and expletives.

"I have a couple questions for you before they get too close," Seth whispered.

"Shoot."

"Is Tal coming?"

"He said he would and asked if he could bring a friend."

"Did he say who?"

"Frank LaRue. That must be Frank Senior's kid."

"You didn't tell Wade, did ya?"

"No."

"He then sealed the deal. "Well, don't; it'd wreck everything. I'm not going to tell Nate either. He could let it slip when they're at the landing site."

Wylie addressed the creatures. "Can ya see where you're going with sunglasses on?"

"Not bad from where we came," said Wade, "but on the cow path, we'd be blind as bats. Tomorrow, we'll put them on as we get closer to the house."

"That's good, because they really make a difference; and with white grease paint, even more so."

Nate removed his bug eyes. "You wackos thought of everything. It makes me wonder why you didn't try to scare me tonight."

Seth was all over the comment. "With your temper, you probably would've marched off in a huff, telling us what we could do with PBS."

"I won't argue that one; I'd've been really pissed."

"Did ya bring the extension cords with ya?" asked Wylie.

"Oh, man; knew I was forgetting something," said Seth.

Wade was in the same boat. "Sorry, I blew it too."

"You'd forget your heads if they weren't attached. Lucky for us I happened to stop and see Gus today."

"Grumpy of Gravel Pit Road?" asked Wade and then turned to Seth. "You know the old fart that taught his dog to whiz on people."

"He does seem to get a big charge from it." Wylie laughed. "Anyway, Gus has something for everything, including eight hundred feet of electrical cord. He owed me a favor, so we're all set for tomorrow. Nate, go inside and plug in the cord by the patio doors. Grab the flashlight on the counter too."

Last night's storm had littered the cow path with fallen branches. It had created a mess of the nice job Wylie had done on Sunday. Each gathered what he could and tossed them over the fence; some would have to wait till morning. Wylie went on to explain that the spotlight guiding them wasn't to be used during their scare; it'd reveal more than what they'd want. A less powerful flashlight could still signal the landing site, signals that should be kept simple. Wade and Nate could see him and whoever coming to check cows, and when he clicked off the flashlight, it would be their cue to plug in the florescent lights. Once his flashlight had disappeared back up the trail, they'd unplug and repeat for the second group of curiosity seekers.

As they worked their way down the path, glimmers of radiance shone from behind wooded shadows, eventually exposing Wylie's contribution. Aliens and earthlings alike stood in eerie silence, awed by the misty glow from beyond. A thin layer of fog swirled in hollows below the grassy knoll. Neither cow nor cricket dared utter a sound in the dense evening air. High heaven was vacant of anything to wish upon, and if there had been anything there, their wish would be to have this night repeat itself the next.

"It doesn't get any creepier than this," said Nate.

Wylie's satisfaction was obvious. "Sure it does. Picture yourselves weaving down the hill, flapping your arms or whatever it is ya think Martians do. It'll be an eye-popping nightmare."

"Should we jog over there?" asked Wade. "You and Seth can check us out."

"We can't be leaving tracks in the field; it'd ruin our setting. When you and Nate are ready tomorrow night, all ya gotta do is follow the extension cord through the woods, hop the fence, and you'll come in from the backside."

"It's been rather wet out lately. What about an electrical short?" It wasn't the possible failure of lighting that bothered Seth; it was the safety of brother and friend.

"Ease your troubled mind, Neighbor. The lights are high and dry. They're secured to plywood, elevated, leveled, and covered with plastic. Connections are wrapped in electrical tape and off the ground. If that ain't enough for ya, the weatherman predicts partly sunny, warmer, and breezy; that should dry up any excess moisture."

"Someone was a busy little bee today. I must admit, it looks the part."

Wylie addressed the green men. "I'll peel off the plastic tarp tomorrow. It defuses the light too much for my taste."

Their return to the cottage was a barrel of monkeys. Wylie spotlighted several of the largest cow pies, fracturing their crusty coat with a tree limb and forcing out their molten cores. Only he would enjoy the slippery retreat of panic-stricken victims, his accomplices elsewhere occupied. Wade and Nate experimented with body movements. Impersonations of such horror icons as Frankenstein, Dracula, and Wolfman all received jubilant applause. In spite of this, gentle flapping of wings had the best field effect, after which a zombie approach would relax tired arms. Seth waited till landing lights were unplugged and aliens out of costume before he began his part of the bargain.

"We should go over the agenda one more time to make sure we're on the same page. It'd help to wear a watch. Nate and I will get Wade at seven, it wouldn't look normal to have his Scout parked here while he's nowhere to be seen. If asked, we'll say he's running late."

"What should we tell our parents?" asked Wade.

"The truth, Wylie invited a few friends over for a cookout. I think Ma will even fix a dish to bring along, and knowing your mother, she would too."

"Nice touch," said Wylie.

"Thanks. Based on tonight, we should have enough time to get you two into costume, including grease paint, and have you out the backdoor before guests arrive. Be prepared to spend ninety minutes out there. Maybe bring a small flashlight, deck of cards, and a couple blankets. Wylie said he'd have a goody basket for you."

"Burgers and brats sound good to me." Nate took a sarcastic turn on the felon who had stolen much of the summer from him. "It'll be like our own private little picnic, Wade darlin'."

Seth spoke before Wade could respond. "No cookout for you guys. We'll need to kill some time before dark. That means the charcoals won't be lit until the first people show."

"Don't worry, Nate," said Wylie. "It'll be a dandy basket, and I'll save some cookout for ya."

"If we remember to synchronize our watches, you'll know when Wylie is coming down the path to check on cows that aren't there. This way, you won't have to keep watch the whole time. It'll be nine thirty, give or take ten minutes, and ten minutes after that, he'll bring the rest of them down. That's when you crop up from behind the hill."

Wade squeezed in. "I thought we'd come out from opposite ends of the hilltop and move forward in a staggered approach about twenty feet apart."

"I don't care if you dance with sugar plum fairies. Just take it slow, even when you look through the windows. Wylie and I want to soak in every bloodcurdling scream."

"I could open the door and let them in then flip the power switch on. That way, Nate and Wade will be able to see the look on their faces too." Wylie winked at the youngest member, and he ate it up.

"I like that idea. We deserve at least that much for wandering around in the dark. Right, Wade?"

"That's for sure."

Seth made it unanimous and went on. "Wylie, try to keep our lambs watching the landing site as long as possible. I need time to pop off battery cables, unplug the phone, and close the gate. Say a couple of strays break away, then you start back and the rest will follow. It's best to keep them herded together rather than scattered all over creation. When their cars don't start, I'll guide them into the house. We'll both count heads to make sure everyone is present. If not, I'll have to go in search of."

"What about calling the cops and cutting power?" asked Wylie.

"When everybody's accounted for, then I'll make the call myself and verify a dead line with whoever is closest: a group distraction and your cue to flip the power switch off. The rest is up to you. Whenever you think the time is right, let our aliens in and shed light on the truth."

Nate cut in. "As always, should you or any member of your IM force be caught or killed, the secretary will disavow all knowledge of your actions. This tape will self-destruct in five seconds. Good luck, Jim."

There were snickers, but Seth underscored the most important issue. "If problems arise that can't be controlled, the mission is to be aborted. Agreed?" They all did.

"I should get going," said Wade. "Football practice starts early, and I don't want to miss a single snap."

"How's the team doin'?" asked Wylie.

"It was damn shaky for awhile; the last few days have been a blast."

This was as far as Seth wanted the topic to go; it was much too close to the Frank and Tal conflict. The mere mention of those names could bust open his can of worms. "Come on, Nate. We should go too. I told Ma we'd be back by now." He succeeded in moving them out the door but couldn't avoid Wade's pep rally.

"Let's bring it together, boys." He fisted a glow stick while egging each to cap it one hand atop the other and began to chant. "PBS! PBS! PBS!" As with their first rally a week prior, they ended with the call of the Timber Wolves. No more practice, it was game time. Wade climbed into his Scout and drove away. Seth and Nate soon followed. Wylie's last words were, "Close the gate."

Nate paused before they took to the porch steps. "Why'd you wait until tonight to tell me about PBS?"

"We did lots this week. I was just saving the best for last."

"It was all of that, and more."

Seth flashed a smile. "Keep your mind on work tomorrow, or I'll have to come out there and kick your ass."

"Huh, a one-legged ass-kicker, now that'd be a neat trick."

"Go catch some shut-eye; it's going to be a big day. We got a ballpark to christen and one hell of a party to attend."

"Aren't ya coming in?"

"Not just yet. I'm going to sit on the porch swing for awhile."

Seth used his ass-kicking foot to push and drag himself into a slow teeter. Although his toe was tender, there had been improvement over the last couple of days and none too soon. Project Big Scare was in play and required mobility. He closed his eyes, drew in a breath, and exhaled. A delicate breeze complemented respiration and sway. Normally, this would've pleased him, but tonight, it was unnerving. The day had been overcast; the air, laden with moisture, had been sparingly pushed about. It was the tail end of a summer boomer slowly giving way to high pressure, except at the landing site. He remembered standing in lifeless calm without nocturnal chatter or the slightest wave of grain; it was as dead as the vacuum of space. It seemed a spark could ignite a chain reaction that would dwarf their florescent lights. Didn't anyone else notice? Nate said it was creepy, but that was it. If his coconspirators found him to be paranoid, which he believed they would've had he told them, then they'd find his next experience to be delusional. Mesmerized by Wylie's fallacy and the climate surrounding it, he'd lingered while the others had headed back. Their calls from halfway up the cow path had broken his spell. As he turned toward their glowing green foolishness, he had heard a sound that was distinct and familiar by description: "Beep, beep." It had jerked his head in the direction from which it had come: the cedar swamp on his western flank. He'd scanned the area with every bit of intensity night vision could give, and there wasn't anything. The others had been into themselves and hadn't even flinched at the electronic echo. A second look had produced zilch, and he'd hurried to catch up. As sure as he was of what he thought he'd heard, an audio manifestation of Marty's story and the newspaper article, so too was he of deception in the human psyche. It could be of his own making, a subconscious fabrication brought on by a number of factors: PBS, unconfirmed testimony, atmospheric conditions. After all, he thought he'd seen a bona fide space alien last Friday night.

Adam broke his reverie. "Seth, hit the lights on your way through; we're turning in."

"I'm right behind ya, Pa."

CHAPTER 8

As his head hit the pillow the night before, having completed the dry run for PBS, Seth's mind had been swarmed by the events of that day, and he'd struggled in his attempt at sound sleep. There were the threesomes Marty had alluded to and his agreement to look in on Penny from time to time, the beginnings of Wickman Field, confirmation of Wylie's invite of Tal and hopefully Frank too, but most troubling, that creepy "beep, beep," echoing in his ears the whole time. He'd awakened early and begun working on his model plane in tomblike silence till he heard his father call Nate from the stairs landing.

"Nate!"

"Okay, Pa."

"Roll out. It's daylight in the swamp."

It was last year when, for lack of anything better to do, Seth had discovered the background of Pa's morning call. Browsing through one of his father's books about logging camps of old, he'd found the relevant page dog-eared. It said an assistant to the actual cook, called a bull cook, was responsible for rousting bunkhouse jacks, among other menial chores. Frozen swamp was where lumbermen plied their trade, and if it was already daylight, they were late. Daylight in the swamp was another way of saying, you better haul ass.

Nate poked his head through Seth's open door. "How long you been up?"

"I'd say about an hour."

He casually took interest in the model plane being worked on. "Can I have a look-see?"

"Come on in." Seth pulled himself from final touch-ups. "*Spirit of St. Louis*, first plane to cross the Atlantic Ocean nonstop."

"I know. It's the Ryan NYP. That's New York to Paris in just over thirty-three hours; I believe it was 1927. Lindbergh won a cash prize of twenty-five thousand dollars for it."

Seth was impressed; he hadn't realized Nate placed any value whatsoever in his hobby. "Where'd you learn that?"

"I picked it up at the library on Wednesday. I may not have the patience to do what you do or hardly as well if I did, but I can research topics other than baseball."

"Can you tell me anything about those?" He motioned at the other two planes suspended in flight.

"You mean the Wright Flyer and Curtiss Jenny? I know more details about either one than Rube Waddell's biography. Right now, I could use some juice and toast before chores. See ya at breakfast." Nate took one last look at the *Spirit*. "Very nice," he said, and then off he went.

The praise was short-lived. Seth knew there were small jobs he could be doing, and his parents conspired to keep him from doing them. He could go gallivanting over hill and dale, yet not be permitted near the barn. Why? Was illness or injury a farmer's vacation ticket? Apparently it could be with proper backup; most times, they lived with it because the cows wouldn't. In truth, vacations were increments of any given day, more in winter than summer and never during fall harvest or spring planting. With milking, feeding, and barn cleaning, every day was a workday. It seemed the only logical explanation for freedom from responsibility was his family's desire for him to taste it, to not have a care, to go about doing as he pleased within reason. The first few days were difficult, but idle hands wasted no time getting dirty. He'd initiated a more elaborate scare than that which had been dealt to him and then went subversive on allies in a selfish act of reprisal. His parents would be appalled if they knew of either this or the things Marty'd exposed him to during his hiatus: gun fighting, breakfast beer, and wanton women. As much as he looked forward to the evening's activities, he was just as anxious for them to end. Maybe by Sunday he'd be on the milking roster, and things could get back to normal.

Between Wickman Field and PBS, it promised to be the best day of young Nate's life. His father's exceptionally good mood during chores produced the outcome he'd hoped for, and out it came at breakfast. "Guess what, Seth? I'll be running a mower over the ballpark this afternoon, if it's dry enough."

"What you doing this morning?"

"I thought I'd pull some of those big weeds along the fence line. There's a lot to keep me busy—plenty of thistle, ragweed, and those candlestick thingies."

"They're called mullein. Curtis says his ancestors tucked the flannel leaves in their moccasins for warmth. They're supposed to ward off evil too. Maybe we should keep a few of them."

"Sounds like you're going to help."

"I am, and you can chip in with cleaning the truck."

"It's a deal."

Their pause gave Martha control of the conversation. "How's Wylie getting along?"

"He's in good spirits. Invited Seth and me over for a cookout tonight."

Seth knew his brother meant well, but he was compelled to correct worried expressions on his parents' faces. No doubt they were thinking of Wylie's age difference and the type of crowd likely to be on his guest list. "It'll be all right, Ma, just a few people over for brats and burgers. I was hoping you'd make something for us to take with." It worked like a charm.

"I have the ingredients for a pan cake. What would you like it to say?"

He couldn't help teasing the subject onto thin ice. "A couple weeks back, Wylie called me over to see a UFO that wasn't there. If I were decorating the cake, it wouldn't be words; it'd be an orange ball of light floating behind those tall pines off his cow path, at night."

Emboldened by his brother's flirtation with disaster, Nate played along. "That'd be so cool, and I know you could do it, Ma."

"Is that really what you want?" she asked of her eldest.

"It'd be funny, tasty too." The benefits of such a decoration bounced around in his head. He believed most of those attending knew of Wylie's sighting, and for those who didn't, they'd find out soon enough. The cake would be an effective conversation starter, at first in playful ridicule, but eventually, Wylie could embrace the "I told you so" defense he so longed to use.

"A trifle early for Halloween," said Martha, "but I'll see what I can do."

"So long as you're fixin' to gussy up the ole truck, check the oil," said Adam.

"We'll go one better," offered Seth. "We'll pull it in the shed and change the oil and filter." He took a drink of milk before setting up his afternoon project. "Do you mind if I use a piece of that plywood we have stacked against the wall? I also wanted to start on the addition Nate and I talked about yesterday."

"Addition? Dare I ask what that means?"

Nate fielded the question. "You could, but we won't tell. It's a surprise."

There'll be many surprises today, thought Seth. At least this one could be reversed with no harm done. "What say you, Pa?"

"Take one, take two, they're small," was a common response in matters that warranted generosity.

Standing at home plate, they looked over the outfield. Center field was in a direct line with the corner fence post separating their corn and River Road, a good four hundred plus feet. Foul lines would be measured at three twenty-five with lots of room to spare. Balls hit left of center could reach pavement, but it'd have to be a mighty swing, and even then, the likelihood of bouncing one off a passing car was remote. Deep balls hit right of center belonged to row upon row of tasseled corn soldiers, barbed wire shielding their ranks. It was nothing a nimble ballplayer couldn't breach and retrieve unscathed. Foul balls were a different story. Their father had taken ten long strides from the garden when marking his spots. Anything tipped high to the rear had a chance of hitting barn, machine shed, or house—although the house had an elm and a white ash protecting its length. Garden workers would have to beware when batting practice was in session. Neither of them expected the backstop to be so close to the buildings. They entertained adult rationale.

"You'd think Pa would've put the backstop further away," said Nate. "We could take out a window real easy."

"Ma certainly had to agree. She's never let us swing a bat anywhere near the house."

"My guess is they wanted a window seat, even if it is asking for it."

"That'd be my guess too."

"Pa could've planted anything here; instead, he kept it fallow. I wonder if he was waiting for us to ask."

Seth pulled on his work gloves. "He sure didn't hesitate on location. Maybe the mystery isn't our love of the game but his. Whatever the reason, it's a short walk to batting practice, which will force us to concentrate on solid contact."

"Something I need work on … I'll pull weeds in right field; you go left."

Weeds piled high, Seth sent Nate for the truck. It'd make transport to the burn pit a one-shot deal and give a young driver some hands-on experience. While loading, he encouraged him to give their field a classic cone-shaped cut along the back, another nice touch.

After the weeds had been pulled and transported to the burn pit, they drove to the machine shed. An oil change led to a maintenance check of other fluid levels and a good opportunity to wire-brush battery terminals and make sure cables could be loosened quickly. Internally sound, their pickup was ready for its school makeover. A little soap and water goes a long way for both man and machine. It had some rust, yes, and dents and scratches, of course; a bath couldn't wash away years of character, though Pa did manage to silence the squeaky door's ability to broadcast it. The interior hadn't undergone such a thorough job in memory. A pine tree air freshener, still wrapped in cellophane, was found underneath the seat. Unwrapped, it briefly appeared on the rearview mirror; its overwhelming potency was its downfall. They stood back and wallowed in their achievement.

"It's not bad, hey?" Nate asked.

"As Pa would say, hay is for horses, but not bad at all. We'll have to take it for a spin."

"I'll let Ma know."

"Tell her we're going to help Wylie with storm cleanup or anything else he might need for the cookout. We'll be home for lunch."

Midmorning was exactly as Wylie's weatherman had predicted. Helios shown amidst billowed titans, and a zephyr swept through summer's last stand, an uplifting respite from several days of obscurity. They proudly escorted their renovated pickup to an open gate. Parting the willows, a day's supply of baled hay was stacked on Wylie's idling flatbed parked in front of the cottage. Driver's side door was ajar suggesting a speedy return was expected. Barnyard divas were insisting on it. Buster blindly guarded his master's entrance, ears perked in awareness of intruders, poised for acquaintance by scent. Undeterred with their arrival, Tony and Elsie kept at a hapless rodent seeking escape beneath shrubbery. Seth gave the sentry his required sniff and a head pat and then called into an open doorway. "Is anyone here?"

"Come on in. I'll be out in a sec."

Under the assumption Wylie was taking his morning dump, they went inside and were immediately set upon by a squawking jailbird. Much to Seth's amusement, Nate got the parrot to repeat "Flip the Bird" several times before he was told to "Shut the fuck up."

"Can't turn a deaf ear to that," said Nate, after which he responded to a toilet flushing off the adjoining hallway. "Speaking of potty-mouth, the tutor has risen from his throne."

Wylie walked into a roomful of snickers. "What's so funny?"

"Flip. Funny he hasn't learned to mimic farts," joked Nate.

"I'm working on it."

Seth stepped in and stated their business. "I thought we'd stop by and see if you needed a hand with anything."

"Good timing. You can help feed the girls; they'll be staying in the barnyard today, and then we can pick up the branches we didn't get last night."

Wylie slowly drove past the barnyard gate and on to the prison's far corner. His cows didn't seem to mind. They obediently followed their appetites inside their barbed stockade, paying particular attention not to bump one another into Old Sparky, the electric fencing. Wylie bypassed his defenses and yanked the binder twine off each bale as it hit ground. Only a couple of seasoned farmhands could handle clearing both fences. He kicked the bales open to a ravenous horde, eased his way through the barricades, and circled his truck back to the cow path. Having done a reasonably good job the night before, it didn't take them long to clear the remaining branches. All three were slugging a soda on the deck in no time.

"Where's the cord for the landing site?" asked Nate two guzzles in. It was to be the bread crumb trail leading Wade and him to their spaceship.

"The patio door wouldn't close, so I ran it out the basement window under the deck."

"I don't see it. How we supposed to find our way?"

"Can ya see that birdhouse nailed to the pine?" Wylie pointed in the general direction.

"Yes."

"That's where it starts above ground. Early this morning, I was sitting out here, and it looked strange having an extension cord plugged inside and running into the woods. Shea is no fool, nor can we expect the others to be. From under the deck, I chopped a shallow trench to that tree and raked it over."

Nate stepped to deck's edge and examined all the closer. "You did a fine job. I should walk over and check it out for myself."

"Why not follow it to the lights? I'll plug them in down the basement, and you can unplug them out there. That way, it'll be set to go tonight."

"I'll be back in a few."

"Stick close to the cord. There's poison ivy ten feet either side of the fence."

"Leaflets three, let it be."

With Nate hot on the trail and Wylie off to his dungeon, Seth surveyed the party stage. It had been hosed off, the grill was cleaned, and there were folding chairs aplenty. He knew his brother would take more than a few minutes to cover the distance. Wylie's return was imminent and favored a sort of fact-finding mission.

"Wylie, tell me a little more about what you saw two weeks ago. You know, when you had us racing over to see an orange ball of light."

"Why should I? Every one of you acted like I was full of shit."

"But I'm the only one coming back for more. That should count for something."

"If ya don't poke fun, because it wasn't that funny to me."

"I can zip my lip when I have to."

Wylie explained that there really wasn't much to add. He went looking for Betty and Tess when they failed to return with the herd. The light was in the same general area Wade was in during the first scare but farther back. It wove slowly through the pines just above ground and then stopped in full view. He couldn't bring himself to shine his flashlight on it, fearing the beam would draw attention. All he could do was watch and suppress the thought it was doing the same. Eventually, it backtracked some and rose behind the treetops. That was when he'd rushed to his phone, thinking it might still be there by the time they arrived.

Of that night, it was the abundance of stars that Seth remembered most. If Wylie's object had performed the same disappearing act Marty had described, he would've mentioned it. However, the intensity of the light could be compared. "Was it a bright light?"

"For as big as it was, maybe twenty feet across, it was rather dull."

That matched Marty's description in both luminescence and mass. This being so, only one question could tie his experience with that of Marty, the newspaper, and Wylie. "Did it make any sounds?"

"I could've sworn it beeped a couple times, but I was quaking like a leaf in a gale. Who's to say for sure?"

Having difficulty foregoing a joke about Wile E. Coyote and Roadrunner, Seth took a swig of soda. The only purpose served with such a wisecrack would've been to distract his resentment for placing any merit in the babble of madmen. He certainly didn't see what they claimed to have seen. The problem was denial of mutual sound effects without second-guessing his sanity. *Mental institutions are filled with people who see and hear things that aren't there,* he thought.

Seth grew tired of the underlying tone and redirected his thoughts. Wylie's story coupled with Ma's dreary cake would further set the stage. "When everybody's done eating, I'll ask you to tell them about what you saw. It'll get the orange ball rolling."

"They'll probably laugh."

"But you'll laugh best."

"I suppose it's not too much to sacrifice."

After bouncing up the deck steps and coming to rest in a folding chair, Nate snatched his bottle and guzzled. "Ah ... This is going be one humdinger of a scare."

"Ya can say that again," said Wylie. "If only we could save it on film."

Mistaken that his sarcasm couldn't possibly be taken seriously, Seth played along. "I could bring my camera. That one shot as you throw the power switch on would be priceless."

"Why don't you flip the switch and take the picture? Then Wylie could have his smiling face among the slack-jawed."

Nate's devious suggestion ignited Wylie. "My flash camera will be on the fridge."

"I was just kidding. What do you think they'd do to a photographer capturing a Kodak moment?"

"You're the one who offered. I'll put it there anyway in case ya change your mind.

"I don't think I will. Is there anything else we can do for you?"

"All systems are go, Houston."

"We'll be blasting off too then, before you get any more bright ideas."

Jumping down from the top step, Nate reconfirmed the meeting time. "See ya at seven o'clock."

"Y'all come back now, hear?"

With an hour to spare till lunch, Seth headed toward town. Normally, this would've brought on a brother's interrogation; it could be a week's worth of hype made the choice another adventure. He slowed down by Fisherman's Ridge and looked for activity. There was none. Up and over the river bridge at Three Corners, he turned east on Mill Road. Their destination: Turtle Cove and the swimming hole they'd visited only twice all summer.

Seth answered a silent inquiry. "No, we're not here for a swim. Marty told me about a fishing spot downriver, and I thought we'd take a look." It was a valid statement but not his primary reason. He was seeking evidence to support or refute the twins' triangle of love. According to

Marty, it had happened Tuesday night. Maybe the thunderstorms in between hadn't washed away every clue.

Field's end was where he began his investigation. Breaking off the beaten path, stretching along the river's tree line, was a set of vehicle tracks forged through virgin meadow. Seth cautiously followed them for fifty bumpy yards, stopping shy of entering the woods. That'd require four-wheel drive. While he was nosing about, more signs of somebody having been there jumped out at him. The spot was protected from pummeling rain, and naturally selected dirt parking bore fading impressions of knobby mud-runners and size-ten hunting boots. Offshore was a patch of flattened grass at the base of a thick cottonwood. Something thought it an ideal place to relax, if not a deer than presumably an angler casting his line this side of the island. Nothing more could be gained by poking around the secret camp, and he wasn't about to retrace Marty's odyssey through the woods. It was on to the swimming hole to see what the lusty trio could've left behind.

Turtle Cove wasn't really a cove, but rather a widening of a river bend. It boasted sun, sandbar, and solitude. More open to sky than Marty's fishing spot, exposure had taken its toll on human presence. Seth would have to look deeper. For those who knew of it, Turtle Cove was a place for daytime swimming, not nighttime parties. An alleged campfire would break an established rule regarding use. The owner graciously ignored overheated teenagers; bonfires and beer definitely crossed a line, yet there was a small circle of scorched earth barely a pickup's length offshore. Extra effort was taken to exceed Smokey Bear's requirements, almost disguising its existence. A casual search of the cove's rugged shoreline proved too much to hide. Forward the umbrella of Marty's vantage willow, a milieu of stones and saturated driftwood held manmade secrets. The smudged faces of campfire rocks attempted to look random and so did charred kindling, some of which was thin-split hardwood diverted from a woodstove or fireplace. His muckraking prompted Nate to interject, "Somebody's going to spoil it for the rest of us."

"And short of posting a twenty-four-hour guard, there isn't a whole lot we can do about it. Check the bushes over there. I'll check around the willow tree."

"What exactly are we looking for?"

"What doesn't belong or disturbance of what does."

The willow's taproots indicated an insecure future. Half were anchored in solid terrain, supporting much of the tree's bulk; the other half slipped into soft beach sand, drawing two heavy limbs closer to a watery grave. Seth circled around and came in as Marty would've done. Matted grass suggested someone had been there, but it was sagging limbs that offered the best seat in the house. A person could inch out over water and gently push aside leafy drapes to get a clear view of the campfire. Mud ground into the lower branch's cavernous bark strengthened Marty's case, and damned if he didn't crack a beer during the peep show. An aluminum tab was crammed in his furrowed armrest. Was it deliberately left behind for a cynical confidant? If the city boy expected him to admit this, he'd be wrong.

"What'd ya find?" asked Nate.

"Nothing much, how 'bout you?"

"Someone chucked a grain sack filled with empty beer cans into those shrubs over there. Last Monday, when we watched football practice, Sara said that Alec and Thomas were just as charming without a beer in their hand. Then there was something about picking up their shirts at her place whenever. You don't suppose the Moellers brought Sara here to party?"

Seth tried to discredit two different occasions, yet accurate speculation regarding the second. "They know the rules."

"Oh, come on. We both know who they like, and this is the perfect place to take her. The mill sack is a dead giveaway, and twelve empty cans seem right for a party of three, not two pigskins in training."

"Secrets like Turtle Cove don't stay that way. It could be almost anybody, and rules aren't for everybody. Lots of people carry empty grain sacks in their pickup; we do. We even have our baseball equipment in one. Anyway, it doesn't really matter who was here because we won't be. School starts Monday, and weekend chores don't allow for swimming, fishing, and baseball too."

"I'll take baseball, but scaring them tonight just became a lot more fun."

As they walked back to the truck, Seth couldn't comment on Nate's jealous spite. Although he considered retaliation on Frank and Tal deserved, it was still vengeance all the same. A pinch of contrition rapidly dissolves in a chalice of villainy. He recalled Nate's last words and made them his too.

They returned home just in time for lunch, which was a vegetable soup, whose ingredients their mother had foraged from the garden soon after breakfast. Each spooned down a second bowl as counterbalance to the coming evening party menu of red meat and soda pop.

With a creepy cake to bake, Martha hustled them out the back door. "I know you men have things to do, so get to it and let me tend to my business."

Together, they moseyed to the machine shed where twelve horses of lawn tractor waited. They adhered to Pa's fetish about checking the oil level, even before gasoline. Seth watched as Nate hopped in the saddle, fired her up, and was off and running. Although mowing grass had been his younger brother's job for the past three years, it had belonged to him before that. Many folks considered it a mindless chore that resulted in hearing loss and carbon monoxide poisoning. Seth thought such talk inflammatory and lacking common sense. If it's loud, you wear ear protection; toxic, a bandanna. He had never had cause to use either, squelching muffler and prevailing wind in his favor. What mowing did do was give him time to think, and watching Nate scoot off to cut Wickman Field brought back the birth of his interest in baseball.

He had been nine years old. With only two weeks left of school, his chums were clamoring on about Little League tryouts. Managing to convince his father a glove was necessary, he was rewarded with a brand-new vinyl imitation. Yellow foam rubber padded the appeasement of what he thought his father viewed as a passing whim. The glove, along with a rubber ball made to look like the real thing, was good enough to practice a couple times against the barn's block foundation. From his parents' perspective, glove tucked under his shirt, he was just going for a long Monday morning bike ride. They were unaware his destination was Oakton. Everything felt right till he reached the ballpark some forty minutes later. No friends showed up. Most boys were two or three years older with leather gloves and cleats. The only one who would play catch with him was a disabled kid bucking for assistant manager / scorekeeper. Between him and the batboy, his experience was seriously deficient, proven so when eventually cast into right field. He hadn't caught a fly ball before but was confident he could from watching others do it. A crack of the bat sent him backpedaling to camp beneath its lofty descent. Not until a mustached man in shades patted his cheeks and helped him to his feet did he realize what had happened. The ball had skipped over his plastic miniglove and struck him in the forehead. If he hadn't been so groggy, embarrassment would've crushed him on the spot. Instead, it gradually took hold as his vision cleared. Neither coaches nor players could fully restrain their laughter while he recuperated in seclusion, a precaution lasting to the bitter end and rightfully so. He'd succeeded only in catching a hardball with his face. The same man who'd helped him up also offered him a ride home. He declined and used travel time to plot his comeback. In hindsight, someone must've informed his parents about the incident because he had a new leather glove and several hardballs within a week, plus time taken from chores to play catch with the ole man—no questions asked.

Reflection on his failed tryout brought on a chuckle as he watched Nate take on the grass straightaway. Unplowed yet cut of hay each year, the tract was a practice field waiting to happen. Many times, he'd seen his father picking up and tossing stones from the area as if grooming it for some special purpose. There was no balking at where their backstop would be. Throw in baseball equipment every Christmas and birthday, and his motive became apparent. Since Seth's concussion, Pa was doing what he could to help a determined second son reach his goal, and Seth decided he would be there to help them along.

Seth turned his attention to the sign they had discussed and began sorting through plywood. There were lots of odds and ends, no sense in cutting into a full sheet. He picked out a piece made to order, measuring two by five feet. With a little glue and a few nails, scraps of narrow molding would frame it nicely. He'd miter the corners. Field markers would be simpler, the only requirement that numbers be legible at their prescribed distance. The entire background would be painted white, like the backstop, and the lettering would be black. Utilizing a fan between coats, he might just finish this afternoon, and then tomorrow, they could officially bring Wickman Field into being. Nate's preoccupation created a strong tailwind that swept his objective to near completion. Seth was second-coating in black when his brother came to inspect the progress. Stepping back with brush in hand, as any painter would do, he waited for comment.

"Pa will be totally blown away." Nate patted the artist's shoulder and read aloud, "Wickman Field, Home of the Fighting Holsteins." He paused and continued, "Pa stopped me while I was mowing and asked what you were up to. I told him to take a guess. Want to know what he said?"

"Sure, go ahead."

"He said he had no more idea than the man in the moon … Go figure … Not exactly the alien I'll be tonight, but damn close."

"Sometimes I think parents have a sixth sense. Let's hope that's the extent of it. Did you tell him about the sign?"

"Sorry, Pops, no can do."

"Good, then I take it you're headed out to milk."

"And I'm holding up the show."

"Take enough time to look respectable," Seth called out. "You're supposed to be going to a party."

Within a half hour, Seth had closed shop and was changing channels on the tube, a rare circumstance at four thirty in the afternoon. He settled on what was left of *Star Trek*, which was followed by an episode of *My Favorite Martian*, another inadvertent donation to the ongoing theme. It was still weird though. There wasn't any better way to kill time in the newspaper. A lawsuit claimed large contributions by dairymen's organizations to President Nixon's reelection campaign influenced his decision to raise federal milk price supports last year. Seth would've preferred the twenty-seven cent increase per hundredweight earned rather than bribed; however, the practice was really no different than oil, labor, or steel interests going about their business as usual. He'd had his fill; it was time to get ready. Nate would be in shortly and didn't need a reason to forgo a shower.

They met at the top of the stairs. Seth had observed his brother's approach and was pleased with the outcome. "We should boogie. It's almost seven, and we have to snatch Wade yet." Nate tried to muscle around him for the lead, but Seth's foot was feeling much better. "Not this time, Little Buddy. Besides, you forgot your watch."

"Dagnabit, I knew there was something."

When Nate returned, they again scuffled down the stairs and entered the kitchen where their mother had prepared them a snack of peaches swimming in heavy cream. The cake Seth had asked for was centered on the table.

"Wow, it's just like Wylie's cow path. There's the pines, the orange light, and look, Seth, I think those are cow pies. Wylie's going to get a big kick out of this."

"I don't see how he couldn't." The cake was magnificent, surpassing all expectations. Gothic in color and texture, even the UFO was dull. How did she do it? Wait a minute, a lone star offered a glimmer of hope, a devout message in the gloomy frosting. It was his mother's personal touch. Putting a knife to it almost seemed a sin.

"Make sure you tell him the decoration was your idea. It's not exactly something I'd enter in the county fair." She covered it and collected their empty bowls.

Seth wasn't going to let her escape tribute. "Especially not when you'd take first place at the state fair." He pushed himself from the table and instructed Nate to handle their dessert with care. "Thanks, Ma."

"What time do you think you'll be home?"

"I'd say around eleven or soon thereafter."

"Well, have a good time, and don't forget you are your brother's keeper."

Seth felt the weight of her words. Most of the evening wouldn't be spent in his brother's company. Pa took issue from behind his newspaper, and Seth didn't know what to make of it. "Keep an eye on Nate. I don't trust Wylie any further than I can swing a bull by the tail."

CHAPTER 9

They pulled up to Wade's doorstep a little after seven, waving to Mrs. Hotchner and daughter Anna, who were gathering sheets from the clothesline. Nate slid over to make room for Wade and a crock of something undetermined. Their fruit bowl had put them back some, and the quarterback was quick to point it out.

"You're late."

"Well, let's hope your sister's not," goaded Nate.

"Shut up, you little twerp."

Not a good start for the alien brotherhood, and Seth was compelled to nip it in the bud. "Stop it, you two. You'll need a lot of cooperation tonight."

"Sorry, Wade. I'm only joshin'. What's in the pot?"

"Ma's baked beans ... I apologize too; it's just that I've been on edge today. Frank and Tal were much too quiet at practice, almost nice. Something's rotten in Denmark."

It was a reminder of what lay beneath his cloak of deception, a keen dagger intended to pierce the backbone of devilry that threatened those he cared about. How would Wade and Nate respond when they discovered his underlying scheme of personal vindication? Would they get satisfaction from it or feel betrayed in their ignorance? Even Wylie didn't know the true motive behind his insistence at Frank and Tal's invitation. Pondering fallout from his actions only complicated a principled cause on the verge of deployment. Seth accepted the consequences. "Don't fret over them. Tonight belongs to us."

"Wait till you see the cake," said Nate, "then you'll forget all about those asswipes."

"I'll need some asswipe when we get to Wylie's. Had to taste Ma's beans right out of the oven, and they've been baking in my belly for awhile." Wade lifted his cheek and let loose a tremendous gas bomb, a real window-opener, the stench of which brought persistent laughter.

Wylie was waiting at center courtyard to guide them to a prearranged parking spot. "Back in next to my flatbed."

Seth followed his directions. It was near the deck but forward the pines, beneath the bows of an oak tree with room for at least two more vehicles. As expected, Wylie had his reasons. An unobstructed view from the north window was desirable for the alien approach. Bearing gifts their mothers had prepared, they scaled the deck steps and were impressed with Wylie's layout. He had a buffet table covered in red gingham; the folding chairs were organized to take advantage of a deep, dark forest; and his grill was ready for the torch. There was more. A portable stereo sounded an 8-track tape with a varied selection of music stacked beside it. The Hanging Gardens of Barone were in bloom, and Flip's cage had a place among them, no doubt to further clear the north window.

Wylie escorted them through patio doors. "Bring the goodies inside. I don't want the flies to eat before we do."

On his kitchen table were two jumbo bags of chips and a generous supply of buns. The stove held a large kettle of brats that'd been parboiled in a concoction of water, beer, and sliced onions. He asked Wade what was in the crock and then warmed the oven.

"Before I put the beans in, you and Nate grab a plate. I've broiled a few brats for ya; they're on the stove. It ain't the grill, but it'll do. Condiments and potato salad are in the fridge; soda, in the cooler. Be quick about it though, no telling who could show early." He took the pan from Nate and set it on his counter. "What's in here?"

Time being of the essence didn't stop them from gathering around Wylie as he removed the lid. His reaction was well worth it; he roared wildly in amusement. "So this is what's meant by taking the cake."

Seth found it impossible to resist, shoveling in a couple mouthfuls of good ole beans, while they bolted down their meal. Wylie scrambled to fill a duffle bag with costumes, blanket, snacks, a flashlight, and playing cards. Seth could see he was nervous about time.

"Better dress at the landing site. Put your clothes in this bag, and bring it back with ya, unless ya want to make a second trip. We can't risk being caught before our plan has a chance to get started."

Sun setting, they synchronized watches at seven forty. Wylie would lure his first victim, or victims, down the cow path between nine fifteen and nine thirty. His flashlight would signal Wade and Nate to plug in; they would unplug when it disappeared back up the path. Five to ten minutes later, Wylie'd return with the rest. Again, his flashlight would signal florescent lights on. A minute of gawking and then out would come the little green men. After the victims began running for their lives, he'd blink his flashlight a few times, alerting Nate to scoot back and unplug the flying saucer; fire prevention being his reason.

"Think I'll have time to disconnect four battery cables and a phone, plus close the gate?" asked Seth. Actually, there'd be five hoods to pop including either Frank's or Tal's vehicle.

Wylie anticipated his concern. "My flatbed is already done, and tools are on the seat. After these guys leave, ya can take care of yours. Keep the tools there, close to those that come later. I'll do the phone before the cow search; I have to come inside to get a flashlight anyway. That leaves two cables and the gate. I bet ya can do it then."

"Suppose I could, if the battery posts aren't corroded as hell."

"That being so, you'd have to let them in on it. Who knows? Maybe PBS will breakdown right then and there."

"Nothing like putting more pressure on me, is there?"

Wade had his last words before taking to the woods with Nate. "If it does breakdown, make sure you let us know. We don't want to be the fools."

His cable slipped off with zero guarantees the others would. He returned to the deck and found Wylie relaxing with a soda. Over the years, Seth had never seen his neighbor drink beer—an occasional mixer, but never beer; he didn't care for the hangovers. This didn't stop him from enjoying one though. In a way, he felt he needed it. He reached in and nabbed a cold one from the back of the fridge; he was forced to pull it out cap first between mountains of hamburger patties and potato salad. There was enough food to feed an army and kegs of ale to quench them. Curled beside the woodstove, unaffected by activity, Buster lay still. Seth took a knee and set his beer down. The pooch was slow to react as he slid one hand under jaw and stroked ears with the other, a pale stare at a familiar smell. The cyst appeared to be getting bigger. Momentary affection was rewarded with a whimper of gratitude, and his reassuring words, honored with a paw on his wrist. "There, there, Buster. Everything will be all right." He left to join Wylie.

Little more than fifteen minutes passed in conversation about Wickman's Field and the presidential scandal. Alec and Thomas were the first to arrive and took the hint to park next to Seth's truck. Much to their surprise, the Moellers had brought a friend. It was Sara Taylor donning a different look. Basketball shoes boasted her last name, loose jeans were snug in the proper place, and a Brewers' baseball cap proclaimed her double-date partiality. If it weren't for obvious jiggles beneath her football T-shirt, she'd look like one of the guys—correction, she could never look like one of the guys. Both Seth and Wylie stood to greet them, raising an eyebrow at one another.

"Hi, Seth," said Sara while taking lead up the steps. "This must be Wylie." She approached him with an amiable smile and shook hands. "My name is Sara … Hope it wasn't too forward of Alec and Thomas to invite me along. I asked them to call first, but they said it wasn't necessary."

"And right they were. Any friend of this crazy bunch is a friend of mine." He winked at matching grins on the guys standing behind her before his eyes came to rest on Sara's T-shirt. "Can I get ya something to drink? I have soda, beer, and a couple jugs of milk?"

What an icebreaker, but it did draw chuckles, including Sara's.

"And just what do you mean by that?"

"This is dairy country, young lady. It's what we do."

"A soda will be fine." Her chaperons mirrored her request and chose the seating nearest Flip.

"Seth, would ya mind?"

"Not at all." Given the convenience of the chest cooler, as opposed to the back of the fridge, Seth figured Wylie was promoting soda over beer, a wise choice. He'd finish his brew and leave it at that. Snagging three bottles from the ice, he cracked a smile over Marty's Turtle Cove story but the north window removed it. A fancy red van was parking next to the Moellers' pickup. Apparently, Frank and Tal weren't intimidated by two unmistakable trucks. It was time to set aside animosity and, as it is said, put on a happy face. That he could handle; their predatory glares would be more difficult. He pulled out another two bottles as peace proposals. The initial shock of the twins recognizing their teammates, and vice versa, was lost to circumstance. Still, he'd most certainly be on hand to receive the newcomers.

It was Wylie who unknowingly pacified the anxiety in its infancy. "Hey there, Tal. Glad you and Frank could make it. The more, the merrier." He noticed extra sodas cradled in Seth's arm. "Look at this, he's thinking about someone other than himself."

Seth wedged two bottle tops between his fingers and held out an offer they couldn't refuse—at least not in front of Wylie. "Have some soda, fellas. We're about ready to fire the grill." He even managed to speak without curling his lip, a tough row to hoe after learning the word *thanks* could be said with such insincerity. "No problem."

For a second time, Wylie's ignorance of an ongoing feud dampened the hostility; his charm was so dominant as to smother subtle clues. He immediately began rambling on about the high-quality lumber Tal sold to him at bargain-basement prices. Seth used the opportunity to deliver his remaining three bottles to a stunned trio yearning for an explanation.

"What's this?" Alec whispered.

"Wylie invited them. I don't think he knows about all that football crap, so let's try and be civil."

"Until when?" Thomas asked and then answered himself, "The second Wade shows his face."

"They're on foreign turf now. Shea and Curtis are coming too; that's way more mind and mass than they could ever hope to have. Smile and be chipper for Wylie's sake." Sara raised her head and straightened up in her chair at his mention of additional reinforcements.

Seth squirmed at the thought of Wylie comparing notes between opposing teammates, unraveling his deception. It wouldn't stop the game, but he'd have a lot of explaining to do later, which he'd have to do anyway once the jig was up. The sudden appearance of Curtis and Shea definitely postponed the inevitable. Wylie introduced them while he went to get what they wanted, a beer. Upon his return, the social climate had relaxed considerably. Host, hippies, and halfback were sharing jokes over a lighter-fuel blaze. Frank was lecturing the twins on defensive strategy, boring Sara into nonexistence. A sigh of relief, a last swallow of beer, and Seth was off to save a damsel in distress.

"Want to help me bring out the food?"

"I'd be delighted," she said and politely excused herself.

Seth took time to acquaint her with the surroundings. As Sara watched angelfish drifting back and forth, attempted to coax a finch onto her finger, and caressed Buster's peppered coat, Seth thought she had more going for her than most. "Here, take the hamburgers. I'll take the brats, and we'll give those cooks something to do."

Together, they delivered meat to the grill and returned to the kitchen repeatedly, bringing forth dish after dish of side fare. Seth noticed each of the menfolk revel in her frivolous burst of energy and unrestrained femininity. Even Frank and Tal managed to muster crooked smiles. Seth had to admit that, so far, things were going remarkably well.

A few minutes from chow time, Sara peeked under the cake lid. "Wylie, the cake is beautiful. Did you make it?" Her question drew some friendly fire from the beer section.

"Me? I'd have trouble with an Easy Bake Oven. Seth's mom has it down pat though."

"Does the decoration mean anything special?"

Talking above the snickers of the five who knew the answer, Wylie responded, "As the cake implies, that tale is best told after dark." A ghostly mime temporarily replaced humor.

The cookout was a complete success. Oakton Wolves gorged as if they didn't know where their next meal would be coming from, and the appetites of Curtis and Shea were every bit as voracious. Sara ate lightly. Wylie did too, like he'd been munching all day. Seth kept it simple as well; the fruit bowl and his earlier mouthfuls had curbed a tendency to overeat as did PBS butterflies. A community waste basket for disposal of paper plates, plastic forks, and napkins made cleanup a breeze. Empty bottles were traded for full. Host and unanimously elected hostess covered sparse leftovers and transported them into cold storage. Sara's endeavor to learn more about the cake met another dead end. However, once she'd finished feeding Flip the crackers he'd asked for and their party settled into leisure, the inquiry resurfaced with new vigor.

"Okay, Wylie. I'm ready for the cake story."

Inconspicuously to all but Seth, Wylie glanced at his watch. A half hour to set the mood before stray cows needed attention. He'd embellish for fifteen minutes, allowing time for questions and answers. "So long as nobody butts in." His request received nods.

Wylie's story was an extended version of the one told to Seth or to anyone else for that matter. Embroidered into the fabric of his personal experience were mythical images designed to stir emotion. Goldie, a fictional blond heifer whose name could've been derived from the infamous Golden Calf or possibly a television starlet, disappeared without a trace on that fateful night and had since not been found. A week passed, and there wasn't the slightest response to his frenzied calls or those of a heartbroken mother. It was as if she'd been plucked from the earth by a giant bird of prey, never to be seen again. Then there was the flattening of standing hay in his northeast field. Deliberately in proximity to their landing site, twenty paces were swirled to the ground in a circle of mystery. The location was inaccessible to cattle and strangely absent of any fence-hopping deer, as evidenced by the lack of tracks, which could indicate a herd's bedding. Finally, in honor of Seth's suggestion, there was speculation about the power station on River Road. Behind a ten-foot-tall chain-link fence, topped with three strands of barbed wire, mammoth transformers hummed with electromagnetic energy. The area, dangerous and forbidden to unauthorized personnel, provided an ideal place for a hovering spacecraft to quench its thirst in relative seclusion. Recent storms hadn't disrupted service, yet in spite of calm conditions after Goldie's vanishing act, there were three notable disruptions.

Having grinned his way through Wylie's yarn, Shea undermined a mesmerized audience. "That's a scary campfire tale, Scout Master Wylie. Please tell us another."

Wylie remained stony despite the epidemic laughter. "I knew I shouldn't have said anything, but there ya have it, Sara, believe it or not."

Seth had to get things back on track. "What leads you to believe there isn't intelligent life outside earth."

S. W. SYLVESTER

Shea continued, "I'm not saying there aren't intelligent life forms on places other than on earth. I'm saying I doubt they're visiting our planet. Debunking Wylie's observations with a variety of natural or psychological explanations isn't of interest to me. However, I can clarify my view in terms of astronautics."

The talking reference library began with Mother Earth, unique among planets of our solar system, neither too close nor too far from the sun. It had an atmosphere protecting it from lethal radiation, thus providing moderate temperatures and liquid water, the building blocks of life. Our sun, which was really a star and a rather average star at that, was one of many billions in the Milky Way Galaxy, which, likewise, was one of many galaxies in the universe. Although this would suggest countless planets in orbit about their respective stars, only a fraction of those would possess earth's distinctive characteristics that promoted life as we knew it, which still could be quite a few. This posed the problem of their location. In this country, distance and time was measured in miles per hour. A NASCAR car traveled two hundred miles per hour, an F-4 Phantom jet about sixteen hundred miles per hour, and the Saturn V rocket engines used in Apollo missions generated almost eight million pounds of thrust in order to escape earth's gravity at, say, twenty-five thousand miles per hour. Out in the interstellar vacuum, it was a whole new ball game. Deep space was measured by the distance light traveled in one earth year, simply called a light year, and nothing traveled faster than the speed of light. At 186,000 miles per second, not per hour or minute, and in the course of 365 days, the expanse was mind-boggling. By comparison, the fastest manmade object in space, Pioneer 10, traveled maybe thirteen miles per second. Such a snail's pace made Centauri, the closest star system and well over four light years away, a fantasy of which movies were made. Who was to say those stars, or any of the other stars scattered over one hundred thousand light years of Milky Way, even had planets in orbit. Science fiction was morbidly obese with star cruisers that defied the laws of physics, overcoming gravitational forces in and outside their craft, darting across space at warp speed; antimatter torpedoes; force fields; transporters—and all at the push of a button or flip of a switch. Such hogwash served only to spark an interest in seeking real truth, which in and of itself was a victory.

Wylie was harder to please. "So what you're saying is if we can't go

156

there, then they can't come here. What a self-centered approach to the universe. Suppose another species isn't a mere century or millennium ahead of us but rather a million years. Or maybe they live a lot longer than we do. Could they make the trip then?"

Before Shea could answer, Seth jumped on board. "Einstein theorized a shortcut by folding space and time. If mastered, they wouldn't need to clip along at light speed for years on end, just slide through a wormhole."

"What you speak of is pure conjecture, without absolute proof, and it brings us right back to what I had no interest in confronting, that being an alien presence, although now that you've forced my hand, I'll comment to mark your futility. Eyewitness testimony may be of great evidential value in a court of law, but it carries no weight in science. In layman's terms, it's called put up or shut up."

It was the moment Wylie had been waiting for. "So physical evidence is what ya need?" He calmly stood and expressed his concern. "That reminds me, better go check on some cows that didn't come back with the others before my whole herd disappears. Anyone want to go with?"

Curtis and Shea declined in favor of another beer. Frank didn't offer, and Tal wouldn't go without him. It was too spooky for Sara, so Alec volunteered in faith that Thomas and Seth would see to her needs. Wylie went inside to get a flashlight and secretly unplug the phone and then, along with Alec, followed a wobbly beam into the night. A flashlight wasn't really necessary, set aside PBS, and was even distracting once a person's eyes became accustomed to darkness. Regardless, nary a soul could deny its use. Much like last night's, the air was still, and the sky overcast so as to conceal most stars. Fortunately, there wasn't a fog hugging the low ground, and Seth believed Wade and Nate would be able to see Wylie's flashlight.

Ten minutes later, as the pair came huffing and puffing back from their hunt for cows, Seth saw that Wylie could barely keep up with Alec, the limber youth having avoided cow pies as though they were everything but dead center on the tire drill at football practice. Lagging behind turned out to be an advantage. Alec exploded onto the deck, put an end to the sound of music, and took complete control.

"Everybody, listen up. This is no joke. There's a weird light in Wylie's back forty. Ya gotta come see it."

Nobody budged until Wylie reached his side. Catching a couple deep breaths prepared him for theatrics and made for a convincing debut. "It's behind the hill, by the flattened hay I spoke of." After a short, quivering aspiration, he resumed, "This one's white and much bigger. I've never seen anything like it."

"Did it gobble up your missing bovines?" teased Shea.

Curtis laughed and guzzled his bottle dry.

"You can sit there smug in your science book or ya can come see it firsthand." Wylie eyeballed the others. "Well ... are ya coming or not?"

It was Curtis who deposed the prince of doubt. "What the hell, Shea. Let's go have a look. Maybe you can tell us what it is, if it's still there."

"Very well, I'll tag along as a courtesy to the host, nothing more."

Thomas felt his brother's honesty and was quick to enlist while Sara chose to stick close at their side. Tal and Frank got up to follow a near united response. Seth took a backseat role in the on-deck excitement, agreeing to douse the grill and join them directly. It was an unexpected safety move that fell nicely into place.

As Wylie led them into the gloom, Seth recalled the feeling he'd had when he had been in their shoes. Memory tugged at his conscience until the flashlight faded away; he had to be sure second thought didn't send anybody back. Coals extinguished, he double-checked the telephone line. It was dead as a coffin nail. His next order of business was battery cables. The van's cable was brand-new tight, and the Moellers was extremely corroded. Both took precious minutes off the clock. Curtis had parked his station wagon cross-courtyard next to the machine shed. It had gone unnoticed when they arrived and consequently became a time trap. Pocketing the tools, he headed for what he thought to be the priority. The gate needed to be closed; Curtis's wagon would have to wait, but it didn't. Running his fingers along the hood in search of the latch, he was interrupted by a distress call, distant enough to stop him from doing what he was doing, too close to press on. Nobody should catch him popping a hood.

"Tal, wait up." The tone was pitiful.

If Seth didn't act fast, Tal and Frank would get to the vehicles before him. He wanted to be sitting in his truck and turning the key of a lifeless engine, pounding the dash of abandonment. When they hopped in their van, he'd switch to Wylie's flatbed, netting the same results. Two expired vehicles besides theirs would be more than a coincidence. Soon after, the Moellers' pickup would confirm the unthinkable; that a power far greater than humanly possible was to blame. In his haste, he knew he'd just have to tell Curtis and Shea about PBS or let them escape. The latter wasn't an option.

"I get nothing," Tal yelled to Seth. "How 'bout you?"

"Me either. Here come the twins. We'll give theirs a try."

Alec and Thomas each had hold of Sara by an arm, scooting along as quickly as her delicate frame would allow. They weren't able to dodge every juicy clump and hence, were splattered with manure from the knee down. Frank wasn't as lucky. He looked like he'd slid into a home plate made of it. Seth could only imagine what the van's passenger seat looked like. Tal was virtually untouched—at least by cow pies.

"Alec, our trucks won't start," the big man pleaded. "Yours is our only hope."

"Hop in back, and we'll get the hell outta here. Those green things are right behind us."

Did he appear then as they did now? Seth wondered. Their eyes were as big as golf balls, and their mouths gaped in horror. Shivers of urgency rattled their bones into a series of jerks and twitches; they were constantly looking behind for aliens in pursuit. Seth hadn't time to question himself; he needed an answer. "What about Wylie, Shea, and Curtis? Shouldn't we wait for them?"

Before Alec could pull his keys from his pocket, Frank and Tal stood backside clinging to the stock bar. It was Frank's last attempt at calling the shots. "Fuck 'em." He slapped the roof. "Get this piece of shit moving."

Alec fumbled through his keys, found what he sought, and laid out the facts as he saw them. "Sorry, Seth, we have Sara to think about. Wylie and his buddies decided to stand their ground. Now be smart and jump in back."

Seth squinted into a cab of desperation. All eyes were fixed as key was pushed into ignition and with each vacant twist, expressions became more dread-filled. Hopelessness was about to be set upon by panic. "Don't tell me yours is dead too?"

Sara leaned forward and spoke for everyone. "Seth, what are we going to do now?"

"Everybody, in the house; we'll hunker down there and wait for Wylie. He'll know what to do."

Logic had defeated sheer pandemonium for the time being. Naturally, Frank and Tal took the lead through the front door. Thomas followed behind his brother and Sara and switched on the kitchen light as he entered.

Seth clicked it back off. "Light makes it hard to see out and easy to see in. There's enough of it from fish tanks to find our way. Go cover the patio door; I'll cover the front. Everyone, try and remain calm. It's going to be all right."

At the end of the cow path, three adult bodies stood dormant, only one secure in himself. The strange light had appeared in front of them and before agreement could be reached as to identity, it went out. The most likely justifications, ball lightning or swamp gas, fell out of favor the moment floating green aliens emerged. Wylie wondered why Wade and Nate didn't turn the light back on with his signal and then come out. They must've had a reason. Nonetheless, it didn't take long for the younger generation to hightail it in double-time. He and his companions held firm.

"Well, Professor, what do ya make of that?"

Shea studied the phenomenon in forced belief, torn from his cynical foundation. "I ... I really don't know ... and don't intend on sticking around to find out." Unable to break visual contact, he spoke to his chauffeur. "What do you say, Curtis?"

"I fear neither man nor beast, but these creatures I've not seen before. We should decide soon though because they're not gettin' any further away. Wylie, you be the judge."

"Missing cows could lead to missing people. Think we've seen enough; let's go."

Shea was off and away in full accord. As he was not the athletic type, his lanky strides resembled slow-motion replays, striving but not quite up to speed. It was most entertaining for Wylie. Curtis was the one he'd have to watch. The forest dweller opted for a cross-country jog, looking back several times as if regretting their choice. A few squashed mounds underfoot didn't result in mishap and just as well. He doubted his ability to keep a straight face in that event. While Shea made a beeline for the station wagon, Curtis stopped, cracked open the woodshed door, and went inside. He'd split wood for Wylie many times and could find his way blindfolded. The ax wasn't where it should be, but the handle to the old rusted blade protruded from behind a half cord of ready oak. With one swift pull, he yanked it from permanence and squeezed out the door. Wylie met his call to arms.

"Just what do ya think you're gonna do with that? Scalp 'em?"

"Not sharp enough, but it'll leave a hell of a mark."

"They're space aliens, for God's sake. You'll be zapped before ya can cock an arm." Wylie relieved him of his weapon and threw it back in the shed; he'd forgotten to latch the door from the inside. "Check on Shea. I'll see how the rest are doin'. They must be in the house." He assumed Seth had fulfilled his duty, and both Curtis and Shea would be along shortly.

In the midst of consoling deranged schoolmates, Seth frequently glanced out the window for Wylie and company, unaware they had streaked by without notice. Everyone converged on Wylie as soon as the door slammed behind him. Seth caught a glimpse of taillights. Oh no, how could he have missed them? Gripping Wylie's arm, he voiced his concern above all others. "Curtis and Shea got away."

Wylie took it in stride. "Nothing we can do about that now."

"Why did their engine start when none of ours would?" Frank was pissed about missing his ticket out of hell.

Wylie jumped on it. "Their car was parked cross-courtyard, hidden and probably protected by the machine shed." Questions began flying at him faster than he could comprehend. "Everybody settle down. I don't see anything coming toward the house yet. Those things could've turned around and left."

"Not so," snapped Thomas from the window. "They're by the barnyard and gettin' closer."

"In that case, we oughta call someone."

What common sense Tal did have was lost in a heartbeat. "Call the army, the air force, the fuckin' marines!"

Wylie rubbed his face with both hands; Tal's seriousness almost blew his composure. "Try the cops. They could be here in minutes. Alec, get them on the phone."

"There's no tone." He repeatedly pressed the plungers. "I get nothin'. It's dead as our trucks."

Seth stood mute at the front door, partially concealed by Wylie, prepared to flip the master switch and blacken five terrified faces. Groans and moans suffocated the click; there was total silence, and then they returned in volume. Sara literally shrieked, poor girl.

"Damn it, would ya shut the fuck up and let a man think." Wylie blindly rummaged through his cupboard, conveniently found a candle, and lit it with an equally handy lighter. "I don't know why the power went out on everything … Maybe it's them. Thomas, where're they now?"

"Still comin' strong."

"Seth, cover the patio door; first, go check on Frank and Tal. I think they scooted into the living room."

The twins were crouched by the window maintaining watch and hugging either side of Sara. Seth admired their serve-and-protect mode in the grips of adversity. He passed by them and tiptoed down the hallway. It was like trying to find shadows in the dark, but there they were, kneeling in front of the couch, chanting prayers of faith. This he couldn't keep to himself; Wylie must be informed.

"They're what?"

"Praying." Seth used thumb and forefinger to pinch his lips, turning his back to the Moellers so as to not be seen. Pinching didn't work. Their smiles broke free, and muffled laughter consumed them, as they snorted to fill collapsed lungs. Self-control couldn't be gained if they continued to look at one another, so Seth wiped away what he could and spun around to take up his post. Any inkling of a grin was removed at the sight of Tal sliding open the patio door, a fact Wylie recognized as well and thought funnier still.

"Better hustle; the altar boy is getting away."

"Laugh it up, Heehaw, the other one is your problem."

Alec, Thomas, and Sara were too engrossed with the aliens to notice their humor or the fugitive. Seth had a few steps to make up on a gifted runner with a head start. There was no railing around the deck; therefore, his break came when Tal decided to jump three feet to ground level, his recovery giving Seth the steps back. While Tal scrambled along deck side, no doubt bound for River Road, he paralleled on boarded edge for the likely pounce. Two hushed calls to stop fell on deaf ears before he took his dive. It was a crash-and-roll blockbuster taking some wind out of the star running back and aggravating Seth's sore toe.

Ass bound and shaking out double vision, Tal delivered a woozy threat. "You're in deep shit now, farm boy."

"Compared to what?" Having scoped the situation, Seth went with the obvious. "You messed yourself worse than a sick baby, and it's all because of a hoax."

"A hoax?" I'm gonna fuck ya up bad for this."

"Before or after you explain your accident to everybody."

"That's cow crap ya smell."

"Who do you think you're trying to kid? Besides, you wet yourself too."

"Then there's nothing to lose." Tal staggered to his feet. "I might as well kick some out of you."

Seth jumped up. "Back off, squishy pants. I have a better idea, and it'll get ya outta here scot-free."

"Talk fast, Wickman."

"Okay, here's the plan. Circle around to your van's side door. Stay low; the twins and their date are watching out the window."

"What good would that do? My van doesn't start."

Seth pulled the tools from his pocket. "These will help get your battery cable back on."

"You really thought this thing out, didn't ya?"

"Not just me. Anyway, do you have something in your van to change into?"

"I always have something to change into."

"Do that first because you'll have to wait for the aliens to pass by and enter the house. Don't let them see you. Stay back in your van. When they do go in, you can do the battery thing. Then toss my tools by the oak tree and quietly drive away with lights off."

"Who are those guys out there?"

"I'll let Frank tell you."

"That's right; what about Frank?"

"He can hitch a ride into town with the Moellers. You just remember the three don'ts: don't be seen, don't slam the hood, and don't leave too early."

"What you going to tell them after I leave?"

"I'll tell them you figured out what was going on, got pissed off, and left. Your secret will be safe with me."

"How do I know that?"

"You'll have to trust me, and I'll trust that you'll not bother my friends anymore. It's a good place for both of us to start."

Tal rubbed the back of his neck, took a couple steps into his mission, and turned about. "You should be playing football. I've never been hit so hard in my whole life."

The flattery was taken with a grain of salt; the possibility that this incident would change Tal was a long shot. Years of nurturing brutality didn't just go away. The most he could hope for was that Tal would steer clear of him and his friends or risk his reputation. He watched a weak agreement blend into the night.

What now? Seth thought. He knew Curtis and Shea would've had to open the gate to get away, but did they close the gate behind them? Chances were they didn't considering their frame of mind, so he had to check. Tal didn't need anything holding him up should Frank decide to go chasing after him. He scurried along bordering pines until he was close enough to verify his hunch, and then he turned back, confident there was plenty of time to be on hand for the reveal.

A swaying among several willow streamers caught his eye; it was movement that couldn't be attributed to a windless night. Out crept the figure of a man with a stick. He wondered if Curtis had decided to stay and make war while Shea went for help. Total shock came when the outline struck a familiar pose, that of standing rifleman in Nate's toy army and bearing down on what could only be a glowing green enemy. His feet responded instantly; his voice was shaken by trauma. With Seth running at full gallop, seconds from contact, the stagnant air was broken by a sound not to be confused with any other. "Ching-chink" belonged solely to a twelve-gauge pump, locked and loaded. Once again, he took flight and T-boned the shooter to the ground, fully expecting to hear a shotgun's thunder. It didn't happen. Thank God, it didn't happen.

There was a short grappling match for control of the firearm before mutual recognition took hold. Marty spoke first. "Seth? … What the hell are ya doin'?"

"It's not what ya think. This whole thing is a hoax."

"Mean to tell me I almost shot a couple practical jokers?"

"Come with me." Seth put the willow tree between him and the lucky survivors. "You aren't supposed to be here."

Lost in his own world, Marty mumbled, "What a trip."

"Marty? Why are you here?"

"I was fishing the ridge when I saw that orange light again. This time, it wasn't on water; it was cruising down River Road pretty as you please. Grabbed my gun and headed for blacktop. That's when I saw a one-eyed station wagon tear out of Wylie's driveway westbound, but no orange light. I followed the action."

"So, Marty Hoffman goes where others fear to tread. Didn't you notice the lights were green, not orange?" Barely into his bitching, Seth could see the hunter's awareness take leave for that which lay over his shoulder. He wheeled around to be seized by everything he doubted. Outside the gate and hovering over the road was an orange ball of light. Not a word was spoken.

Marty slowly began to raise his weapon. Seth pushed it back down. Then in a most spectacular fashion, the object appeared to acknowledge his gesture. The color changed from pumpkin orange to deep yellow, and three black dots formed an inverted triangle within its soft glow, the lower dot stretching into an upward curve. It was making a smiley face like the one Penny had stuck on Marty's rear window. Inertly stunned, they observed it clear the expression, return to its original color, and with a "beep, beep," scoot off toward Oakton.

Although Seth was thoroughly amazed, Marty wasn't. "That alien bastard is toying with me. I'm going after it. Are ya coming?"

"I can't. There're things to take care of here." He latched onto Marty's wrist. "Meet me at the ridge in the morning. We have to talk about this."

Marty jerked his hand free and was onto the chase without comment, leaving Seth unable to tell whether or not the message had gotten through. He hoped it had. With Nimrod pursuing obsession, some relief was expected, yet it didn't come about. Confusion abstracted truth; he didn't know what to believe. Wade and Nate were closing in on the cottage. His decision to go for the front door rather than the patio doors was a poor one, inviting another unpredictable slant. Next to Wylie's entrance sat a whiskey barrel and on that barrel, a watering can. Catching his bad toe on the entry slab, he reached for support. As it turned out, the barrel was empty and unstable and the watering can, full. Both tumbled on top of him as he hit ground for the third time in ten minutes.

Wylie stepped outside and closed the door behind him. "Didn't your ole man ever tell ya to pick up your feet?"

"No less than a thousand times."

"Are ya okay?"

"Oh, I'll be all right."

Attempting to control his laughter, Wylie offered a helping hand. "Ya look like a drowned rat."

"That makes me feel better … How are the others doing?"

"They're all scared shitless. Where's your buddy?"

"I had to tell him the truth. He's in the van waiting to split as soon as the aliens go inside."

"Doesn't he want to see the ending?"

"Let him go; he's really pissed."

"Whatever ya say." Wylie didn't have time to argue; Wade and Nate were getting closer. But he did have one last scheme. "As long as you're wet, act like you're hurt bad. Don't say anything; I'll do the talking."

"Are you going to flip the power on then?"

"Of course, you're mortally wounded."

With Seth's arm draped over his shoulder, Wylie dragged him inside. The candle had since been blown out to avoid alien detection. Alec and Thomas helped ease Seth down while Sara slammed the door. Frank was trembling in a fetal position underneath the table. Wylie used Seth's wet shirt and the near total darkness to his best advantage.

"He's bleeding, and I think they got Tal."

Sara squeezed between the twins and cradled Seth's head in her lap while Thomas gripped hands with the dearly departing. Alec was more optimistic about Seth's chance of survival. He removed his shirt and pressed a makeshift bandage on a nonexistent stomach injury in an attempt to stop the hemorrhaging.

Franticly checking for a pulse, Thomas blurted out his prognosis. "His heart stopped. I think he's dead."

Wylie rose from a horribly funny death scene and prepared to further anguish the emergency medical team.

"They're coming up to the house. Nobody make a sound." His command was obeyed, that is until Wade and Nate roamed from north window to front door and began wiggling the knob.

Seth's noggin hit the floor as Sara withdrew in dread. Alec released pressure on a bogus wound, and Thomas let go of his hand, each choosing to defend the living over the lost. Between Sara's gasps and Frank's whimpering came shouts of warning, growls from cornered animals. "Get outta here!" and "Leave us alone!" were popular at first. When these demands weren't met, "What do ya want?" became a plea for mercy. Seth felt it was time, as did his neighbor apparently.

Wylie flung open the door, surrendering his castle to alien invasion. And then there was light. The spacemen had clearly practiced their finale. In unison, each held out their sunglasses, took a step forward, and went with a classic; "Ta-da."

Seth hopped to his feet and skimmed over the room, better to get a little piece of everyone's reaction than to focus on just one. Wylie exploded in tears of laughter. All openmouthed and white, the victims spoke with their bulging eyes, even as one crawled out from under the table. In a blink, identical complexions shifted from flushed to feverish, each spouting a string of profanity not to be outdone by the drunkest of sailors. Wylie's uncontrolled cackling soon coerced a pair of awkward smiles. Sara actually cupped Nate's face with her hands, asking if it was really him and, after being convinced of such, rubbed the grease paint off on his chest. Nate seemed to like that. By far, the bleakest undertones lay in scorching glares between the quarterback rivals. Wade fumed as to why Frank was there, and Frank condemned Wade for it being so. Seth moved quickly to defuse the mounting fury.

"Wylie invited Tal," he whispered, "and Tal invited him."

The remark didn't escape Frank. His short-lived smirk proclaimed a right to be present. A bold stand yet somewhat diminished by his duck-

and-cover response while guised in manure. Wade brought things back into perspective for him.

"And just where is Tal?"

Seth hopped on the bandwagon. He'd noticed Tal's van silently drive by the kitchen window with a minute to spare. Mocking Frank's contempt for rural folk by exaggerating his country accent, he added, "I reckon he done left without ya, once he got his bat'ry cable back on." Frank pushed him aside and raced out the door.

"The second I saw Tal's van, I knew something was up," said Wade. "I just don't know whether to hate it or love it."

"Probably how your coach feels when you call an audible and it scores a touchdown, which reminds me, I should go after your backup before he hurts himself." He snatched a dishtowel from its rung. "Here, wipe the paint off your face. It's hard to take Pubie the Clown seriously."

Seth could tell his brand of justice had boosted Wade's mood, evening the score for the previous week's scare and single-handedly dividing the bad boys. As he skirted around the ruckus of the other members, who were naive to their borderline conflict, he felt fortunate to be going after Frank; the others seemed to be unearthing his hidden agenda.

Wade shouted at Seth before he got to the door, "Wish I would've thought of it myself!"

Frank was bumper stuck to the Moellers' pickup as Seth approached with care. "Hey, Frank."

"Wickman, you planned this, and I'll get you back if it's the last fuckin' thing I do."

"You'll have to stand in line." Without Tal, violence wasn't a concern.

"Suppose they're all inside having a big laugh on me?"

"It's only a little cow shit."

"That's easy for you to say."

Seth let ride the dig and offered a solution. "Wylie has a faucet below his window over there. Let's go hose it off."

Frank perked up. "I guess it's better than sitting in it."

"Sure is, but let's move. They'll be coming out soon." He couldn't believe what he was about to do with complete immunity.

"Okay, enough already."

"Try and lighten up, Frank. Laugh at yourself for a change."

Wylie, missing two guests, led the remaining lot outside. "Seth! Where ya be?"

"I'm around the side, washing off."

"When you're done, get some chairs off the deck. We're gonna hang out in the courtyard for awhile."

Most of the talk was familiar to Seth. Jokes relating to what was said, what was done, and plotting future scares. When his undercover intrigue finally did surface, fate intervened. In the rapid fire of events, he'd forgotten about the ones that got away. A lone headlight pierced the willows and behind that, a complete set followed. Each pulled to within twenty feet and doused their headlights. By the looks of it, Curtis and Shea had brought extra troops from the Lumberjack Saloon. Eight doors swung open in uneven succession and slammed shut in kind. Black leather, facial hair, and tattoos numbered six behind the leaders. They looked astonished beyond words, unable to pry their eyes from Wade and Nate. Seth had no idea what to expect next as nervous giggles circulated around the lawn-chair assembly.

Before the bamboozled could utter a sound, Wylie spoke. "Don't ya know it's not polite to stare?"

Shea seemed less than enthusiastic with Wylie's devil-may-care attitude. He turned to his partner in disbelief. "What an asshole."

Curtis, on the other hand, broke into laughter far greater than Seth recalled from their trout-fishing expedition. His sizable influence dictated that if he thought it was funny, it was. The loyal entourage spontaneously concurred, Shea reluctantly joined in.

"Take your alien brother and get the cavalry some beers," Wylie said to Seth. "I think they could use one."

While glow sticks were being passed around so to were peace offerings. Nate was the party's life, fluttering about like a fairy as he handed out his quota of four to Curtis, Shea, and the two bikers beside them. Those two happened to be saloon proprietor, Jack Harding, and his bouncer, a big bruiser who answered to Harley. Apparently, the alarmists had been persuasive enough to draw them away from their roost, which was not an easy feat.

Seth delivered his bottles to four unknowns leaning against the rear fenders of a battered Impala. Whatever prompted him to glance inside their car, he'd never know, but it threw him for a loop. A tattered flannel shirt didn't quite cover a sawed-off shotgun, nor did an oily pillowcase hide the rifle. He tried hard to ignore this as well as the two of them who were packing a pistol inside club colors. Whiskey voiced appreciation for drink attempted to conceal the fact that they'd come to do serious business, to take matters into their own hands and with much less to go on than Marty'd had. Regardless of all the precautions taken to avoid disaster, PBS came ever so close to being just that. No one knew this more than he. A tad bit of anxiety left when they finished their beers and returned to the gang's home away from home, having bagged a wild barroom story if not a couple alien corpses. However, Seth counted the minutes until brother and friend would be far removed from this place.

"We've milked this for everything its worth. I'll put the battery cables back on. Wade, take Tinker Bell inside and make sure he gets all that stuff off his face. It'd be tough explaining that one to the folks."

Nate petitioned for more time around Sara. "Aww, come on. We can stay a little longer."

"I said I'd have you home by eleven. Let's not ruin it for the next time." He knew there'd be no next time, at least not for them. "Get your clothes too, wherever they are, and change."

"Do as your brother said," Wade added. "I'm ready to hit the sack myself."

Alec and Thomas also had reasons to be on their way. They might've had mixed feelings about the hoax—being annoyed yet amused—but not about Sara. They seemed anxious to get her off to themselves. Frank was forced to ask them for a ride into town.

"Why do I have to ride in the back?" Considering Frank's reliance on their sympathy, Seth was amazed that conceit still held reign.

Alec laid out his terms. "It's our truck, and we won't allow a lady to ride back there."

"A lady?"

"Be careful what ya say," said Thomas. "It's a long walk to Oakton."

Sara flashed the first of two satisfied smiles. "Go ahead, Frank. Jump in. It'll be fun." The second grin came with something she whispered to Thomas.

Seven miles of country road in a pickup bed, even with foam rubber and sleeping bags, wasn't going to do a body good, especially when the slighted driver knew every pothole along the way. That realization was plastered across Frank's face as Seth and Wylie watched them leave.

"Looks like the rich kid never rode buckboard before," said Wylie.

"There's a first time for everything. Let's go inside and see how they're coming along." Seth was less concerned with Frank's comfort and more with Nate and himself being presentable under kitchen light, the conditions under which their mother would likely see them. His wet clothes could be tossed in Wylie's dryer for a few minutes, but his brother needed closer inspection to please a discriminating eye.

Aside from shitty shoes, which were not unusual for country boys, they appeared as they had arrived. While they tried to gain some resemblance of normalcy, Wylie busied himself washing the cake pan and bean pot for immediate return. A note on each thanked his neighbors for their contribution. That being done, they all gathered to crow like cast members after a standing ovation. The only thing missing from their backstage egos was a desire for a repeat performance. Once was more than enough.

Leaving Wylie in his taillights and having the most vital interests sitting next to him, Seth felt a gush of relief wash over him. Nothing could've prepared him for the loss of brother and friend. As he was longing to bestow gratitude on something other than Lady Luck, his high beams illuminated another possible alternative: the very spot where he and Marty had witnessed their close encounter. Such an outlandish suggestion raised more questions than he was willing to tackle at the moment. Postponing judgment until he'd talked it over with Marty made better sense. What about Marty? Where did he go, and what was he doing? When they parted, a piece of him had wanted to run with the prowling man/beast, although not necessarily with the same sinister intent. He drove slowly past Fisherman's Ridge and strained to see through the darkness, actions that gained nothing more than Nate's attention.

"Thinking about fish tonight, are we?"

"No, just looking." It was a blind response covering an imperative that Marty show in the morning. If not, he'd have to hunt him down.

"Looking for what?"

Wade broke his silence. "Skip to the important question. Ask him about what we heard."

Nate went quiet, gleaning the courage to speak of it. A dry tongue did its best. "We were by the chicken coop when we heard it."

"Heard what?" Seth feared the worst.

"The ching-chink of a shotgun. Talk about scared, we didn't know what to do."

"While you were out talking to Frank, Wylie told us you had to run down Tal during the scare. Whatever it took for Tal to abandon Frank had to be huge." Wade's insinuation made their point clear.

"So you think Tal pulled a twelve-gauge out of his van and was about to blow your heads off, until I caught up and gave him the lowdown?"

"Something like that," said Wade. "Well?"

Their theory held a minor flaw that enabled Seth to bury his secret deeper, a secret that was between Marty and him. "Tal didn't have any such thing. Stopped him back of the deck and filled him in. What you heard may've been his van's side door; that's where he steamed off to."

"Pissed or not, I can't picture him leaving Frank behind."

"You'll have to ask Tal about that. He did what he did."

"Frankly speaking, ha-ha, I'm glad the big ape left. Without him, Junior was curled under the table. What a couple of pussies."

His fellow alien's ridicule brought on a wide smile. "Worse, Sara showed more guts." It didn't really matter why Tal split, betrayal left a scar. Add that to Cow Pie Frank and his role as quarterback gained some big yardage tonight; it was almost a happy ending. "Sure sounded like a shotgun though. Didn't it, Nate?"

"Sure did. I thought we were dead meat."

With Nate's words echoing in his ears, Seth came to rest at Wade's doorstep. "Tell your ma the beans were great."

"Will do. Same for your ma's cake." Slapping hands with both, Wade paused before easing the door shut. "I'd be honored if you guys could make it to a few of my football games. Things are going to be different now."

Nate left no doubt they were fans for life. "If I get my way, we'll be at all of them."

Driving back to the farm, content his friend was safe at home and his brother nearing the same fate, Seth kept glancing at Nate's face. PBS could've gone so wrong. He reached over and patted his shoulder to make sure things were as they should be.

Nate turned to him with a half grin. "What?"

"What you said to Wade, it meant a whole lot to him."

"With your driver's license and this old truck, how could we not?"

Reward came swiftly. "Bet Sara would like to ride along with us."

CHAPTER 10

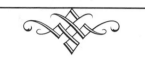

Between conclusion of PBS and his early morning appointment, restful sleep couldn't be had for Seth. The folks were already in bed when they got home the night before, having placed complete trust in him to look after Nate. It was a failure that weighed heavily on his conscience. Not only did he spend such a brief amount of time with his responsibility, but those fractions of the evening he did spend, at least in the beginning of the scare, could've easily been his last.

A quick note for his parents and he was out the door, abstaining from breakfast in favor of food for thought. Turning on the trail to Fisherman's Ridge, he noticed the reflection of his headlights off a chrome bumper, indicating he wasn't the first to arrive, if indeed Marty had left at all. Seth shut off his lights and inched closer. In doing so, he realized the truck wasn't parked for tailgate fishing. The monster's eyes were closed but prepared to brighten the river at a moment's notice. A determined penumbra sat patiently behind the steering wheel, gun barrel sticking out the window. At no other time did NRA and smiley face stickers take on such profound meaning. Their dichotomy went beyond human terms.

Marty knew who it was. He'd sit tight, watch, and wait for Seth to come to him. When the passenger door opened, he spoke without eye contact. "Hop in."

Everything about the scene told Seth this was as serious as it got.

Marty was panning the watery highway, periodically poking his head out to survey a dubious heaven. His trigger finger rested on the safety button of a twelve-gauge, and an open box of shotgun slugs lay next to him. He was battle ready. "Have you been sitting here all night like this?"

"Pretty much."

"I take it Happy didn't come back."

"So, you saw what I saw … Now do you think it's real?"

"If it isn't, then we had the same hallucination at the same time. Doesn't seem likely, does it?"

"Not in my book. Maybe it was a chapter out of the one you and your buddies wrote."

"Guess I have a few things to explain." Seth began with Wylie's amazing glow stick and how it sparked, not one, but two scares. He kept Tal's incontinence to himself; otherwise, the story unfolded as it had befallen them. At times, Marty was amused, at others, indifferent. Either way, not a word could pry his eyes from the watch.

"That's quite the caper you planned. I don't think it could've come any closer to blowing up in your face."

"Too close for comfort. In hindsight, I should've let you in on PBS long ago."

"There's no way you could've known that I'd show. By not telling me, you were keeping the deal made with your friends. It makes me feel better about our arrangement."

"Friends … Huh. The same friends I used to get even with Frank and Tal."

"You had just cause. Those punks wouldn't last five minutes in my neighborhood. I'm surprised they didn't shit their pants."

Seth wanted to comment, but he didn't.

A few minutes passed before Marty addressed what did bother him. "About last night, before you knocked me down, I clicked off two rounds at your aliens. Both were misfires. The first shell was ejected by the willows; the second is in the glove box. Take a look at it."

Seth inspected the primer; the firing pin had indeed met its mark. He was under the impression a blindside tackle had stopped any shots from being taken. In truth, Marty had already squeezed off one dud, pumped in a second shell, and came up blank again. Shivers ran through his spine. "Two in a row; what are the odds?"

"Not good. I buy only the best and have never had a problem, even in rain. Both rounds came out of that box next to you, and the handful I used before last night sounded off."

"Think Happy had something to do with it?"

"That's why I'm here, to find out."

"Things could've turned out so bad."

"Fortunately, you stopped me before I emptied my gun."

"And nobody would've blamed you for it, especially not me."

He looked at Seth for the first time. "But it didn't happen, so there's no sense in dwelling on it."

First light came upon them in silence; each was in his own world. Marty continued to search for that which presumably had lost interest. It was a last-ditch effort at the impossible, and he'd tough it out. Seth might've seemed like he was involved, yet nothing could've been further from the truth. Taking his friend's advice, he welcomed in the new day. A rather dreary week had given way to a grand sunrise. Before breaking vista, the underbellies of scattered clouds blushed with anticipation, straining to remain dark in plumage. A sky of blue ushered in a fireball of color that changed with each passing moment from red to orange to yellow. It bleached the tea rose and blueberry from cumulus veils, leaving clean sheets to the wind. Not only was everything all right but his father's hollow words had found meaning. There were many occasions when reference to color had come up, for whatever reason, and Pa had his favorite all-purpose response: "sky blue pink." Prior to sunup or after sundown, there was a smidgen of time when the two mingled as one. It was silent eloquence in full bloom.

"Marty, I don't believe our UFO is coming back. How 'bout I buy you breakfast at Tiny's Truck Stop?" Getting him to join his family for a meal always fell short. Changing location could do no less.

"It's a tempting offer, but ..."

"No excuses. It's the least a civilian can do to show appreciation. Then we can go visit Penny."

Marty sat silent for a moment, apparently thinking about it, and then began ejecting unspent ammo from his weapon. "I might just as well. That thing's probably not going to give me another chance.

They'd each take their own truck, mostly because Seth didn't want to make an appearance at home. Popping in with Marty at breakfast time would only complicate matters. However, there was one nagging detail that needed attention before their feast could begin. "I'd like to take a quick walk over to Wylie's and retrieve that shell you ousted by the willows. We can't have him running across it when he walks down to get his mail."

"You didn't tell them about me?"

"No, and I'm not going to. What occurred between us and Happy should stay put."

"By all means, I'll walk with you though and take a look around in daylight."

Marty roamed outside the gate while Seth, cowering in secrecy, went to the willows. They effectively shielded him from cottage view as he combed the grass for the shotgun shell. There it was. He latched on and hurried back, recognizing it too had a dented primer. Marty was standing in the middle of the road gazing upward. Emulation intensified his curiosity. The canopy had been hollowed out, not opened to sky but domed in wilted leaves and bent twigs. Larger limbs had been avoided completely. It was as though something round and considerably warm had nestled in for a spell. Seth knew what the answer would be, but he asked anyway.

"What do you think caused that?"

Talking more to himself than to Seth, Marty let go. "Why that sneaky little shit. It turned off its light and burrowed into the trees directly above my head."

"Happy Face?"

"Damn straight. Took only a few seconds for me to hit the road with gun in hand, and it was nowhere to be seen. That's when I saw the station wagon tear out of Barone's driveway. I must've run right underneath it when I went to investigate."

"This is getting way too weird for me."

"Weird or not, it's the only evidence that proves what we saw was real, unless you have a better idea of what made that crater."

"Your guess is as good as mine ... Let's skedaddle before someone sees us."

Within twenty minutes, they were seated at the roadhouse counter waiting for Tiny, who was not really tiny, to create his famous Mighty Meal: a he-man-sized platter of steak, eggs, and spuds fixed to their liking, two slices of homemade toast on the side, and a bottomless cup or glass. It was more than anyone could possibly consume, but many tried. They'd be no exception to the many. Seth paid forward his pledge while Marty left a generous tip and a wink for the waitress. Sated in daily bread, they were off to see Penny.

No matter how much he tried, Seth couldn't ignore the yellow sticker in Marty's rear window. Mass production had plastered the irritating smile on just about everything from here to Timbuktu. Was the UFO merely duplicating an image it deemed commonplace among earthlings, a positive expression for the nonviolent choice of ultimately pushing the blunderbuss down, or was it taunting Marty, a visual metaphor intended to provoke Elmer Fudd and his ineptitude at killing the Wascally Wabbit? Given the fact that the first two shots had been duds, Seth was drawn to the former. There could be a way to test his theories, not with absolute certainty, but few things could be. It'd require a favor from both Penny and Marty.

They backed side by side in front of Jake's garage; thunder from Marty's steed alerted the living he had arrived. Penny was harvesting beets at the far end of her garden. Sun bonnet, gloves, long sleeves, and bib overalls minimized her exposure to ultraviolet light. The only freedoms taken were bare feet guiding her and a basketful along a well-trodden path. As she walked toward them, Marty enlightened Seth on her less controversial talents. He boasted of her pickled beets, applesauce, and frozen creamed corn—not to take away from the many other fruits and vegetables she preserved. He said she baked bread, pies, and special brownies that made him crave one after another. "She doesn't like eating animals yet can make them taste good for others; she can even chop wood and change the oil in her car." Seth cut him off before she got too close.

"I know Penny's not fond of your shotgun but would you ask her if we can empty the rest of your shells into the woods?"

"You want to see if there are any more duds in the box, don't ya?"

"Yes."

"Good idea, the thought crossed my mind too." He stepped forward to relieve Penny of the produce and, using his own brand of charm, worked himself into the advantage. "You fit right in with the Garden of Eden, even though you're overdressed. Wouldn't you agree, Seth?"

Seth went with something less suggestive and more family friendly. "Prettier than a shiny red wagon."

Penny recouped from a giggle bout. "Okay, what do you two have rolling around in your head?"

"We really just came over to visit," said Marty, "and ask a favor."

"That is?"

"I ran across a couple duds in a new box of shotgun shells. I was wondering if you'd let me shoot the rest into the woods; can't take a chance there aren't others."

Reluctantly, she gave consent. "I suppose … Give me a few minutes to crank some tunes and jump in the shower." Penny took back the basket and turned to leave; shaking her head at Marty's parting words.

"Jumping in the shower? We wouldn't be hurtin' if you left open the curtain."

While Marty disappeared through the garage service door, Seth was instructed to get the gun and box of slugs. He took great care in making sure there weren't any loose shells lying around, particularly the one in the glove box. That was added to the one he already had in his pocket. Marty came out holding a flap he'd cut off a cardboard box, a hammer, and two roofing nails. These things were destined for the decaying fencepost just this side of the wood line. They took the walk, tacked up their target, and returned to a spot not far from where Penny had been collecting beets. Out of the original twenty-five shells in the box, there were thirteen left. Five were slipped into the Remington 870, and their experiment was set to begin.

"How far do you think it is?" asked Marty.

"I'd say sixty, maybe sixty-five yards."

"You'd be right. I stepped it off myself, and the target?"

"It's about the size of Ma's cookie sheet."

"Do you want to do the honors?"

"No, thanks." Seth could hear music vibrating from the house. "Shoot 'em up quick though, for Penny's sake."

No sooner said than done, and there came five ear-popping explosions separated by the "ching-chink" so described by Nate. There was a pause for reloading and five more; another pause, and then three. All thirteen shells lived up to their purpose, lead balls shattering the sound barrier in a flurry of concussions and airborne casings. This wouldn't be the end of it. Seth pulled the two duds from his pocket.

"Give these two another try … I have to know."

Marty snatched them from his hand. "We both do."

"Ka-boom, ching-chink, ka-boom, ching-chink." Seth scrambled to get aftershock empties. The firing pin had tapped over the very same spot as it did the first time, with different outcomes. They were like any others scattered on the grass. He tossed them to the shooter and gathered the rest. "I was hoping that wouldn't happen."

"Obviously, it can happen but that doesn't mean the Sundevil made it so. I still lean toward a manufacturer defect," Marty stated.

"You could be right," was the response, which carried no more weight than its counterpart.

"Let's go check the target."

As they walked toward the target, Marty explained, "Accuracy with a firearm is influenced by a number of factors, such things as type of gun, distance, shell load, wind speed, gravity, and, of course, steady aim. For instance, let's consider shooting the Colt last Tuesday. Given the short distance and shooting from the hip, I suppose the determining factor could be classified as a steady aim, but I prefer an intuitive ability to point the barrel directly at the tin can. Today is different. Using a shotgun slug at sixty yards brings the other factors more into play. Most of the time, when hunters kill deer with a shotgun slug, they do so from less than forty yards away to minimize nature's elements." Approaching the cardboard target, Marty pointed and said, "Look at that. I only expected about ten holes."

Seth counted fifteen, a perfect score. "You're one crack shot, Marty."

"I know, but it's always a boost to hear it from someone else."

As impressed as Seth was with his friend's marksmanship, whether it was handguns or shoulder weapons, there were implications to such proficiency. Distance to target was similar to last night's near catastrophe. He tried to ease his mind by placing some doubt in the capacity of anyone to repeat the score at night. However, if anyone could, Marty would be the one to do it, and a glowing green target would only have made it easier. The lives of Nate and Wade boiled down to a couple reincarnated shotgun shells. As foolish as it sounded, his theory seemed more plausible than Marty's.

"You're a plant man, Seth. See anything different along the wood line?"

"Ten minutes ago, when we were nailing up the target."

"And you didn't say anything?"

"Like UFOs, cannabis is something you pretend you don't see, least of all to others."

"Damn good answer. Now I won't have to kill ya." Marty laughed while tearing away his scorecard and a little more after Seth's nervous attempt at finding humor.

When they had the gun secure in its case behind the truck seat, Seth followed Marty into a kitchen filled with the aroma of brewing coffee. Penny was at the patio door wrapped in a white cotton robe and drawing a brush through dampened hair. Warm sunshine and a gentle breeze aided each golden stroke.

"Behold, an angel stands before us," said Marty.

Although Seth didn't think a true angel would arouse a man's passion as Penny did, the vision was close enough for him to respect Marty's conviction. "From cloud nine, I suspect. What do you suppose she wants with our heathen hides?"

"I don't know. Why don't you ask her?"

"I'm not going to ask her; you ask her."

Penny responded to their back-and-forth exchange. "Do you really want to know the answer to that?"

Seth blushed and looked down, unable to reply, aware that Marty was laughing at him.

"Would you like a cup of coffee to think it over?"

"If you please," Seth finally uttered. Without thought, Ma's words had fallen from his mouth. He didn't even like java. Still, it was a small fee to escape an awkward moment.

Marty suppressed his mirth long enough to say, "There's no if about that; she pleases."

Penny retrieved cups and saucers from her china cabinet, which, to Seth, seemed unusual for such casual company and then poured their coffee. He watched her go through her condiment ritual: one scoop of sugar, a slosh of cream, and the rhythmic spoon chime that united them. She skimmed swirling clouds from a brown vortex and sipped them away. "Tell me, Seth, do you hunt as well?"

"Not really, even though Black Bart here did get me to shoot his pistols a few days ago."

"And it was fun too, wasn't it?"

"It was, but a tin can is a far cry from the living."

"Not that far when protecting or providing for. The point is you weren't afraid to use it, and better yet, it was fun."

"Would you men like some breakfast. I have meat in the fridge; didn't kill it myself but somebody had to."

"No thank you," Marty said, laughing, "Seth treated me to a big plate of aggression at Tiny's."

An hour flew by in the grip of a discussion about people who'd influenced their lives. For Penny, it was Jake and before that, an elderly professor she had admired during her two years of college. Marty spoke of street people in the city, some good and some not so good. Seth had his family and a few friends. At times, he felt unworldly in the diversity present company had experienced, but it was swept away by sincere interest in what to some extent eluded them. At any rate, the coffee clutch was winding down. Two cups of caffeine wasn't enough to keep Marty from burning out. Seth assumed his tired friend was very near where he wanted to be, the bedroom.

"Think it's time I should be getting back." Seth stood and took his cup to the sink. After dumping most of the bitter brew and rinsing, he politely acknowledged the hostess. "Should you need anything, I'm only five minutes away."

"Your offer is thoughtful, considering Jake's gone much of the time and Marty will soon be fitted for uniform … Yet, I'd worry about how your mother would take it."

"You're our neighbor, and lending a hand is the neighborly thing to do. She'd probably bake something for me to take along. In no time, you'd be swapping recipes and coupons with her."

A genuine smile parted Penny's lips. "You really think so? That'd be wonderful."

They walked Seth out, but Penny took leave halfway to the pickups. "Don't go anywhere until I get back. I have something for you."

Marty gripped Seth's hand tightly. "It's been a hell of a week, huh?"

"Without a doubt, Marty."

"I appreciate the breakfast, and what you said to Penny. You made our day."

"Do us a favor once in a while and send a letter. Let us know how you're doing."

"And you keep your eye peeled for the Sundevil. If it ever comes back, I want to know about it."

"That I will … Despite the distance between us, it's the tie that forever binds. I still don't know what to make of it."

They shifted their focus to Penny's bouncy approach, and Marty added, "Maybe you can tell me what you make of that." A lusty grin accompanied his candor.

She had her hands pulled behind her back, like a schoolchild waiting for a mate to choose one. The taut robe proved her to be far from it. "Pick a hand, Seth."

"Don't you mean a handful?" Marty asked.

The comment tore away Seth's erotic gaze that was sure to have been noticed. He tried to hide ripening modesty with a tap to her shoulder. It didn't matter which hand he chose, either was going to produce a gift, but what? Pinched between thumb and forefinger, every bit as jubilant as she, a smiley face sticker was held out for his approval. Whether it was intended as an innocent gesture of good faith or the mark of new territory mattered little; it generated a twelve-hour flashback that rendered him voiceless.

"Mind if I put this on your rear window? … Marty let me put one on his."

"Sure, go ahead." What else could he say? As she placed it in the same spot as on the truck next to it, he traded a surreal nod with Marty.

Driving down the lane, Seth cast an eye in the rearview mirror. He could see Marty playfully tugging at Penny's robe sash, catering to the notion that a farm boy could be watching. Seth would never know if their impromptu burlesque show unfurled; he'd voluntarily returned his eyes to the road. Was he tempted to look? Definitely, everything about her was a yes. Marty's personal endorsement covered all the bases.

What brought about his decision was a gut feeling that perhaps what she really needed was a female friend and not another lover. It was why he'd pulled his mother into the picture; Penny seemed very excited about the Betty Crocker idea. Time would tell. These three words also held true for Marty, answering glum intuition that he'd never see him again. War had a way of making it so. As for now, there was one stop to squeeze in before heading home.

The only physical evidence to support what Marty and he had witnessed the night before required a second inspection. Seth parked a few lengths from Wylie's gate, stepped out, and once again studied the withered dome. It'd be safe to assume passing traffic wouldn't notice. Wylie might if he happened to look up while shuffling through his mail, which wasn't likely, and in the months to follow, autumn would strip the canopy clean leaving no trace of anything ever having been there. He salvaged a broken limb roadside to fling at the damaged foliage. A closer look was a must. Some leaves were floppy, partially drained of moisture; others that were nearer the heat source had crumbled under pressure. Whatever did this was very warm but fell shy of igniting combustion; the leaves were dry cooked not burned, with a faint odor that supported his observation. Fearing that Wylie, or anyone for that matter, could happen by and question his motives, he climbed back into the truck and drove off.

Seth saw Nate in the corner of left field, thumping down the first of three markers with a hand maul. Each short tap brought a smile to his face. A gentle breeze moved the corn, which he thought of as standing room only for thousands of fans that flocked to be a part of this historic event. As if on cue, Nate stood up and yelled into a maul posing as a microphone, presumably the official announcer for the Fighting Holsteins, "Ladies and Gentleman, it's my pleasure to introduce to you today, the promoter, club manager, trainer, and team physician, not to exclude batting, pitching, and fielding coach … Let's give a big round of applause for Seth Wickman." The crowd went nuts, aided by a gust of wind.

Pulling his cap back into place after waving approval to the packed house, Seth wondered what else little brother was mumbling about. It couldn't be that bad; the kid was grinning like a fool. "How'd you get the foul line so straight?"

"Pa helped me line it from home plate, the others too. He thinks markers were the only things you worked on yesterday. I can't wait till he reads our sign."

"We'll do that soon as we get the other two set. It'll be ready when he comes in for lunch."

They carefully hoisted the sign up parallel ladders, secured it with four lag screws, and stepped back to admire their accomplishment. There was talk of adding a small insignia in the left-hand corner. Maybe a muscular bovine, steam shooting out flared nostrils and eyes red with rage as it squeezed a Louisville, would add character. It was all in fun. That was unless Pa said it was okay.

Their mother laughed when she came out to see what their proclamation to the world said. "Wickman Field, Home of the Fighting Holsteins."

Nate wrapped his arm around her shoulders, "Well, Ma, say what you think."

"I'd like to see the look on your father's face when he reads it."

"I'll go get him."

"Hold on thar, Bubba Louie," said Seth, "He'll be coming in for lunch within a half. We can watch him from the kitchen window. There's no way he'd pass by it and not walk over to take a peek."

"That's better yet," said Nate and moved to adjourn in favor of their mother's chili.

"We'll be in to wash after we're done putting things away, Ma. Nate, grab a ladder; we don't want to be late for the revue."

It wasn't long before they watched Adam exit the milk house, glance at the backstop, and stop midstride. With one set of knuckles on his hip, the thumb and forefinger of the other hand lifted his cap just enough to enable the remaining fingers to scratch his scalp, as if to ask, "What on earth have they done now?" Wrought with anticipation, the three of them continued spying from the casement window as Adam walked over to the sign and began laughing. When he turned to the house, they scattered to avoid detection; the heirs took their place at the Round Table while Queen Mum ladled bowls full of chili. All appeared normal when His Majesty entered and cleansed battle-hardened hands. Neither bread be broken nor cup raised until he was seated. Even then, idle spoons waited for spoken word.

Eventually, Adam asked, "What?"

"You know what," said Nate. The pause didn't last long. "We watched you check out our sign from the window."

"Same window you'll be fixin' several times a year?"

"We'll try our best to keep it in play … 'Beware of Foul Balls' will be our motto."

"Thank God that wasn't written on it," Martha said.

Initially taken aback in disbelief, Seth exchanged blank stares with Nate and his father. Then Adam laughed, prompting his boys to follow in rip-roaring fashion. None of them thought such a comment would ever cross her lips.

Two bowls later, Nate was anxious to take to the pitching mound. Seth wasn't. He agreed to play some before chores, but a sleepless night determined what he'd be doing next. His repose was briefly interrupted by a ringing phone. The message was for him, it's content, saddening. He dragged himself to his room and found solace in feather pillows, a curious sibling close behind.

"Who called?"

"Sara, to tell me they're moving."

"They're moving, when?"

"Right now. Apparently, her Pa couldn't find a job around here, so they're going to stay with her uncle and his family."

"Where's that gonna be?"

Typically, this would've been the point at which he'd end his brother's badgering. However, the week had brought about a significant change in attitude. Nate had stepped up to the plate in more ways than one, both on and off the farm, and to think lightly of it was not possible, given the fact that it could've been lost forever. "Texas. Said she had a real good time last night, something she'll never forget. She also wanted me to give you a big hug for her, but it just wouldn't be the same coming from me."

Nate bowed his head and mumbled, "Wish I could've talked to her." And then he turned to go. "Guess I'll go see what Pa's up to."

Sara also wanted him to give Alec and Thomas the bad news, something she couldn't bring herself to do. Sniffles saturated her short adieu. "Sorry, Nate, we're all going to miss her."

Feeling that Nate would eventually get over the loss, Seth tried to clear his head so that his body might rest. Although his injured toe had been aggravated the previous night, it was well into recovery and didn't interrupt. Distraction lingered elsewhere. Those involved in PBS would carry the incredible story wherever life took them, spreading their version as they saw fit. Neutralizing Tal's muscle by threat of blurting "Shitpants" may've temporarily improved Wade's football aspirations, but it didn't guarantee anything. The contemptible pair went back a long way, and the thirst for revenge would be no less potent in them than it had been in him. Watching out for each other became more important than ever before.

It was the flip side of Project Big Scare that drew most of his concern. The only way he'd ever make any sense of it would be to start with the beginning and take it one step at a time. He simply couldn't deny what Marty and he had witnessed. His vision was perfect and faculty at that moment, on high alert. Alone, he might've rubbed such a sight out of his sockets or stuffed it into the attic of disregard. The eyes of a skilled predator confirmed it and prevented contradiction. In a strange twist of priority, physical evidence played a secondary role. There wasn't any exchange of family photos or lovely parting gifts, no space-beer containers strewn about or glowing skid marks on pavement. As for the withered dome outside Wylie's gate, there could be other possible answers. He just couldn't imagine what they'd be. Accepting that what they saw together was real had to be the first step.

What was it? In many cases, he knew people could look at the same thing and interpret it differently. This didn't afford him that luxury. Whether it was Wylie's portrayal of what he'd seen two weeks ago, Marty's observation at Fisherman's Ridge, the article in Tuesday's newspaper, or the anomaly of last night, the description remained consistent. Each occurrence showed the object to have a sense of direction. It could weave between tall pines, hover silently in midair, or glide the middle of a country road. Marty claimed it could retrace its own path and blend with the environment in doing so. Was that not evidence of intelligent design?

One other feature connected the stories: electronic beeps. All of them had heard it and suspected the same, a feeling their presence was being monitored. The beeps that caught his ear during Thursday night's practice run seemed to pad Marty's account of a chameleonlike quality. Try as he did to find the source, only darkness lay in his search.

Before Seth could possibly settle on the inevitable, he had to give natural and manmade explanations their due. Nearness to the object eliminated many from both categories. Stars, planets, or asteroids offered no more than aircraft, weather balloons, or satellites. Perhaps it was a secret military weapon spying on Nowhereville? He entertained the thought anyway. Whether from home or abroad, technology-wise, Happy Face made the Space Age appear Stone Age. As a hoax, there was even greater disparity. Ball lighting and swamp gas were phenomena Mother Nature had yet to show him. Supposedly, ball lighting was small and only lasted a few seconds after a strike. Swamp gas, also known as methane, was a byproduct of decomposition; it was colorless, odorless, and flammable. If it could self-ignite, could it smile at him too? Were precisely timed sound effects that of a daring field mouse testing the competence of a screech owl, or maybe a paranoid sparrow with a sleep disorder? Whereas skepticism often rewarded him with viable options for the unbelievable, this case left him penniless. Doubt was a comfortable bed to sleep in until one was awakened.

Starry-eyed in revelation, he took it to the next level. It always seemed odd to think man was alone in the universe. Contention arose with alleged earth visitations. Having wiped that slate clean, speculation was boundless. As Wylie suggested, superior intelligence could easily be a million years' worth of understatement—either in civilization or mortality. Suffice to say, our galactic neighbors could do what they wanted, when they wanted to do it, from the very beginning of mankind.

Purpose was a tougher nut to crack. Hell on earth could be going along as planned, or it could be a pathetic sideshow on the way to somewhere else. Without a meeting of the minds, the question of why our blue planet would be of interest to them fell impotently into the lap of human assumption. It helped to stick with what was given to him. The probe, in redefining the object and Happy Face, happened to be in the right places at the right times—at least in relation to glow stick activity. According to the Fisherman's Ridge report, it disappeared in the direction of the first scare and returned shortly thereafter. In Thursday's dry run, it privately flagged his audio radar. Opening Night apparently justified personal attendance. Based on the premise they were there and therefore infinitely more knowledgeable than we, it wasn't a giant leap to presume the probe was aware of everything going on. Most important, it chose to become involved.

Marty said it came from the east on River Road, "Pretty as you please." It'd be a short hop over the pines to get a bird's-eye view of Wade and Nate mocking, of all things, space aliens. Putting this aside, it lured an armed earthling out of ambush and into an extremely dangerous situation involving mistaken identity. Although Marty might've accepted manufacturer defects regarding ammunition, Seth didn't. Out of a box of twenty-five shotgun shells, two were initially duds, the same two that spared precious lives. Would this not be enough to support the probe's interference? That morning, they had discharged without incident. Was that still not enough? When he pushed down Marty's gun, it changed color, smiled, changed back, and with a "beep, beep" went about its way. If Marty maintained that the probe teased his ignorance with the facsimile of a window sticker, it would be his story to tell when war dogs gathered at the canteen. Seth was hard pressed to think the message of the gods was "Naa, naa, na na, naa." For him, the meaning had been elucidated by example: taking lives is not good; saving them is. It bore a striking resemblance to the Sixth Commandment.

He hadn't expected that a review of the sighting would take a pious turn. To imply the probe could be the Almighty, or an emissary thereof, constituted blasphemy in its most despicable form; unless it was divine, in which case a traditional approach would've worked much better. Should he have been contacted through a burning bush not consumed—wait, cancel that one—say, a booming voice from on high accurately prophesying events in the near future, no matter how unlikely or insignificant, now that would go a long way toward theological commitment. With respect to religion and its ideals of love and compassion, he couldn't dispute the warmth such virtues brought to his heart nor the sorrow brought by cruelty and suffering. The problem was the absence of communication, and not for lack of effort. Due to an unrelenting silent treatment, he gradually thought the existence of God and a Soul as unknowable. Trying to live a moral life was an acceptable safeguard to his free-thinking. For if there were a God, he doubted that such an entity's ego would be so unstable as to be slighted by those in the flock who admitted to themselves that they just didn't know for sure. They were the ones who needed a boost, not a slap on the ass. It stood to reason that constant torment between faith and science was punishment in itself, till death did they part.

There was, however, his understanding of the probe's implication: "Thou shall not kill." It was a best-guess hypothesis loosely supported by a smiley face, two unpredictable shotgun shells, and a feeling. Intellectually sharing a single ethic, the probe in practice and man in thought didn't necessarily make it a Godsend, nor did it mean that other beings zipping around out there held the same values as dear, but it didn't slam the door shut either. Given the chance to correspond on a more intimate level, provided he could overcome a sense of impending doom, to know Happy's take on how all things came to be would certainly top the list—solving the enigma of an afterlife, a close second.

The impossible dream of learning ultimate truth was rather selfish; he wouldn't be able to tell anyone. How he came to know it would bring on the hecklers. This was a fact, for he used to be one of them. Pointing out his shortcomings didn't stop there. He imagined what the probe's controllers might think of our species being force-fed a heavy dose of humility. There seemed to be no mystery why honest communion wouldn't be a part of the equation. In the first scare, when he assumed Wade to be alien, a metal fencepost soon found a pair of willing hands. During PBS, while under the same assumption, Curtis latched onto a woodman's tomahawk, Marty bore down with firepower, and it didn't take long for an armed mob from the Lumberjack Saloon to mobilize. Granted, some of the victims took flight, but there sure wasn't a shortage of defiance. Little green men weren't the menace; it was man's fear of the unknown. On a much larger scale, fighter jets had been scrambled and troops dispatched in response to UFOs, a lot of something for nothing that posed a national security risk. It seemed the "kill first and ask questions later" mentality of the naked ape, in general, would discourage any meaningful dialogue.

Bearing the weight of creation's rotten kid served no useful purpose. Seth attempted to move on. As far as actual close-up encounters, there had to be others, many others from many places around the world, military and civilian alike. Did most of them, as he intended to do, keep their mouths shut to avoid ridicule, or were they silenced for other reasons? If solid evidence were available, why would any government keep the most important discovery in history to itself?

The question brought to mind a story he read about Orson Welles's 1938 radio version of *War of the Worlds*, by author H. G. Wells. For thousands who didn't catch the program's opening disclaimer, its realism invoked widespread panic. City dwellers packed up their families to escape alien attack while country folk shot at suspicious-looking water towers, the latter reaction sounding very familiar. Mass hysteria seemed to provide a reasonable cause for a government to withhold information or furnish disinformation, but if Martians weren't here to lay waste to our planet, then what was the problem? Mankind could sure use a helping hand—or tentacle. The strongest argument was that of control. Politics and religion, bound together from the beginning of time, stood the most to lose. Public awareness would jeopardize their authority as never before, splinter them into an ever more complex array of nonnegotiable differences, and possibly urge a submissive populous to seek divine guidance from the new masters of illusion. The status quo must be secured at all costs; terrestrial aristocrats depended on it. Keeping the masses struggling for survival left no room for them to contemplate whether or not other intelligent species visited earth. As a lowly farmer, a peon in the hierarchy of wealth and power, there wasn't a thing he could do but wonder why the probe even bothered with him when there were much bigger fish to fry.

His mind was becoming weary; his body, heavy. With eyes closed and hands folded topside, his last thoughts faded into slumber. He would've liked to figure out whom to thank for the lives of his brother and best friend. All he knew for sure was that he didn't know—a common ending for many of his deepest reflections.

"Crack!" It woke him out of a dead sleep. Was it the screen door slamming shut? "Crack!" There was only one thing that sounded like that, and he could almost feel it in his hands. Seth jumped out of bed and lunged for the window to see his father send yet another pitch roadside. So what if Nate had snuck in while he was asleep and took his Louisville, the sight of the ole man swinging lumber was good enough reason. "Crack!" No time to lose, Pa did this once in a coon's age. He checked the closet for his glove and discovered Nate had made away with everything, except his cleats, and time didn't allow them a second look. Sturdy railing posts top and bottom, their caps worn with reliability, slung his body downstairs and into the kitchen. The shifty-eyed wall cat read three fifteen, forty-five minutes to chores. Opposite, his mother was content with a press box view of Wickman Field. A clap from the screen door was followed by another crack of the bat. He slowed his pace, rounding the back porch. He didn't want to appear eager. Who was he kidding? They probably were betting how many hits it'd take to bring him out.

Curling his fingers in the chain-link fence, a backstop no-no, Seth watched his father take the next pitch low and outside. "Can anyone play?"

Adam looked over his shoulder with a half grin. "Don't ya know people die in bed?"

"Give me a few practice throws with Nate, and we'll see if I can get one past ya."

"You're on." He called to his youngest, "Nate, warm up your relief. Seems to think he can do better than you."

"He can. I'll fetch balls from the outfield first."

After his brother had collected the balls Pa had driven deep into Wickman Field and dropped them off at the pitcher's mound, Seth began his warm-up. On many occasions, his father had scouted his talent and, to a much lesser degree, took hold of a bat. The last time the ancient one faced him, he hadn't had any more stuff than what Nate threw, but things had changed since then. He watched his father study him from behind the chain-link, tossing only off speed junk and the less-than-full speed that Nate was accustomed to. However, when Pa was standing at the plate, his real heat would show no mercy.

"Batter up," said Nate, and he took his place behind the backstop; it was where he should be when catcher's equipment wasn't in the budget. Calling balls and strikes would still keep him in the game.

Seth ran the count full, using power pitches. Somehow, Pa managed to stay alive with a couple foul tips and a sharp eye. Tempting as a knuckleball was, he went with the twice successful slider. A check swing and the umpire gave the batter a walk. "You're blind in one eye and can't see out of the other; not to mention the batter broke wrist on his check swing."

"Don't argue with the umpire … Man on first, no outs, next batter."

If the preferential treatment from a biased umpire wasn't enough, a gutsy batter knocking the crap off his boots with his prized Louisville was. Pitching from the stretch with a man on first, the next throw was a bullet right down the pipe. He couldn't believe his eyes when the ole man laid down a bunt, a nice trickler down the third-base line.

"Safe at first and second, no outs," ruled the judge.

Flustered about having two ducks on the pond, Seth went into his windup and delivered in the same spot that had previously led to a walk.

"Steee-rike."

"You're eyesight's improving, Ump." He shouldn't have smarted off.

"Your game isn't though. Because you used a windup instead of a stretch, there was a double steal on that toss. What you have now is men on second and third, no outs, and one strike on the batter."

How could Seth not be disturbed? "Would it be okay to stick with my windup or you going to call a double steal of third and home too?"

"You made the mistake, and I made the call. In this case, advantage goes to the pitcher, so use your windup if you want."

"Quit your bitch'n', and let's play ball," Adam said.

Nate chimed in, "Yeah, quit your bitchin'."

It was clear they were in cahoots as Seth hoofed dirt in front of the rubber. He needed this strikeout and was determined to get it. Looking one in, a swing at a high and tight fastball, a clumsy reach at a hard breaking curve, and the out belonged to him.

"Men on second and third, one out," hollered the arbiter.

The next at bat, Seth lucked out. Pa was catching up to his power and again ran the count full. A rocket line drive snapped into his glove, and a quick fake throw to third doubled outs to end the inning. No runs, one hit, and one error. Swaggering back to the mound, playing catch with himself, he adjusted his cap and spat. "Care to go another round, ole-timer?"

Adam chuckled away the comment and submitted to age. "You're right about that. I'm no spring chicken anymore, so let your brother have a shot."

"How 'bout a few more, I'll throw some off-speed junk? See if you can put a club to it."

"Go ahead, Pa," said Nate. "Tear the hide off."

Tapping the plate with his bat, Adam gave way. "Ya got ten pitches. Make the most; I won't take a swipe at anyth'n' bad."

There were several times during the last series that he fiddled with the ball's stitching behind his back, on the verge of letting go a knuckler or screwball. The few curves he did throw were hard, not the off-speed slop intended to mess with a batter's timing. His decision to stay with heat in the first round turned out to be a wise choice. Ten pitches later, he and his brother were sweeping roadside grass for a boomer that cleared leftfield. Another was in the cornfield. Pa's fluid stroke resulted in two homers, a double, and an infield single. Considering two pitches were wild, four of eight throws met the sweet side of Hank Aaron's signature, a triple-crown performance. There was an upside, though; he did catch him looking at one and swinging at air a couple times. It fostered his strategy for the next outing: mix it up, keep him guessing.

The ribbing he tolerated from a prejudiced umpire didn't affect his sensibility on the mound. He threw what his brother was used to hitting. It allowed for a respectable showing, a chance to shine in the eyes of a proud father. With Pa clapping and pacing, Nate time and again squared off, wiggled the top of his bat, and took a healthy cut. Half a dozen rips to the short fields had him standing tall, but the high long ball that squeaked over in left center had the kid jumping up and down. Seth thought it such sport that he cared not for his time at the plate. It was all good, and it got better.

"Nate, round up the gear and don't lollygag. Your brother and I'll start chores." Adam looked at Seth. "Unless ya forgot how to do what it is we do 'round here."

"Forget? I'd sooner forget my own name." He trotted to the batter, handing his glove and a low five. "You swung a mean stick today, Little Brother."

"It runs in the family," said Nate. Everyone knew that eventually Seth would return to starting lineup in the barn, and that was just fine with Nate. His worth had been established, his effort recognized in both farming and baseball. He made a damn good alien too.

In the barn, Seth was greeted with resounding approval from many of his parlor girls. Each held her cud to bellow as he strode down center aisle. A scratch here, a pat there, a tug on the ear—it was quite a reunion. Delma received special attention, for it was she who had put him out of commission, and trust had to be restored. When Nate arrived, he surrendered rank, claiming his injury needed to be broken-in gentlelike, an exaggeration, as proven by Wickman Field. It went unchallenged. He was glad to shovel manure and watch them milk the herd. Teamwork had them all at the supper table in no time, salivating over fried chicken with mashed potatoes and gravy. As Seth admired Wednesday's red rose in full bloom, he fancied Mini-Golf Mary doing the same with her pink one.

Ringing phone or not, there'd be no plans tonight, other than to help clear the table. Looking into their living room, he saw Nate's butt hanging on the edge of couch cushions, an indication the Olympics would eventually fall prey to NFL football. If only there was an easier way to change channels, then maybe the sports fanatic could relax. Pa was several pages into his newspaper and getting a charge out of whatever. It sure wasn't the front-page headlines: U.S. planes bombed some bridges near the Chinese border. Marty was right about that. With his mother's back turned to drying dishes, he leaned over and smelled the rose.

"Anything else I can do for you, Ma?"

Martha replied, "Thank you, but I can handle the rest. You go watch the games."

"Maybe later … Think I'll go sit on the porch swing awhile."

"Do as you please."

Seth thought the evening was much like the one he'd had a week ago yesterday. "Sky blue pink" had given way to the witching hours; a soft breeze flattered his face with a country aura, and crickets chirped background to a whip-poor-will's lead. The Big Dipper hung low in the northwest, its cup upright as if to hold water, and directly above, an overturned Ursa Minor seemed to be filling it. Polaris crowned the farm's twin silos, yet to be replenished. Eastward was the Great Square of Pegasus, the Winged Horse, flying topsy-turvy over Wylie's pine monarchs. For him, this was where similarities with that first alien night ended. The healing process now allowed both feet to rock him in nature's symphony, and the shadows of Wickman Field promised many good times to come. Drawing breath at having survived eight straight days of turmoil, none for the worse, he exhaled in solitary gratitude, but for whom? It was the unanswerable question that he'd fallen asleep on, the one that would forever be written on the faces of Nate and Wade. It'd be waiting for him every time he drove by his neighbor's gate, interrupting each platonic visit with Penny. Some middle ground had to be found, a compromise he could live with.

Synthesizing God and aliens wasn't his idea. He'd read some things about it at the library, eventually walking away entertained, not necessarily convinced. From prehistoric man to modern man, the ultra-advanced technology of visiting life forms would, for all intents and purposes, be godlike. They could create or destroy, manipulate or ignore, be seen or not be seen; the orange ball was in their court. Darwin's earthly evolution of our species might've fallen short of possible cosmic influences, but they too had to come from something and that something apparently had a message to pass on: live and let live. He returned to the North Star atop their silos and made it a focal point of appreciation. Although it wasn't the brightest star in the sky, it was fixed, never setting, on an oath to always be there. This feature would best symbolize thankfulness and continue as a reminder till his dying day. He didn't expect his blessing for Happy Face to get a response any more than church the following morning; yes, he'd decided to swing by God's house. Ma and Nate would be thrilled. Pa, Wade, and Anna would be shocked. The Moeller twins, given the news of Sara's departure, would probably be heartbroken. It couldn't hurt to put in a good word for them and Marty too. Wylie should be fine; he had the Pud Lady going to bat for him.

"How's your toe coming along?" Martha asked.

Seth refocused. "It won't stop me another day."

"I gathered that much." Standing behind his gentle sway, she laid her hand on his shoulder. "Is there anything else that's bothering you?"

With a reassuring smile, he reached up and patted her hand. "Everything's all right, Ma." Her exit brought a final thought before he went to join Nate at the tube. "Or as right as it can be."

S. W. SYLVESTER earned a BA in philosophy/humanistic studies from the University of Wisconsin-Green Bay. As a lifelong resident of the Badger State, his narrative transpires within said boundary, although it extends well beyond such geographical limitations. Writing has been and continues to be a lingering passion.